Thirty Degrees – Portal to the Afterlife

Thirty Degrees
Portal to the afterlife

Miguel Angel Camiletti Sáez

Translated by Jennifer Yaeggy

Thirty Degrees - Portal to the afterlife
1st edition: August 2021.
Santiago, Chile.
ISBN: 9-798409-615314

Total or partial reproduction of this work by any means or process, including reprography and computer processing, is strictly prohibited without prior authorization of the copyright holder. Likewise, the distribution of previously unauthorized copies is not allowed and will prosecuted.

THIRTY DEGREES – Portal to the Afterlife

Copyright © 2020 Miguel Ángel Camiletti Sáez

All rights reserved.

Translated by Jennifer Yaeggy

Get your copy by calling +569 92753792 – Santiago de Chile.

DEDICATION

I'd like to dedicate this book to my children, Miguel Angel, Ignacio, and Gabriel, and to Paola, my ex-wife, all of whom I love and have affection for. Also, an honorary mention for my niece Catalina. She's one of the people who encouraged me to explore this public literary adventure.

My children were and still are a fundamental pilar in my life, product of a project that ended, as all good projects do.

"You can change the world's consciousness, but never your children." This is something that time has made clear in my concept of existence. How could I not be proud of them?

I can say that with the launch of this novel, I am lucky to have written my second book. There is no purpose behind it other than to leave my family, friends, or whomever reads it a message of an intimate human experiences, perhaps hard to believe, that marks a before and after in this existential journey where, with varying intensity, body, mind, and soul intertwine.

CONTENT

Dedication vii

Acknowledgements iiii

Prologue 1

Chapter I: The reason behind it all 5

Chapter II: Encounter with a spirit 19

Chapter III: The Spirits' clinic 29

Chapter IV: Christmas 833

Chapter V: "glasses," back home 999

Chapter VI: Hostile Hologram 1099

Chapter VII: Uncle Victor 11155

Chapter VIII: Graciela's Grandmother 1199

Chapter IX: Gustavo Cerati's Concert 1255

Chapter X: Bright Light 1277

Chapter XI: Mental Power 1355

Chapter XII: Portal to the afterlife 14141

Chapter XIII: Energy of the Living 1477

Chapter XIV: The Medium 1533

Chapter XV: Investigation and technique 1633

Chapter XVI: Theory 1699

Chapter XVII: Yamil, Guardian Angel 18787

Chapter XVIII: The Presentation 1999

Reflection on the Pandemic 2099

About the Author 21111

THIRTY DEGREES – Portal to the Afterlife

ACKNOWLEDGEMENTS

I'd like to thank my friend Agustín Mas Layi for helping with key details in the book and his constant push to deliver a high-quality literary product.

How could I not treasure our long and interesting philosophic conversations, from Viña del Mar to Santiago de Chile, during the global pandemic?

To María Luisa Cordero Velásquez, psychiatrist, for her respect, affection, and professionalism. In 2006, it would have been almost impossible for me to abandon the dark, dead-end alley that I found myself in without her help.

PROLOGUE

I once heard someone say that life is a stretch of intertwined backs and forths where anything can happen; an unforeseen event plagued with emotions that ends with a fantastic flight towards eternity. Due to inevitable and sad circumstances in my life, my first and only marriage ended in an abrupt fashion. My three children were adults at the time. It wasn't easy to go through, but there was no other choice.

A friend offered me a room in her modest house for the time being. It wasn't fancy and the cost of living there was well within my budget. Yes, all of a sudden I was back at the beginning of my life, though older and a bit wiser.

As is the case with many others, the blows received during my existential journey had made me grow, leaving gaping wounds on my body. There is no other way to polish your consciousness and ensure its evolution and growth with perfect purpose.

One sunny day at the beginning of March in 2019, my friend, a thin, divorced, blonde woman in her early fifties, who I had met through her son, welcomed me into her home with open arms. I'd seen her just a couple of times before that. "You were so dejected when you arrived. Your face and your eyes were so sad," she commented a few months later, after the three of us had become closer friends through sharing a living space for a time. Her closest friends called her Lali. She was a wonderful and marvelous woman.

Leaving my home had been an odyssey. I suppose that after twenty-eight years of living together there is no way to avoid collateral damage during a marital separation, no matter how amicable it may seem. My case was no exception. My entire family suffered a great deal. As for me, well, I lived with the damage and consequences of that decision in the flesh.

Anyway, every cloud has a silver lining, as the saying goes. I hoped that the road I had chosen would change everything for the better, both for her and for me. Paola, my ex-wife, an exemplary mother, was able to accept the designs of fate though it hurt her.

Sometime after I'd left home and had been renting rooms in different places where I met and spent time with wonderful families, I decided to write this book. I thought it was necessary for me to do so because of several reasons. The main reason was not to take with me to the grave a mysterious and special secret, in particular for those of us who have asked ourselves, "Why does that strange feeling come over me in the dark, as if something is watching? Why does an unpleasant shiver runs down my back for no apparent reason? Are life and death what we believe them to be?" It may be pretentious on my part to try to answer these questions, but I had two options: either I stayed silent forever or I wrote it down and shared it with the world.

Whether it was the right decision or not, I felt that I needed to share it. I chose to write without fear of being criticized or branded in a cruel fashion. After all, who am I? What was the worst that could happen? To be judged or chastised by society? No. That wasn't relevant in this literary journey that provided very necessary catharsis during the global pandemic. In the beginning, this book was a way to get things off my chest, intended for me and no one else to see. Then, after reflecting on it and through the encouragement of the people dearest to me, I decided to publish it. What with Covid-19, I had no idea if I would still be part of the existence on Earth I had placed so much value on. That is, until I saw a secret and surprising revelation with my own eyes.

I never believed in spirits or energy. My critical thinking and rational upbringing wouldn't let me. However, I received specific signs one spring day in 2005 when, after a long and arduous period of work and suffering from strong emotions from various sources, I had a breakdown due to severe stress and then fell into a deep depression.

I lost the notion of time and space; right there, in the place where my life had gone on with the hypocritical normality characteristic of our culture. Maybe I had overestimated the size of the existential load that my relative youth could bear.

I was thirty-five years old at the time. The tsunami of everyday activities I carried out occupied my entire life. I had reached the point where I wished that each day could last longer than twenty-four hours.

It's not an easy task to become aware that life is a finite road where our bodies are the vehicles and time is the fuel that drives us. It's an ephemeral and irreplaceable asset that we don't value until it runs out.

In general, it's not until we're on our death beds when we start to regret everything that we didn't do and left for later. That's why there are some who, after death, victims of their own lack of evolution, return from beyond with the healthy goal of finishing their tasks or asking others to help them with it. By then it's too late because, except for specific cases, it's not possible to change the way things will work out.

Maybe, because of this, there are others who live, even if it's in an unconscious decision, as if each day were their last, almost as if they don't want to leave anything undone. They're not good role models either because living like that isn't living at all. It's like trying to swallow without chewing. "Everything at the right time and in the right measure" is a wise phrase. Wanting to speed up or slow down when things happen is to try to defy established laws. It's an intent with no effect, much less meaning. On the contrary, it's an important waste of the fuel used on Earth that no one in their right mind would want to lose; time, invaluable and even more precious than gold.

CHAPTER I: THE REASON BEHIND IT ALL

My name is Daniel Antonio González Ruiz, and I'm 50 years old today. I'm an average person. I was sunk in a world that I'd crafted, framed by the current social constructs of the most tragic era of Chile's history.

I was born in 1970, a decade that produced a generation where most of us were much less militant than before. Pinochet's period brought with it not just physical but mental confinement as well. It was a lockdown that dragged on for two decades, more or less.

In 1985, as a teenager, I faced overwhelming terror at the possibility of dying in the March 3rd earthquake. A year later, I saw Halley's comet. In 1989 I watched as the Berlin wall came down. Then, in 1997, I was amazed at the UK's decision to give Hong Kong back to China. In 2001 I was taken by surprise by the attack on the Twin Towers.

The tsunami in Indonesia made me cry in 2004 and I was left speechless by the earthquake in Chile on February 27th.

And now, in 2020, I find myself confined to a small wooden room, trying to protect myself from the Covid-19 pandemic.

Looking at things as though the glass is half full, I've lived a privileged life. In my short life span I've witnessed great milestones in human history. I don't know what else there is for me to see.

At the beginning of the nineties, after I graduated as a computer technician and with a wife and son to feed - living in a society marked by chauvinism - I become a workaholic.

From the beginning, starting in school, we were taught that everything we wanted to achieve could be obtained through hard work and persistence. However, after a few decades of living in this long, thin, pepper-shaped stretch of land, life had shown many Chileans that reality was quite different.

During that decade when dreams were the order of the day, the most important thing for me was to see my children grow up with all the commodities in life. I wanted them to live far from the trauma and lack of affection and finances that I suffered through as a child. I'd prepared myself for that. Today I know that the idea was a fool's dream, but the ideals of a person with aspirations such as mine (which were so high as to be absurd) had been ingrained in me since birth. I was the son of a difficult, though at the same time enriching in every sense of the word, populist environment and I did my best to provide what I thought my new family needed.

In the world of capitalism's social costumes, I had some luck in obtaining my superficial objectives. I became a manager and part of the board of directors of some smaller-scale companies, though they were large enough to understand the essence of the market's productive cells and its speculative polarities.

And so there I was, naivety personified, with the profound and almost philosophical thinking of the poorer classes, both in economic and spiritual terms, who were victims of the unfulfilled promise of a system established at the beginning of the eighties.

Given the results, it seemed that it was the best that the Chicago boys could aspire to, trying to make Chile into a lab for the creation and implementation of a new economic, political and (I say this without fear of being wrong) much less social system in which inequality would show its worst aspects, not just in my country, but across a large part of the globe. I'm not alone in this line of thought. Innumerable international studies, biased or not, prove what the majority of Chile's citizens know, live, and suffer through every day.

It's probable that more than one person will take my words as the normal complaints of a malcontent. It wouldn't be strange for them to be seen that way. But, if we analyze things in detail, I can't be classified as one. My life has been one of privilege. I had access to higher education. I enjoyed comforts that I never imagined. With my ex-wife, Graciela, we were able to raise our children so they could live good lives within the current system.

Though my thoughts may contradict themselves, making me appear to be ungrateful, it doesn't mean that I should agree with how things were established. I paid a high price for my excessive lack of worry, blindness, and ignorance about the lifestyle I had chosen to create, seduced by the materialistic awareness of greedy individualism postulated by the economic model I lived in.

In some ways, ignorance isn't that bad. However, when we become aware of it, it our minds can't be indifferent to it any longer. It wakes us up and can lead us to suffer from intellectual anxiety. Then we open our eyes to reality, revealing the subtlety with which some have tried to disguise their slavery by making it look like a laudable symbol of personal growth but that, deep down, is nothing more than cheap make-up that hides their deepest desires and that they use to emulate a high-class lifestyle, exposing their spiritual emptiness.

Part of the latter is reflected in a few phrases of a pop song that says, "You can't go where the others go 'cause you don't look like they do. That's just the way it is. Somethings will never change."

Without being a communist, it is still evident that uncontrolled capitalism contributes to creating a society that is discriminatory, stressful, unjust, and segregationist, where a few define the rules that the majority has to follow. It doesn't just numb the mind; it numbs the spirit also in order to focus on the production of "wealth" as an implacable goal that ends up devouring our time, environment, and love along with its purest instincts.

In Chile, we're going through the largest social rebellion that has occurred within recent memory. People have started to ignore the role of the State and its hierarchical imposition as well as current institutionalism. It's as if anarchy is gaining ground, taking advantage of an awakening that screams for social restructuring and a substantial change in the rules of the game.

Anarchy as I see it isn't chaos or the lack of justice, but rather a means of collaborative, horizontal, organization and self-management necessary to get around what many see as the incompetence of the traditional political class and a worn-out institutional system that seems to be distant, arrogant, and indolent with those who have long-standing, legitimate, and unsatisfied demands.

They see their politicians as protectors the wealthy but full of contempt towards the unresolved rights and needs of more than ninety-five percent of the population. How will it end? In a regime different from the one we know today, one where there is no place for us to decide for ourselves, but rather where less sensible people decide for us on a whim?

They say that everything is based on cause and effect. I soon found myself facing the effects of the causes that I had crafted in my youth, on which I had built my thoughts and both conscious and unconscious actions according to the conditions of an incipient neoliberal model that, in the long run, structured the most sensitive aspects of Chilean culture and, of course, my life for forty years.

It's because of this that it's difficult to remove the lens of politics when we talk about how to structure our lives. Though there are people who deny it, human beings are political by nature.

As a teenager located on the median of a Gaussian distribution (statistical term) without a set political identity, the economic/political model that started in the eighties molded me in its image. Like most everyone, I took in its precepts without protest, the same that were necessary to carry out the great blue plan which focused on the structural change of a society that was as beaten down as a wild animal in a circus.

It was a Disney-like concept of life, encouraging the creation of a Prince Charming who would woo the princess, get married, have children, and live happily ever after. In the meantime, the motto was work, work, and more work. Get the most money and most material goods as possible because that was the one thing that society praised; a conservative society that was used to lying to itself since colonial times, and to make itself out to be something that it never was. Maybe it's a symptom of the capitalist model or the pseudo-capitalist models that try to emulate it but just turn out to be defective copies that weren't quite able to meet the standards of quality control. In other words, these are the mercantile models that were designed to maximize gain at a low economic price while paying a high social cost.

I don't know. The single point that is clear to me is that the effects crushed me like an enormous steel ball, or like someone stepping on a poor, unsuspecting bug.

Despite everything, I will never regret what I lived through to reach where I am today, the lone protagonist of my life. Now I live a different existence, far away from the stress that ate at me like cancer and that I had to endure for so many years. It almost killed me. Yes, it had me against the ropes, absorbing my life like a sponge, but most of the guilt lies with the person who feeds the beast rather than with the beast itself.

To be fair, I can't deny my part in it as my perfectionist personality was one of the factors that always worked against me. More often than not I felt frustrated for things not turning out how I wanted them to, even though I know that "perfect is the enemy of good."

How stubborn I was; how unwilling to look beyond the tip of my nose. Maybe there was a logical explanation for the persona I projected to others. A friend took it upon himself to let me know.

"You're my friend, and I've got to say it. I've been watching you since we met. I would bet that you have Asperger's" he said without any reservation.

"So now you're a doctor or something? You're just an engineer with a degree in math from the University of Chile," I laughed.

"No, but I know people like you who have been diagnosed. You share many of the same traits."

"You're crazy. Though, truth be told, it's not the first time that someone has mentioned it to me."

As I write this, I live in the Maipú area in Santiago de Chile, a place of historical battles and a fervent spirit of the fight for freedom. I find myself writing a personal story that I'd wanted to write for a long time and that, if not for the insistence of my niece, Josephine, I would have waited to start writing in my old age.

That girl is better than any control system in existence. I've known her since she was a baby, and she's the embodiment of her grandmother who was a sharp woman with a determined personality.

Maipú has been my home for some time. I arrived here twenty-five years ago. After a short while, I knew that I'd stay here for the rest of my life. It's like a small town within the limits of the big city, and I like country life.

In 2016, tired of my own inertia as a citizen and of being witness to the corrupt regime du jour, I decided to try my hand at politics.

I dedicated myself to study the internal workings of a subject I had understood just in theory, guided by literature on the subject and what I saw on TV.

Who knew it would be such an astonishing experience? To my amazement, I was asked to run for a spot on the city council. Not without reservations, I accepted the challenge. Even with the risks to my personal and professional life due to being in the public spotlight, which were well known, it was worth it to try to work towards the better good, to change the ungrateful destiny of the people in my community with the firm hope of bettering their conditions of living.

I got involved, wanting to work towards a goal that I thought was genuine and worthwhile. This happened at a time when people had lost faith in the institutional and political apparatus due to massive fraud and acts of corruption that had become public knowledge across the country the previous year.

My political party ran its campaign using the slogan "Change our reality." We decided to fight for what seemed to be a true utopia, the possibility of having a say in the decisions made by the town council and later in Congress, in the case of a victory in the parliamentary elections.

At the beginning I felt that I could make a small contribution to calming the waters among the entropy of the political system. However, I soon learned that the dynamics involved are much more complicated than the common citizen believes. I learned concepts, terms, culture, customs, tactics, and strategies. At last I understood why it's said that politics is a very inexact science.

The implicit precepts can't be learned from one day to the next. As with most things, in order to excel, you have to have something more than a certain degree of talent or charisma. Understanding, assimilating, and applying these ideas take time. Some people learn fast. I learned with agonizing slowness.

The surprises of my excursion into politics continued since, after just one year of participating and through a democratic internal vote, I received the great responsibility of becoming the coordinator of Maipú, the council president of my community, during an election year when the party I represented didn't have any congressional candidates that could represent our area.

It was a difficult time. The stress of my full-time job and my political inexperience coupled with an unstable internal environment made for treacherous sailing through heavy storms for my team and I, which my unstable guidance almost caused us to capsize in. As fortune would have it, with the help of several volunteers who believed in the essence of the political experiment our group had started, we were able to make it through. We received, and I admit it, a huge prize as a result of our actions.

The joint effort of our district bore fruit. We managed to gain some seats in the then disreputable Chilean parliament. It was an invigorating experience that made me feel satisfied with the work done by everyone who helped make it happen. But, on the flip side, and as always, my self-criticism left me unhappy with my performance. I just know that I pushed myself to dive into the deepest part of the river without knowing how to swim. I still don't know how I managed to float on the furious current of swirling waters just waiting to drown the hopes of someone as ingenuous as I was.

Party politics, as most things, can be both sweet and sour. It's cyclical, and no one has a magic potion for success. Even so, the best strategist is the one who has the best possibility of success. Juan Domingo Perón in Argentina knew this well and was able to read and charm the masses as well with his charisma but was also able to attack the Achilles' heel of his rivals and bring them down, making them abandon their pride and arrogance. I don't point him out as an example to follow - he's not my role model - but as a point that needs to be paid attention to.

Who would have guessed? I lived life in a series of roles, some of which I was "successful" at and others that were debut and goodbye in the same breath. I always wanted to try different facets, not to delve deep in them or to look for success, but to live as many experiences as I was able to, such as writing novel.

I was willing to do anything to avoid communing with dreary routine or to avoid the age-old question, "What if…?"

I guess that no one can tolerate leading the life of an automaton which, in the end, kills off all human essence, motivation and joy in favor of heterogeneous situations. Life in and of itself doesn't have meaning. Each person gives life their own meaning, or at least that was my premise.

This time I want to touch on a less explored facet: that of an author. Though I have written another book, this one is special because it will be shared with the public. Why not? I was never a singer, but I dared - though now I laugh at myself - to sing for a number of years in an amateur rock band. I feel embarrassed now just mentioning it.

I wasn't the one behind it but rather the musicians who believed in me enough to insist on having me join them though I didn't have the qualifications to do so. I won't say that I was the worst either. Keeping everything balanced, my limitations and expectations, I believe I did have some high points. Not many, but they did exist, and I still laugh at myself over it.

I was caught off guard the first time I was offered money to sing. I wouldn't have paid a cent to see one of my performances, though to each his own. It's just that it would have bothered me to see myself up there, trying not to be me.

A good friend used to tease me and say my singing was off-key and insipid, but I was a good actor. Maybe doing it from the heart provoked certain emotions in the audience that, on occasion, made me feel like an artist. I always believed that I had a good amount of sensitivity that made me see things from a more sentimental point of view.

The high point of my stint in music came about on an eighteenth of September, Independence Day in Chile, when we played for around three thousand people in the official celebration in Renca. How very daring of me, seeing so many people dancing along with the music and my shrill voice blasting from the giant speakers.

The most amazing and incomprehensible part was hearing the audience shouting for the encore. They were all drunk, the guitarist would laugh when talking about the event later. Years later I was invited to sing in a higher-class neighborhood. There I got a more indifferent reception from the public, though there were one or two indecent proposals thrown in. Some people think that their money gives them the right to treat others like objects to do with what they will.

Anyways, when I was a child I lived in my own world. Some sad events at the beginning of my life had marked me in a profound manner and I was a very shy person. Maybe that's why I enjoyed drawing so much. It helped free my consciousness. I could spend hours on my bed, creating stories for my friends and classmates who, short on patience, would ask me over and over again to hurry up and finish so I could read to them the long graphic adventures of teenage footballers, either created or copied by my childish innocence.

To tell the truth, none of it was very original. The most popular storyline of my comics had been copied from a famous Chilean collection called "Barrabases." In this story, Guido Vallejos, the author, shared the adventures of a soccer team made of promising young Chilean talents. Jorge, the oldest son of one of my mother's friends, had shared the story with me on a visit to his house in the La Reina community, a high-end neighborhood in Santiago de Chile.

I remember that each winter at the beginning of the eighties I dreamt of seeing the unending streets and alleys of the Pudahuel neighborhood transform into ornamental sand surfaces and beautiful, well-kept public gardens.

I wished that I would no longer see the brutal contrast between the architecture of La Reina and Pudahuel. Even today, we can travel from west to east and observe how, in a matter of minutes, a drastic change occurs in the vegetation, architecture, and anthropological landscape of the city, going from horrendous poverty to illuminated affluence, both next to each other but very ignorant of the other's reality. It's as if they were two worlds living face-to-face but never looking each other in the eyes; dreams and reality together like two panoramas within a schizophrenic landscape.

Half-way through the seventies, when I was between four and ten years old, I lived in a humble campground called Villa El Sauce, in the Cerro Navia neighborhood, near the hill that bears the same name. There, within four walls made of rough-hewn wood and a tar-coated cardboard ceiling, life was hard on my family. However, it showed me what reality was, which is always hard to see, though some people forget after they've obtained a certain level of economic success.

During the winter rains, the mud and frost in the early morning outside our rudimentary abode would congeal around enormous pools of murky water which the slippery and hungry worms called home.

They single spigot we could get water from was almost always out of order because it was frozen. It painted an indelible memory in my mind, which I still have today. It wasn't because of its extreme nature, but rather because, for me, it was one of the most representative symbols of poverty and precariousness in one of the many facets common in Chile back in the day.

The first time I read the "Barrabases" magazine, I was astounded by its stories and illustrations, which provoked in me varying feelings of freedom. I saw myself in the stories and in more than one character as at the time I was part of a pee-wee soccer club in my neighborhood in Pudahuel. The club was called the Arenal, or Sandlot, because there was more than one sand and gravel quarry near where it was founded which were very characteristic of the area around the capital city.

At the time, money was scarce. There were families who couldn't afford to buy food, much less comic books, so I made them myself in my used notebooks. I shared them with whoever wanted to read them. I enjoyed seeing people smile as they read them. Those were the happy and innocent days of my childhood.

I tried and tried to make my drawings look like the original, but after a lot of trial and error, I gave up and adopted my own style. It was less refined than the original, but judging by my readers' interest in my stories, it was just as entertaining.

With varying detail, the adventures I described would shorten our long summer or winter afternoons with their unending rain during the eighties. At every chance they got, my friends would snatch my notebooks out of my hands so they could read the fanciful stories. They'd ask to read them again and again.

The storylines were diverse, but my then fixation on height (I was short as a child) made me focus on stories related to extraordinary characters. One in particular was over four meters (12 feet) tall and I named him Flea.

"Daniel, please, finish the story soon! We want to know how it ends. What happens to Flea? Does he die?" my classmates would ask.

Hearing other people insist on knowing what happened in those illustrated adventures drawn using pencil and crayons was a symphony to my twelve-year-old senses. Among my closest friends I began to feel like I was important, a kind of celebrity, which was a different feeling from the cruel periods of bullying that I was victim of in elementary and part of middle school. I spent most of my time alone at school or with my female classmates, trying to avoid running into the more bothersome bullies who were ruthless with their taunts, cementing the silent development of my low self-esteem.

Maybe because of this I never thought things came to me in an easy manner during my first stages of life. Quite the contrary, I always thought that I had been born under ill-fated stars, which meant that I had to work twice as hard if I wanted to change the hand ungrateful destiny had dealt me. I suppose that it explains to a great extent some of the behavior I had during my teenage years, such as always trying to measure myself against my peers.

The torment at school didn't overshadow the congratulations that I received from some of my family and close friends who would praise my creative achievements, no matter how small. I'll always be thankful for that.

However, it was never enough for my permanent teenage need to be recognized for something. Some psychologists claim that this attitude stems from the absence of a father figure during childhood and puberty. If it's so, then that would be my case.

As an adult and after having graduated from a technical degree, the academic requirements to get a better job got steeper. So, seeing as that at the time I had two children with my then wife and a third on the way, I decided to go back to school. If I didn't, I thought, it would be more difficult to give them a better future like we had promised we would work towards giving them.

I meditated on it a lot. I thought about studying something like law. Debates and legal complaints seemed like something I could do, thinking that I was skilled at rhetoric, but, as the saying goes, cobbler to your last. Without planning it, I had specialized in computer science and the cost of starting over from scratch in a different field was incompatible with my role as a father and provider for my family and the inherent economic responsibilities that stemmed from its increasing size. I decided to study engineering. I knew it was a demanding and time-consuming career choice, which I was used to, but all in all it was well-viewed by others. It was a specialization which could provide the income that was in tune with what my family budget would demand in the mid-to-long term.

And to think that as a child I had wanted to become an obstetrician, dentist, or some other medical professional. I was interested in biology. As I grew, I understood that blood and I don't get along. My inquisitive nature led me towards the scientific-humanistic side of academia.

That was my true passion. After all, everyone builds their destiny as they best see fit, or so they say. What I ended up doing in my professional life didn't seem to be in my hands, however, but rather in the hands of an unkind sociopolitical framework where we had to study what was available and not what we were passionate about.

Let's agree that up to today the situation hasn't changed and was one of the reasons behind the social upheaval in Chile that started on the 18th of October 2019. It was an unprecedented rebellion that, considering the history behind it and its immutable dogmas, would take a long time to digest and, of course, settle down.

At the beginning of the century. life, at least in the economic aspect, started to smile at me. But everything has a cost, and in this economic model nothing is free, much less a right.

Among others, too much work and my disciplined upbringing joined together to ensure that any spare time I might have spent with my children and then wife was relegated to small periods of fun and education. This happened to the detriment of the most profound and essential feelings whose absence, sooner rather than later, can come at a rather steep price.

Looking at the facts, the social, political, and economic model reigning in the country, it's clear that it wasn't made to encourage relationships between people. This is a function of the development of an ideology that restricts time to think more and more and focuses the mind on the paradigms of aggressive, stressing, and predatory "progress" based on the culture of sustained "economic growth" portrayed as infinite in a deceitful manner. It's a paradigm that prioritizes the creation of money and wealth over socialization and collaboration.

The progress is based on cannibalistic competition that brings with it a superficial society based on the premise of giving value to human beings according to the amount of economic success they achieve rather than spiritual realization and the necessary bonding intrinsic to human relations.

The explicit and implicit repression of culture also did its part, cooling creativity and artistic expression in its deepest essence.

Add to that the events of my life that at times took twists and turns, attacking without mercy at the moments when we least expect it. Just when you think everything is under control, something happens that mutates a problem which needs to be solved as soon as possible, before it gets out of hand.

How we face problems depends on our level of personal growth. Those who have ascended to a certain level in the spiritual evolutionary pyramid know that there is no problem that can't be solved. On the other hand, people who haven't reached that level shouldn't worry about what can't be solved or else they can overload their central nervous system. This, in turn, generates unexpected effects on their health and, as a result, their every-day lives, many of which are lived on autopilot, walking along flat and boring paths that then weigh on them like boulders in the dusk of their unnoticed and apathetic existence.

With time I confirmed that these barriers are in our minds and not in the physical plane that we live in, holding the reality that for good or ill, depending on how you look at it, we make, define, and in the end, put into practice for ourselves.

In this context I recognize a series of episodes that marked my path of highs and lows, hitting me until I was dazed, disoriented, and on deaths door. They were bitter experiences that ended in a sad feeling of shame due to the blindness and gullibility that defined me for so many years.

Today I believe that I'm less ignorant as the failures and forced landings that life dealt me motivated me to move forward a few centimeters on the path of spiritual growth, which is something I treasure as a precious asset. Those small steps aren't easy for us common mortals to assimilate.

One of the events that started my awakening was the accident that resulted in the death of Cristian, a dear friend, who had gone to do military service in Los Angeles, where he was from.

Circumstances were such that on the 18th of May 2005 he, along with forty-three other young adults and an officer, lost their lives in a tragedy in the foothills of the Antuco volcano. It was later called one of the biggest tragedies of the Chilean army during times of peace, receiving the name of the "Tragedy at Antuco."

A year earlier, my then wife had been diagnosed with pancreatic cancer. That year I had also decided to help out my mom in starting a business that we knew nothing about and, due to that and other reasons, didn't prosper. My friend's death was the catalyst that took me to hell but at the same time opened the door to something fascinating and incredible that changed my life in a radical way.

I don't know at what point I adopted the attitude that I had to solve other people's problems. A lot of the time I was gullible and naïve. Sooner or later maturity hit me, not with cotton and rose petals but with thorns and sharp rocks.

Boldness comes at a steep price, one that I paid in spades in 2005, the despicable period that I called the year of inflection. I fell into a deep, severe depression due to enormous strain at work, extreme emotional upheaval, and an incomprehensible lack of motivation to find a way to relieve the stress I was under. Up until then I had read about something like this but had never seen or experienced it. However, let me make this clear: when going through it in the flesh, it can be a silent death sentence.

Who was I? A simple person just like any other. However, contrary to what I had thought my whole life, there was a little bit of good luck waiting for me, something much more valuable than an overvalued material good or trivial social status, ephemeral, and volatile as a piece of data stored in a bit or a byte on a computer.

Despite the personal cataclysm I endured, 2005 was the most meaningful year that I could have ever imagined. It was difficult to accept; digesting it was nigh impossible and understanding it even more so.

It meant various things at the same time and among them, and maybe even the most profound, was an enormous shift in my perception of existence.

It was a dramatic change that awakened in my closest social circle some insurmountable prejudices against me. I don't blame them. Anyone with a fervent neoliberal mentality would have reacted in the same manner to someone as depressed as I was.

Even though my awakening wasn't related to conscious changes in my ideology, it's undeniable that several concepts related to the matter were, without intention, brought into question during my rethinking of values and principles.

I wasn't a follower of communism either. I have friends who are, and I respect and love them, but I don't share their ideals. I don't follow anything that approaches an ideology or doctrine that restricts, either in full or in part, the rights and freedoms of anyone, though some may see that as inevitable.

I dare say that about eighty per cent of the population lives on the path of endemic ignorance. The remaining twenty percent is made up of the elite and those who understand and participate in politics as a matter of routine, some from their very first breath.

My serious demeanor, as well as the paltry, superficial, and overvalued neoliberal achievements reached at the age of 30 mattered little to none to me during my depression. My family couldn't believe this, even knowing that in my depression I had, to be honest, reached rock-bottom.

In the eyes of those who had known me in my "successful" phase, I had transformed into someone stigmatized and considered emotionally unstable. But how was I to mend the decayed image everyone had of me? In Latin American culture, which is individualistic and materialistic to the extreme, there didn't seem to be a way, in particular within our prejudiced social circle, or at least that's how I saw it. Therefore, I did nothing to repair it. I thought it was a lost cause, a waste of time. Besides, the convenience of being able to say my honest thoughts, without filters, under the guise of not being all there in my mind, is priceless. It's a prize of inestimable value that makes us free.

Some people can suffer a radical change after surviving a tragic accident,. Others couldn't or wouldn't change a single iota of their inflexible personalities even if they were born anew. I belong to the first group, the ones that were forever changed, though, in the end, it meant that I was discredited by my loved ones and, why not be honest, by myself at times. Waking up is never easy, nor is renouncing everything that we were taught as children. However, if we want to live to the fullest, it's a necessary step that needs to be taken, no matter how hard it is. The soul is grateful for and values that step because with it, it can break the chains that bind it. The chains I refer to are the heavy, invisible, and oh-so-resistant chains that are set in the mindset of the poor and make them stumble over and over again in an interminable paradox where few win and the losers are always the same.

In certain cases, when a person undergoes a tragic accident, something both physical and psychological happens in the brain. Maybe, like we say in IT, it undergoes a reset. In truth, I wouldn't know how to define the process, but nothing is the same as before. Everything is transformed in both the conscious and subconscious mind. It's an overwhelming psychological earthquake.

To describe it just a little, I could say that it's like hitting your head against the concrete floor. All the concepts of life that you've learned up to that moment fall apart and are lost forever into the ether, giving way to new premises. It makes you question everything and consider life in the widest sense, without restriction or censure. You reproach yourself for everything you think you might have done wrong, without fear of facing yourself, as many times as needed and for however long you think it's convenient. It allows you to examine in depth the role you play in the herd, trying to elevate your thinking above what you're used to.

Free from paranoia, we reach the conclusion that there is no other way to escape the shoebox that we've grown used to, as if it were a hidden technique to domesticate us or the use of dubious biological mechanisms that treat us as if we are animals.

Finding the words to define this state of reflection is a difficult task because it's as if we're traveling on a high-speed train at the same time that our lives go on. We focus on our arrival and don't stop to think at all about the journey nor if we're doing things in the correct manner and whether we'll arrive at our destination how we would like. As saying goes, "It's not the destination, but the journey that matters."

Before the "year of inflection," my life went on as usual. Of course, normal within the limits of what can be expected as an average person of the middle class in a society and country such as mine. Afterwards, my life, how I looked at it and how I handled it, changed with no possibility of going back.

I learned that there is no more efficient way of evolving than to be broadsided by a large-scale emotional and physical assault capable of moving the most hidden neurons and affecting the slipperiest atoms in the body.

Today, this is happening on a global scale due to the attack of Covid-19 and its geopolitical effects. Now each and every one of us is learning a great lesson. Could it be the opportunity needed to rethink our systems so we can begin to evolve?

CHAPTER II: ENCOUNTER WITH A SPIRIT

As a child, I had heard all the common ideas about the afterlife. I knew about spirits but, as a result of rational thought and structured education, it was unfeasible to give myself enough space to delve into the topic. Because of this, I never stopped to think about or question the existence of beings of light, imps, or divine specters other than in selective and occasional thought processes related to the matter.

I knew of psychics, some famous, others not so much, but nothing sophisticated enough that would allow me to conceptualize the matter, or at least gain consciousness of its energetic and supernatural qualities. The closest I had come to studying energy was what I had learned in school about Einstein.

At the young age of six, my mother took me to visit the south of Chile for the first time. We went to visit my grandfather, who had lost his wife when he was young and my mother hadn't reached five years old. Grandma had passed away in her before her mid-forties. Her premature departure must have been a devastating blow for such a young girl as well as the rural, chauvinist family she left behind.

My grandfather's house, located in the countryside in the small town of Hijuelas Canteras on the outskirts of Los Ángeles, the eighth region of Chile, near Quilleco, was a small and rustic-looking abode. It sat in the middle of about seventeen acres of fertile fields planted with enough wheat to feed a family of four for a year. It was a common occurrence in the rural area of that zone for people to emigrate to the city in search of better opportunities, escaping from relative poverty.

My grandfather also produced honey on his farm. Together with one of his oldest daughters, Marta, the third of eight children, he did everything he could to survive the icy winters there. In addition, they raised poultry and other livestock which they would sell in Villa Mercedes when they felt it was necessary.

Grandpa never missed the opportunity to tell his grandchildren, whenever they visited for their end-of-year vacations, scary stories during the warm summer evenings around the stove inside the shack where the kitchen was located. It was a ramshackle structure made of dry wood and used to cook food in, to toast and separate the wheat from the chaff, or just to heat water in.

The bedrooms and the main dining room of the old house were in a separate building, about sixty feet away from the shabby kitchen. Around that time (middle of the seventies) there was no electricity or running water. All our basic survival needs were provided by nature. How lovely!

Drinking water came from a twenty-one-feet-deep well using an old mechanical iron pump.

The lack of electricity was palliated by candles at night or by a small, empty coffee can with some paraffin and an improvised wick. The wick would peek out from a hole in the middle of the lid that closed the coffee can. Lighting the wick turned it into a pretty efficient lamp.

The years went by fast and Ramón, the youngest son, as many other young farmers who were bored with working the fields, moved to the city to look for new opportunities. Marta got married and went to live with her husband. Like magic, the prosperity found in my grandfather's house disappeared with her. The old man's alcoholism made any other end improbable.

She had studied in the Catholic University of Chile to become a teacher and was able to find a job in the solitary rural school in the area. The school wasn't too far from her father's house, so she lived there for some time along with one of her older brothers, Mario, who was also an alcoholic.

The relationship between father and son had its highs and lows but was stable in the long run. In his youth, Mario tried to become a self-taught auto mechanic since it was one of his passions. Despite the intense disagreements between both men, my mother was able to maintain the tradition of visiting them every summer. We would spend the hot summer months there, from January to March, just before the new school year would start.

After the sun set, the large trees and exuberant vegetation gave the old house a macabre feel. It was the kind of place where you could imagine the most disturbing horror story playing out. The old man made sure to instill this in our innocent, childish thoughts.

One night during the beginning of the eighties, after a hot and muggy day in the country, Grandpa, Mom, and Uncle Mario drank mate while engaging in an enthusiastic conversation. We were in the kitchen, the run-down, rough-hewn shack. It was dark inside, and at times even gloomy. Soot had impregnated the roof and left little space to see the wooden beams that held up the battered roofing, deteriorated by the inexorable passing of time, rain, and sun. Mi cousin Patricia and I washed our feet in the aluminum basin next to the rustic stove. There, in that ramshackle room, we listened to the adult's conversation with interest, interrupted at times by hoots of laughter as they told their stories.

"That's when I said to don Segundo, 'Where are you taking that bottle?,' the old man looked at me in an acerbic manner but didn't say a word. I knew he was going to Villa Mercedes to stock up on red wine. The problem is he always comes back with an empty bottle because he drinks it all on the way home," said Mario between loud sips of the metal straw in his piping hot cup of mate.

"Wine has something that only the gods can comprehend and the devil ignores. But in the end it ends up making even the sanest person go crazy," replied my grandfather.

The glow from the fire in the stove and the candles on the table illuminated the pale faces of the people in the room. It was a few minutes before ten o'clock at night. After we had drunk our customary glass of fresh milk and eaten some bread, my mom spoke.

"Alright children, finish eating and go to bed. It's way too late for you to be up." That was a common phrase in the conservative culture of the eighties and nineties.

At twelve years old, my childhood mind ran amuck, inventing and creating horror stories based on the movies that I often saw on TV.

I remember that I wanted to see a ghost, though the idea frightened me to no end. How would I react? I was sure I'd faint or at least pee my pants, I thought.

To be honest, I couldn't even comprehend what could happen to me in that situation. Maybe my cousin, two years older than me, had similar thoughts running through her head related to close encounters with people who had passed on.

For some reason, I don't remember why, that year I had gone to the countryside determined to learn more about my grandmother. She had died young, when my mother was still a child, so, to our misfortune, neither her daughter nor I, her grandson, had ever gotten to know her.

I would ask every relative I saw about my grandmother. I was convinced that one of them would say, "Yes, your grandmother was beautiful, tall, with light-colored eyes and thick hair. In fact, I have a picture of her here with me. Take it." To my chagrin, this never happened, never mind how much I wanted and hoped it would.

"Now that you've finished eating and washing your feet, off to bed. Take this candle with you to light the way."

"Auntie, it's really dark outside and there's a lot of wind. The candle isn't going to make it," Patricia replied, uncertainty coloring her voice. Just like me, she was terrified of the idea of walking out into the dark with a simple candle to light our way.

"Shield it with your hand and you'll be fine," said my mom, not letting us question her instructions.

The distance between the kitchen shack, the dining room and bedrooms wasn't too far, but it was far enough to provoke terror in young and innocent souls such as ours at that age. Sixty feet was long enough to give us heart attacks because the dark hid the unknown. The incessant chirping of crickets and the swaying of tree branches in the wind crated a sinister and disturbing atmosphere.

Just before staring the walk to the bedrooms, we stopped for a few seconds in the old kitchen's doorway. We shut the door in a timid manner and looked at each other with fear in our eyes, ready to run the gauntlet. It was a frightening path, a walkway of unending anguish.

"Patricia, please, don't let the candle go out, or else I'm running back." She smiled though she was nervous but didn't hesitate to start walking.

"Don't even think about it because I'll faint on the spot." Patricia was an intelligent girl with a beautiful smile and beautiful, almond-shaped brown eyes.

Her long brown hair fell down to her waist. She was taller than I was, but at the moment, it seemed like she as more afraid than me.

We started to walk at a slow pace. As we did, we kept our eyes glued to the small, flickering flame that rose from the candle. Every so often we would look at each other, trying to find something that would mitigate the unpleasant feeling of dread.

After what felt like an eternity, we made it to the main house's door. We pushed it open using little strength and it let out the loud creak it always made. The silence of the still night amplified the sound two-fold, which just made our unease crank up a notch. It was a perturbing sound.

We made it into the hallway. The door slammed shut behind us, making us jump. Whether it was intentional or not, the door was designed in such a way that it always swung shut.

We kept walking. We stopped in front of the dining room door. The effect was the same. Despite its crude fabrication, it also always swung shut. We walked along the hallway to the doorway that led to the bedrooms. We'd been assigned to one of them. It had two beds separated by a screen. The candle illuminated a space about six feet around it, which was just enough to see by.

The rough wooden floors made a characteristic sound when trod upon, generating even more unease in our fearful mind, pumped up on adrenaline due to the situation. We left the candle burning on the dresser so we could change and get into the narrow beds.

We could see the beams a few feet above us holding up the old and worn shingles on the roof. Sometimes the thick beams acted as worn catwalks for huge mice that would start to fight amongst themselves as soon as the lights went out. At times they even fell and bounced off the beds. These aggressive rodents had long lost any fear they might have held towards humans.

The next few minutes passed in silence. Without saying a word, I saw my roommate lie down and pull the covers up over her head. Then, with a deep breath, in less than a second, I blew out the small flame. I too pulled the covers over my head as a way to suppress my deepest fears, now so close to the surface because of the dark.

That year I had been given a watch during the end-of-school-year party. It had two buttons, and one of them turned a small light on and off. It was the closest thing to electrical lighting that we had had for a few weeks as we'd been there for over a month at the time, using candles or lanterns in my grandfather's house.

The heat of the summer night wouldn't let me sleep, so I played with the watch under the covers, hoping that at some point I'd fall asleep. Without warning, a strange and new sensation came over me. It felt like something was watching me from the doorway. Never in my short life had I felt anything like that. I didn't pay much attention to it at first, but soon after it was almost impossible for me to concentrate on what I was doing. I stopped playing with my watch in an instant. Almost without noticing, I found myself trying to listen harder so I could figure out if the sensation was just something in my mind or if something strange was in truth happening out there.

I heard footsteps in the room, the tell-tale sound of the floor giving them away. Lying on the bed, my feet faced the door. The steps started to move in a calm but sure manner towards my pillow. They were loud and deep. I supposed that whoever wore shoes big enough to make such a racket would have to be taller than most. I had ruled out my cousin, Patricia, since she was as scared as I was during our walk there. I didn't think much of it for several seconds. It didn't matter to me at all who it was. I pretended to be asleep, rolling over to get comfortable. In my mind it was a clear sign to the person in the room that they should stop with their intention of playing a possible joke on me since it wouldn't work. I even added a light snore to and a deep breath to my act, still on my side with my head facing the wall.

"I'm sure it's Uncle Mario, trying to play a prank on me. Nothing out of the ordinary," I thought to convince myself. Even so, there were some things that wouldn't let me believe it one hundred percent. It boiled down to a few questions that I couldn't answer. Why had he decided to leave the kitchen, leaving behind the mate that he had been drinking a few minutes earlier? Besides, how had he gotten into the house without making any noise? I knew the three doors that had to be opened to reach our bedroom creaked loud enough to be heard several feet away.

How was it possible that the sound of steps had started at the bedroom doorway? What happened to the normal noise that should have been heard from the front door to the bedroom door? No, there were several things that for sure didn't add up. Something wasn't right.

All these thoughts left me feeling unsure, paralyzed by the fear that engulfed me. I didn't understand what was happening and started to sweat buckets. In the meantime, the steps kept moving forward until they reached my pillow. Once there, I heard several repeated knocks on the floor under the bed. It sounded like they were made by the heel of whoever wore the heavy foot ware that caused the stepping noise. It was eerie beyond belief and I couldn't have been more terrified than at that moment.

The sound seemed sinister and unstoppable. In an instant, I heard heavy breathing coming closer and closer to where my head lay on the pillow. The disturbing sound came down from its original height to just above my head, still covered by the blanket.

I couldn't believe what was happening. I started to feel desperate. The first thing I that occurred to me in the midst of my panic was to reach out and hit whoever was breathing like that square in the face. I hesitated because, if it was Uncle Mario, I'd probably break the scant few teeth he had left and then I'd be in trouble. That made me change my mind and I decided I'd rather scream until I was out of breath. Yes, that would make my mom and Grandpa come rescue us and catch the old mechanic with green eyes and a wizard's face right in the act.

The agitated breathing of the entity wouldn't stop. I was still frozen with fright. The uncertainty of not knowing what would happen next ate at my insides. Having decided to scream with all my might, I took a deep breath in, but when I exhaled to scream, I couldn't. The scream died in my throat and I couldn't make a sound. I knew that wasn't normal, and I was at the mercy of whatever this thing decided to do to me. I didn't have any other options but to lie still and expect the worst. In my innocence, I even thought that this was the end. In the back of my mind I was also surprised because my cousin Patricia hadn't moved a muscle and her bed was less than three feet from mine. How could she not hear anything?

A few minutes later, it seemed that the entity decided to desist in its actions. I think that it wanted me to see it or at least acknowledge its presence. After waiting it out, it must have been obvious that my intentions were quite different from the ones it had. I tried to ignore it altogether.

Then I heard it start to move away with great slowness, carrying out its actions in inverse order. First, the agitated breathing went away and then the steps sounded again, this time walking towards the bedroom door. I still can't explain it to this day, but once it reached the doorway, I felt that it turned to look at me one last time, as if it were saying, "Fine, if you don't want to see me, I'll leave."

A few seconds later, the entity's energy dissipated, taking with it some of my fear. I sat up in bed as if I had been spring-loaded and let loose a deafening scream of terror like none I'd ever made before or since. I made such a ruckus that it wasn't long before my mom reached the bedroom.

As she walked into the house, the three doors creaked as loud as rusty gates. That just furthered my conviction that the strange visit I'd had wasn't normal.

"What's the matter? Why all the fuss?" asked my mom as she entered the room. Her mouth was covered with an improvised scarf and she held a candle in her hand.

"Mom, someone was in the room. Was it one of you?" I asked between sobs.

"What are you talking about? We're drinking mate. If we go out into the night just like that, we could get a stiff neck." It's a common old-wives' tale that the abrupt change in temperature could cause that. "You made me risk that to come see what you were screaming about."

"Patricia, did you hear what I did?" She had just sat up in bed, her face lined with fear.

"Yeah, I heard everything. It's true. Someone was in the room with us. It wasn't Uncle Mario, was it?"

"No, you're uncle has been with us the entire time. He hasn't left the kitchen at all. How could he? He's drinking mate too. Besides, we were all sure that both of you were asleep." My mom couldn't understand what had happened. The next day no one spoke about it. We still had to spend several more nights in the new house of terrors.

A few weeks later, back in Santiago, my young mother confessed that at the time she'd felt as much or more panic than my cousin and me.

"I couldn't show that I was scared, or else everything would have all gone to heck."

Five years later, in the same room, she would live through a similar experience to the one we had. The difference was that she was able to react and shine her flashlight towards where the eerie sounds came from. The loud steps and agitated breathing almost gave her a heart attack.

"I turned on my flashlight and pointed at where the sounds came from. I screamed but couldn't see a thing. There wasn't anything there to see," she later recounted.

Many years later, on one of the rare occasions when we were at the house at the same time, my Uncle Miguel, one of my mom's older brothers, and I were talking about it. I led him to the room where the events took place and told him the story.

It was around noon when we stood in the dark room, destroyed in part by the effects of time, erosion, and termites. Together we looked for any possible mementos that might have been left behind in the ruins.

"This is where I had my first paranormal experience when I was twelve. Uncle, I wanted to ask you something I've always wondered about. Do you know where and why Grandma died?"

He sighed and after a few moments looked up to study the old roofing tiles. Then he lowered his gaze to the floor and started to tell me part of the story that took place during the fifties.

"Your grandmother's physical ailments started in this room. She became sick with aggressive pneumonia. She couldn't breathe right. We would help her to get up and move about, but she was in a bad way. She'd shuffle her feet when she tried to walk since, despite her limitations, she had always been a strong, active, and independent woman. She insisted on trying to follow her day-to-day routine as if nothing were the matter. When we were at last able to take her to the hospital, it was too late." As soon as he finished I had no doubt about who it was that had visited my mother and me. The question was, though, had she visited us or had we invaded her space?

Without having asked him, Uncle Miguel took the time to describe in detail what had happened in that room decades before when Grandma passed away. I appreciated the gesture because, despite the many years since then, thinking about his mother's passing had to have been hard on him. For me, it answered a question I had has since I was a kid.

The young mother had moved on though she was worried - and she was right to - that her absence would have an adverse affect her children, in particular Uncle Ramón, who was a very young six months old at the time.

Enthralled by the tale my Uncle Miguel, an old army officer, related to me, I didn't speak for a few moments. In my mind I asked several questions. Why do people who die in a tragic and unexpected manner cling to the places where their emotions were strongest? Do they not realize that their lives have ended? Or is there an external force that stops them from leaving?

If that's the case, what happened to the process where God is supposed to take them to their place of eternal rest? Is a person just an insignificant material conduit that transports a miniscule portion of divine light whose purpose is to make a brief stop during a long celestial voyage, only to return to the vastness of space?

Could it be that we're like butterflies or bees that go from flower to flower where each flower is a different dimension? What is the meaning of existence as we know it? In actuality, how much free will do we have in our physical and spiritual existence? What does the Bible say about it? Could there be one or more parallel universes? And if so, who lives in them? How does time work in them? Does it move forward or backward?

There were too many questions that flew through my mind, and I've carried them with me since.

Philosophy is the study of these and other questions that deserve to be studied. As the years went by, I had more than enough time to investigate, though, as with the majority of people absorbed by the whirlwind of work and everyday life in a society that rejects in-depth thinking, I never looked into it. Metaphysics was one of the curious and intriguing subjects that lit up the shadows of my existential thinking.

CHAPTER III: THE SPIRITS' CLINIC

At age thirty-five, my life had gone down a materialistic, superficial, and individualistic road, just like the morals, principles, and social model that had been ingrained in me required. I didn't think about anything other than making money and living comfortably, believing that it was how I'd find what had been described as happiness. In some manner, I wanted to achieve what I felt that life had deprived me of as a child. I didn't consider myself obsessed with money, but I turned it into an objective that, to tell the truth, wasn't what I wanted. However, it was expected of me so that I could satisfy the demands of a society that was harsh in its judgements of economic "conformity. In other words, it was a dumb fear, worrying about what others would say and the madness of showing off my fleeting and arrogant "success" in front of my friends and acquaintances.

Many will think about having a textbook family that lives in comfort, though they'll never admit to wanting to maintain appearances based on needless sacrifice, foolish pride, and an incessant need for social approval. I understand, because they are ashamed to accept that they grew up in underprivileged neighborhoods and faced the lack of several necessities at a time when things weren't going so well in both social and economic aspects. But, please, what kind of madness is the fictitious idea of social mobility when the vast majority of people can lose in a couple of months of unemployment what it took them years or decades to build up? Then they become another statistic in our country's growing list of people who live in poverty. Maintaining the current system going based on debt is a cruel and heartless strategy.

The entire social model is based on hypocrisy that does no more than propagate the delusion of well-being of an obtuse and ailing society whose weak structure was exposed thanks to the appearance of COVID-19.

The unhealthy belief of promoting competition in all aspects turned us into materialistic machines, upholding "values" and "principles" of a destructive neoliberal society that, under the premise of privatizing, reducing taxes, and eliminating the social state, made the rich richer and the poor poorer. It created a fantasy to placate the potential discontent and eternal frustrations of those caught in its web. Everything was, in theory, necessary to carry out a prosperous social and economic restructuring driven by the military regime at the time who saw in Friedman's model the solution to the critical structural problems the nation faced before and after the 1973 military coup. It was an adverse scenario, exacerbated by the global recession at the beginning of the eighties.

I know that my ideas may sound like the repeated rhetoric of left leaning, even revolutionary, political claims. "Irrefutable reality," ten percent of the population would say, in particular those with red tendencies. Another ten percent, those on the blue side of the political spectrum, would say, "Lies, as it was a necessary intervention." Nothing could be further from that. If it is true that, from our earthy perspective, it makes sense to condemn loathsome creations and actions, it is no less true that, in essence, from the spiritual perspective, that condemnation lacks value and substance.

To recap, when someone does skydiving, they know there's the possibility that they may die, but they are conscious of the risk. If they die, they can't complain and they accept that. To live life on Earth as we know it is tantamount to jumping out of a plane.

At the beginning of the 2000s, my economic future looked wonderful. I had formed a company with a couple of partners who I met by chance and in whom I came to trust with blind faith. They had shown me loyalty beyond reproach, but, as my grandfather would say, not all that glitters is gold. A few years later I would be betrayed in the deepest way possible, proving the truth behind the saying.

I suffered the indignities of betrayal when the fledgling technology firm that we built together started to grow and the revenue became more generous. Greed has a thousand disguises to hide itself from the unsuspecting.

My supposed friends took advantage of the deplorable state I was in regarding my health and tricked Graciela into signing a fictitious sale where I gave them my part in the business. According to the books and "gentleman's honor," my part was worth about two million dollars, which vanished into thin air.

Despite the callousness of this action, I didn't think it was such a big deal because, more than the money, for me, a young and ingenuous man, what mattered was the challenges inherent in an working toward an interesting objective. In a way, that company had been that objective. Perhaps in the eyes of individualistic conscience it might seem incomprehensible, but just participating in the creation and growth of the company left me with various and unforgettable life lessons that are priceless.

We started with around three million Chilean pesos (a little less than eight thousand dollars today) but our administration of the company was so efficient that we made three million dollars in the sixth fiscal year after starting, which was extraordinary growth. The best part was that we were able to reward our workers for their loyalty and commitment to the company by means of salaries and benefits never before given by companies in the field. In addition, our competitors started to copy our offers, sacrificing a part of the juicy profit margins that they were pocketing before our debut in the market.

Judging by the company's financial results, the three founders of the project made a great team, but their greed and excessive confidence were the death sentence to my participation.

I assume that everything was calculated by one of them in a cold and precise manner. He was a complicated, dark, and cunning man. I don't judge him. Just like me, he had worked his way up from the bottom. The difference is that he loved money more than he did himself. The other person, from a wealthy family, turned out to be pretty unreadable and pretty far from transparent with his intentions, which served to bring about the fraud they perpetuated.

In 2004, Graciela was diagnosed with pancreatic cancer. We had three small children, one of which, the youngest, was born with Asperger's syndrome. Asperger's was a new diagnosis for the time and for the most part unknown to the specialists in the country. This brought with it several challenges to our daily lives. None of the neurologists that we visited wanted to venture a diagnosis. "The child is too young for a precise medical opinion. We need to wait," they said. Because of all this, we had started to consider emigrating to Canada. There, we were told, the resources and experience in regards to childhood developmental problems were much more advanced.

Several of the sources we consulted said that our son's condition was due to genetic predisposition aggravated by the vaccines administered at a young age, which had an excess of mercury or undefined toxic components, brought to light by non-official scientific studies. I could never rule these elements out because there were also credible precedents that cast doubt on the reliability of these vaccines.

For example, after sending soldiers to United Nations missions for years, the Italian government started to suspect that the vaccines they gave to their new recruits weren't one hundred percent safe. This was because after receiving the six inoculations required by the UN, the soldiers would return to their country with serious oncological and immunological problems.

They then formed a scientific health commission to do an in-depth review the content of said immunizations. They were surprised to find out that the vaccines had sixty-three toxins they couldn't identify and so made a public complaint that caused innumerable losses to the pharmaceutical industry. I don't know what the consequences of the Italian's audacity were, but they must have paid a high cost for it. Some experts say that no one can go up against that industry because, according to them, it's even more powerful than the mafia and drug cartels. Who knows?

Something similar happened with an Austrian scientific report that detected pig genes and other toxic components that, according to some non-official sources, were used to stop the propagation of both porcine and bird flu.

The attention deficit and hyperactivity of our child didn't allow us a respite to regenerate the scant physical and emotional energy that we, as a couple, had left. We had started our middle-class family project way too young. This then became another fundamental reason that drove my need to produce more money and ensure the well-being of my family, thinking that it would mitigate our suffering in some part. We kept thinking that outside of Chile we could get the urgent help that we required, but in the end it remained a pipe dream due to the bonds of hearth and home.

It was a feeling impregnated with internal rage, since even trying to show a certain level of calm, Graciela's anguish and anxiety were making the cracks in the emotional ties between us grow.

It wasn't easy for either of us as young parents to accept the condition of our son. We asked ourselves what could have happened, considering the two older boys were born healthy.

Uncertainty, lack of information and immaturity contributed in no small measure to the feelings of confusion, impotence, and sadness that didn't help me at all in making good decisions. I had become a ticking bomb that was destined to explode. I didn't know when but it was just a matter of time.

Graciela's cancer was another bucket of cold water for our family. Faced with an imminent and unavoidable surgery, the doctor, just hours before the operation, let us know that her probability of survival was not much more than fifty percent. When I heard that her odds were the same as flipping a coin, it shattered me. I couldn't believe that my life partner would be in a life-or-death fight during her surgery when a few weeks ago she had been fine. I was overcome by fear though I did my best not to show it. However, I lived that profound pain deep within my inner solitude.

The tragic information hit me so hard that I was in shock. As best I could, I made it to a nearby park to decompress. At that time, it wasn't easy for me to cry. Even so, the emotional impact was brutal. I couldn't hold it in, so I sat down under the shade of a tree, lifted my face to the sky and cried until I was worn out. Some passers-by watched the sad scene out of the corners of their eyes.

It was one of the most distressing moments that I have experienced in all my life. If luck wasn't on our side, our life project, the one that I had placed all bets on and had been built through hard work, would come crashing down around our ears.

Thousands of tragic thoughts ran through my mind in a few seconds. I imagined my young children crying over their deceased mother, resting in a coffin. Hopelessness is a cruel and unpleasant companion.

I meditated for a few hours, waiting for the decisive moment that we were about to go through. Sitting in the park, wrapped in my misery, I clenched my fists and my teeth before gathering myself and walking back to the hospital, just in time for the surgery.

I was there two and a half hours, pacing back and forth, sometimes sitting down, trying in vain to control the anxiety that gnawed at my insides. I waited for the surgeon to come out of the operating room and tell me the results. I think the stress of not knowing if she had survived or not generated such tension in me that to this day still I don't have the words to describe what I felt at the time.

The waiting room chair became the single support I had so I could maintain my dignity. I had to hold on to something tangible. Those were the longest hours of my life.

At long last the experienced surgeon came out of the operating room, sweating as if he'd run a marathon, and his face red as the ripest tomato. His face showed the extreme pressure he was under.

"Doctor, how is she? Please let me know she's alright!" I exclaimed with desperation. He lowered his face mask, took off his cap, and, after a long sigh, finally spoke. I felt like it took him forever to get to that point.

"Don't worry, your wife is fine." The stocky doctor hugged me like a child. I shivered so much I felt like I was in a refrigerator. I was so nervous that my jaw dropped and I couldn't stop the tears from falling again, but this time they were tears of happiness. I dried them with a handkerchief that I had with me and that I hadn't stopped holding since I got to the park. Graciela had cheated death.

"You have no idea how grateful I am! If there is a higher being, may you be in his favor! I don't have words enough to thank you for this.

"Don't worry, it'll all be alright. You should go home and give your children the good news. Go rest and relax. I know you need it.

After a firm handshake I left, headed to the parking lot to get my car. Once seated inside, I rested my head on the steering wheel and crossed my arms, trying to decompress my fears and the enormous stress I had been under. I stayed in that position until I fell asleep. When I woke up, it was dark. I felt as if the Schumann resonance had reached its peak. Time sped up. I turned on the motor and drove home.

Days went by. Some friends called me to ask about the situation, worried about us. I spoke to them as if I were a zombie, product of several day's insomnia. My body had been affected by the tremendous impact of both stress and strain.

To my misfortune, our problems didn't end there. In May of the next year the biggest tragedy in the history of Chile's army occurred. Forty-four recruits and a junior officer died on the foothills of the Antuco volcano in the south of Chile. In all, forty-five people died. Unfortunate political and administrative decisions taken by the people in charge at the time sealed the fate of several small-town youths.

Among the recruits was Cristian, a dear friend, the youngest son of Aunt Sonia, my mother's best friend from childhood. They had both lived through poverty together during more than a decade.

Cristian had a very peculiar relationship with my grandfather. They had become great friends starting when Cristian was little and lived with his family in my mother's country home next to my grandfather's old house.

When Grandpa died, Cristian was five years old. At the funeral, the young boy grabbed on to a chestnut tree and cried inconsolably. No one could cheer him up. Being so small, his wracking sobs grabbed everyone's attention. They asked him what was the matter. He told everyone that he had seen a man with huge wings and who was dressed in white take Grandpa in his arms. Everyone was surprised by the young boy's innocent reply.

There was a large age gap between him and me. He was fourteen years younger than I. I had taken care of him as a baby, and he was like a brother to me. His mother called me the same day that the tragedy occurred. I didn't hesitate to travel from Santiago to the south to at least be there to give her support and help in whatever way I could.

Two days had passed since the tragedy and no one had any news about the soldiers who, according to the news, were still missing. They had been caught by the white wind, a very unusual meteorological phenomenon, while they were doing training exercises up in the mountain. Their light gear didn't stand a chance against the ferocious gusts of wind and snow that hit their defenseless bodies like needles. They fell victim to the extreme cold and died of hypothermia on the ice-cold mountainside.

Aunt Sonia lived the agony of not knowing the fate of her second son together with the rest of the recruits' families of the 18th regiment in the cold city of Los Angeles. No one knew what had happened to the unfortunate youths. No matter how much the families demanded, none of the authorities present would give any information about their loved ones.

We'll never forget those moments of stress, uncertainty, and sadness.

After at long last finding out about their fatal end, and as a product of the stress I was under during the wait, my body started to cramp all over to the point that I had trouble walking. It had been just about a year since we had gone through the Dantesque experience of Graciela's fight with cancer and now I had to face Cristian's death. My luck didn't seem to be improving in the least.

The bad emotional streak I was living through was merciless. My nervous system had suffered relentless punishment, but I still wasn't aware of the consequences of having ignored the effects of those disconcerting blows.

I never looked into getting psychological help, much less psychiatric help, after so many events, even though I felt I needed it. The prejudices and social stigmas associated with it made me dismiss the possibility out of hand, which just paved the road to the cliff I would later fall off of.

That same year, my parents' sentimental relationship was on the rocks. My mother had started to think about definite separation from my father. She had been planning on living in the south of the country. She decided to settle down for the rest of her life in the land where she was born.

One Sunday over lunch at her house, we were talking about her plans. She had been talking about a project for some time and she took the opportunity to mention it again. It involved a partnership with two other people. I didn't know them, but she assured me that they were honorable and trustworthy people.

"You know how bad things are between your father and I, right?" she said in a low voice.

"Yes, but I thought you were willing to work things out. Or am I wrong?" I replied before taking a sip of hot soup.

"He always wants to stick his nose in everything and I'm done with him," she replied.

"So what are you going to do?"

"I want to go to Los Angeles. I already have a house there. I just need to set up a business so that I can make some money and live independently because your father pays for everything here, you know." Her expression lacked conviction, though. I knew that, deep down, she wasn't convinced.

"But what kind of business would you set up there? There aren't many jobs, and it would be even harder for you since you're almost sixty," I replied, trying to curb her apparent enthusiasm. She had always been stubborn and reticent of showing her true feelings, more so to her closest friends and family. I had always thought this stemmed from having lost her mother at such a young age.

"I have two possible partners for an interesting project that we could start there. They want to talk to you and I'd like you to listen to them. They want to know if you could finance part of the project, but only if you think it's good. There's no pressure," said my mother, her eyes shining.

I grew up watching this woman sew clothes in her old sewing machine, straining her eyesight by staying up until all hours of the night, and suffering intense breakdowns, all so that she could provide food for her two small children. How could I refuse to help her with her project? It was time for me to pay her back for everything she'd done.

I agreed to finance the majority of the project. The sole condition was that I would be the person in charge of the business's finances, and the income would be split eighty-twenty, proportional to the initial investments made.

Though she considered those people her friends, under no circumstance was I going to risk leaving money in the hands of people I didn't know. With time, it became apparent that it had been a wise decision. My idea was that once the business could stand on its own, I would give my share to my mother as a way to thank her for her years of unending sacrifice.

At the time, money wasn't a problem. I had a good job and my business was flourishing and had been giving excellent results for some time.

The following week I met with the prospective partners. I wanted to know the details about this business venture. When I met them, I noticed they both had strange personalities. The first thing I did was ask to see the financial projection to make sure that the business was viable. When I saw the numbers, they seemed reasonable. The investment could be recovered in a decent amount of time.

They talked about their past experience in the field and assured me that it wasn't the first time that they had led a successful project of the same magnitude.

"We have everything working in our favor. Your mother has known us for a long time and knows that we're responsible and take things seriously. We'll make a lot of money," one of them said. My reaction was to think that as long as she was happy and had enough to live on, that would be enough.

There was a possibility that things wouldn't go well, of course, but the combined enthusiasm of my mother and her would-be partners was contagious. During the beginning of the nineties I had lived in Los Angeles, a commuter town (even the native Angelinos called it that), and so I thought I knew enough about its night life. However, there was one variable that I hadn't considered, and that was that it had been at least a decade since I had lived there. Everything had changed in the interim.

Not long after starting and contrary to what they had said, my mother's partners started to show their lack of skill in managing this project. They had said they were experts in the entertainment industry, specializing in night clubs for young adults. That's when the project became a living hell that I couldn't escape from.

Administrative problems cropped up everywhere and became insurmountable. We started bleeding money. Without a doubt, it had been one of the worst decisions that I had made, caught up by my emotions instead of using the cold light of rationality. Without knowing it, my head had already gone down the path towards disaster. I still hadn't realized what a grave mistake it had been. There was little to nothing I could do to stop the runaway train that had started its course and I had no other option but to hang on until it reached the inevitable end and either derailed or crashed.

Pressure and stress overwhelmed me. Just the thought of the eventual failure of the dream I had built as a means to thank my mother had a merciless effect on my health. Several times I found myself stumbling about as I were drunk and my nervous system was on the brink of collapsing due to the strain, but there was no way out. I had frequent dizzy spells. I also often forgot things, and through it all, shed mor than a couple of tears for no apparent reason. My intuition told me that the project would go belly up and there was no way to avoid it.

The warm-up to the worst part of the experience arrived. My mother's partners decided to quit one day when I faced them to tell them that they had lied to us, that they had no idea what they were doing.

"This is terrible. We've spent money that we don't have and the returns are a disaster. We need to make a radical change now, otherwise we're going to go down the tubes," I exclaimed during an improvised meeting with my mother's partner and the personnel we'd hired.

"Daniel, businesses take time. You can't make such a harsh statement when we've only been open for a month. Besides, your condition was that you'd be in charge of finances, not the logistics or the technical side, which is what we're in charge of," said one of the partners.

"Because I'm in charge of finances is the exact reason that I don't plan on throwing more money away, so I'm demanding we make a change now, before it's too late and we won't be able to. None of the auspicious scenarios that you presented on paper have come about," I replied, my anger showing. The shocked workers just looked on at the passionate and heated dialogue.

"Fine. If you're going to be involved with everything, then we have nothing more to do here. We quit. Here are the keys. You can take care of everything now. Is that what you want?" From his tone of voice, I knew that the older of the two partners wasn't going to move an inch from the commercial strategy that they had implemented. Without a doubt, they were testing my then unyielding pride, and I wasn't about to allow that.

"Fine. If that's your decision, then there's nothing left to say. Let my mother know that you won't be working with us anymore."

One of the bartenders who had been listening to the unpleasant conversation spoke up. "Mr. Daniel, you're right. They don't know what they're doing. I have more than ten years of experience in this field and we, all of the workers, have been witnesses to their inexperience and horrible decisions. They don't know anything about the business and they don't know the city. Mistakes were made starting on the first day, but we thought it was prudent to not voice our opinions, since we're not paid for that. If you want to continue with this business, we'll help you out, even if you can't pay us for a time. We want this to work so that we can have stable employment and we're willing to do what it takes. We've already talked about this and we're all in agreement." The rest of the personnel applauded the young woman's speech. The amount of determination and generosity I saw in her was such that I had a hard time - again -hiding the tear that rolled down my cheek. In that exact moment I realized that my feelings were overwhelmed. Everything made me sad, which was the polar opposite of my otherwise serious personality. It was another sign of what was to come.

"Thank you so much for your support. It means a lot. They're not bad people; they just misjudged what they could do in this undertaking. I don't think it's fair that you should work without pay. It's not necessary and I won't accept it, but I will be frank. If things don't turn around during the next month, we won't be able to keep the doors open. That being said, let's get to it."

My mother's partners were shocked into silence. I don't think they ever imagined something like what they had seen would happen. They took their belongings and walked out the front door, under the disapproving gaze of everyone else there.

We worked together during the next few weeks to try to get the project on its feet, but the demands that I was under were inhuman. At that pace, my energy took a nosedive, as did my spirits. I had to juggle four different aspects: my family, my full-time job, my technology company and now the night club, the latter in a city about three hundred seventy-five miles from where I lived. I made the six-hour trip every Friday, stayed there Saturday and came back on Sunday. I'd arrive in Santiago exhausted. Only a lunatic could have agreed to such a demanding schedule.

One day, I fainted in the back of the club. I tried to cover it up as I felt that I couldn't show any degree of weakness at all to the people who trusted in me and my unwavering strength. After all, I had always tried to be Superman to my family. I was the cornerstone, the person they all looked to for answers when there was a complex problem that needed to be solved.

In my mind, I always thought that I had a ready and effective answer for everything. Time would prove how wrong I was. It was clear that I was far from being someone strong. On the contrary, I was sailing in a paper skiff over an artificial lagune that was emptying itself at a rapid pace and that would soon take me right into the maw of the whirlpool were it drained, down the unending and disastrous precipice. The most tragic part was that I didn't know it and so I continued on without a stop, oblivious to what would happen. I placed all my trust, without limitations, on an ever more precarious vehicle that was my physical and psychological integrity at the moment.

Everything has a limit, though. Time makes sure that all debts are paid in the end, and when a person's vehicle breaks down, it does so in a total and complete manner. Well, it was my turn and nothing could stop the count countdown that I had started. The inevitable disaster struck and I had no way to avoid it.

It was a normal afternoon when I was at my full-time job, around three p.m. After a relaxing lunch I sat down at my desk to continue the work that had been left unfinished before I went out to eat.

I remember that I had been testing the information security systems that the company I worked for had in place. I had heard the people in charge of IT say that they were spying on users and the websites they visited. They had already found out about certain "unsavory" preferences of some of the C-suite executives in the company. My foolhardy IT colleagues had no idea how delicate this subject was in a legal sense since it was tantamount to invasion of privacy. They didn't seem to care about the risk they were taking.

Disputes between the IT specialists and us. the program developers, were common. Everyone defended their own interests and, when called out by management, would throw blame on each other.

Sometimes in jest and sometimes in earnest, a few of my coworkers and I would try to access sites of dubious moral quality to see if we were also victims of their espionage. The cold war between our two factions had been going on for a while. Our efforts were aimed at verifying if our actions were detected, blocked, and then reported by people who were supposed to be competent professionals. Our goal was to obtain any evidence that would demonstrate the contrary and then show their incompetence to the upper management. I don't know when or why I devolved into that infantile and absurd behavior. I couldn't understand it. Maybe it was another unequivocal sign of my impending mental and physical breakdown.

Out of nowhere, an overwhelming impulse came over my and I got up from my desk and walked to the parking lot. Without letting anyone know, I got in my car and started the drive towards the Sol highway, the road that leads to San Antonio in the central Chilean coast and to my then home in Maipú. I remember I sped along without any control, reaching speeds of over one hundred thirty miles per hour.

The other motorists along the way just watched me whiz by along the road. Their cars seemed to be wind-up toys next to mine as it shot like a bullet along the highway. No one could stop me. I wanted to end my life, and that was a fact. I was totally out of control, out of my mind. I had decided to crash head on into the first wall that crossed my path and end everything. Thousands of thoughts wandered through my head, none of them coherent.

I couldn't explain what happened to me. I just felt anxiety so brutal that, according to me, the sole possible way to end it was by my death. Maybe that's what everyone who contemplates suicide feels when they make that decision and no one knows why.

The driver of a huge truck laid into his horn as he saw me pass by. It was so loud and stentorian that in that instant it felt like I had woken up from a bad dream. I realized that I had been in a kind of trance less than three hundred feet away from ramming the car into a bridge's containment wall near Quince Mountain in Maipú. My subconscious had already decided that this would be the wall I would crash into.

Thank heavens for the truck's horn. I took control of myself again and looked at the speedometer. I avoided the wall by mere inches and got back on the highway at a hundred and thirty miles per hour. The trucker and his infernally loud horn had saved my life.

As I tried to regain my composure, I started to cry and nothing could console me. Frenzied tears welled up over and over again from my eyes. I slowed down to a normal speed and I made it home somehow, though I'm not quite sure how I did it. I parked the car and got out as if I were sleepwalking. I half-heartedly knocked on the door, waiting for someone to open it. Graciela answered the door. She didn't understand what I was doing there.

"What happened? Why are you home so early?" she asked.

Without a word, I headed to the master bedroom and threw myself face down on the bed. My gaze was vacant; my mind lost to reality or coherent thought.

I felt that something in me changed forever that day, though I don't know what. My brain had entered into a lethargic phase that it wouldn't be easy to wake up from. Shattered thoughts floated in my head and I still couldn't comprehend what they were. I just experienced a new and strange sensation in my skull. Never, in my then thirty-five years of existence, had I felt anything in any fashion similar.

It was as if my cerebral cortex had detached and was floating free.

Weird and senseless thoughts had taken over my consciousness. I observed things around me and couldn't make sense of my surroundings or the people near me.

Graciela tried to talk to me several times to find out what happened, but all I heard was babbling. I tried to take control of the situation but at this point it was out of my control. Not even the worn-out sentiment "do it for your children, they need you," had any meaning for me.

No, at the moment not even thoughts of my children were enough. I couldn't see any way out or how to get rid of the tremendous weight that I felt crushing my body and that didn't let me feel motivation, hope, empathy or have a reason to live. It was the end.

As the days went by, my health took a turn for the worse. I couldn't go to work, so we went to see a specialist. After he saw me, he didn't think it was that bad and just recommended a couple of days to rest.

Despite my perturbed aspect and visible disorientation, within me there were mental states where I could think with clarity. I knew that something wasn't at all right with me but, to my misfortune, I couldn't find the words to explain it.

I wasn't happy with the results of the visit to the first psychiatrist. The almost uncontrollable urges to end my life remained, so we managed to get a referral to someone else. Otherwise, I was sure that the outcome could be fatal.

We must have visited at least three psychiatrists. None of them took more than fifteen minutes to try to understand, guide, or much less try to solve my case. None of them figured out what was happening to me. A pessimist would say that being in Chile, and everything had to be done "as best possible, within our means."

A friend suggested that we visit a famous Chilean psychiatrist. In those days, she didn't have the best reputation when it came to ethics.

"When I was depressed, she stopped me from killing myself. Take Daniel to see her. She's the one person who can pull him out of this," a worried friend of Graciela suggested.

The doctor's name was María Luisa Cordero, an expert is psychiatry, who had been judged in a harsh manner when she found herself involved in an very publicized and high-visibility case in volving falsified medical licenses. This had gained her trial proceedings and the possibility of a suspended license.

Even so, we trusted in our friend and went to see her. Her clinic was on Salvador Avenue in Santiago. The mental image I had of her was just of a medical professional that had had seen the limelight and wanted to be a part of it.

Speaking of which, that reminds me of a story from 2003 when

Ricardo Álvarez, director of the Miriam Hernández Singing School, called me to her office to ask about some information. I had attended a singing workshop there, and I wanted to see if I met the requirements of the Channel 13 Talent School, the channel's first reality TV show.

"How old are you, Daniel?"

"I'm thirty-three."

"Do you have any children?"

"Yes, three, and I'm married."

"Wow, you don't look your age! You look much younger, maybe late twenties. You have a certain charisma that's an exact fit for what we want for a new TV show, but your age and the fact that you're married and have children complicates things. I would have liked to suggest you as a candidate to work with us in this challenge."

"Are you kidding me? If what you say is true, you should know that not even if I were single and had no kids would I have considered getting into entertainment. I think that I don't have enough talent. Besides, I already have a degree and my job. What you suggest means to start over from zero. In my case, I'd say it's impossible.

"I thought you could be a part of the Channel 13 Talent School, but your age works against you, plus your kids and even worse, being married, won't work for the reality show.

At three p. m. on the dot Graciela and I sat in the doctor's waiting room. My condition worsened every day and I looked to be in a sorry state. I could have fallen off a cliff without reacting and I found it difficult to walk. The doctor's vast experience didn't take long to show.

"But how is it that you're in this situation? You look like a dead man walking," the specialist said. She lowered her glasses to the tip of her nose, looking me over from head to foot without believing what she was seeing: a human being turned into a zombie, without expression, unkempt, and, in the eyes of everyone around me, at death's door.

"Doctor, please help him. We don't know what to do. We've already seen several specialists and none of them have helped," Graciela begged. I didn't have the strength to talk and sat there slack jawed.

I paid attention in a sporadic manner to the conversation held between them. The headache I felt centered between my brows was unbearable; apathy wouldn't let me do or feel anything. Everything was indifferent to me.

"He's in a very bad state. Tell me, what happened?" asked the doctor. I had seen her on TV before, where she always had a somewhat belligerent and irreverent attitude. When I heard her talk, I realized that her real personality was far from the insensitive persona that she showed in her public appearances.

While Graciela and the doctor talked, my attention wandered to the roof or the floor of the clinic. Indescribable anxiety had taken over me, provoking shivers that wracked my body which I couldn't control.

"I want to leave. I don't want to be here!" I exclaimed.

"Calm down, we're here to help. You're suffering from severe depression and need help as soon as possible."

I didn't reply. I didn't pay much attention to her and sunk back into my self-absorption. I heard a few words here and there of what Graciela said. I think that she talked about most of the events that had been the apparent causes of my current situation. I understood some phrases, though most of her words were no more than babbling to my ears.

After listening to her story, the doctor prescribed a significant amount of medication. It felt more like what someone with a terminal illness would need to take, and I almost felt like that was my case. In any event, if it was for my good, I was willing to do what was needed so I could get out of the fog of my depression.

"Come see me in two weeks. If things haven't improved, we'll have to take more drastic measures," said the doctor.

"Doctor, I'm not sure that I'll be able to give my husband so many medications according to the schedule. We have three children with attention deficit and I can't handle them on my own. And now that he's sick, I'm afraid that things are even more complicated," Graciela said with worry in her voice.

"Ask your family for help if needed, but you need to follow the prescription to the letter. Try it for now and if things don't work out, come back and we'll see what else we can do," she reiterated.

"Yes, doctor."

"This is my personal phone number Call me whenever you need to; it's no trouble for me to take the call," said the experienced professional.

The next two weeks went by after our visit to the doctor. It was no use. The plan failed and the treatment couldn't be carried out with the necessary discipline. My sad and taciturn state as well as the inordinate amount of activities Graciela had with the kids were a preemptive strike against the strict therapy.

We were back in her office before the two weeks were up. My situation was worse. There was no way we could follow the treatment at home, much less expect a successful outcome. I had stopped eating, and my face looked even more worn and my body even more ragged.

"This is bad, very bad. It doesn't look like we'll be able to get any results with you at home," said the doctor, shaking her head from side to side and pressing her lips together in disapproval.

"What other options do we have then? I don't know what else to do," replied Graciela. She was well aware of the enormous problem my sudden illness represented.

"Is there anyone else that can take care of him so that he can follow the treatment as prescribed? A parent, friend, someone you can trust?"

"No, there's no one else."

When the white-robed doctor heard that, she thought for a few seconds. She stood up and looked out the window. "Then the only alternative I can see is to admit Daniel to the hospital so that he can follow his treatment. If no change is made, I don't even want to think about what could happen. I know of a place that I can recommend. It's a comprehensive rehab center. They can give him the medication and take care of his basic needs. They'll treat him well," she suggested.

Graciela looked at me as if asking what to do. I was skeptical because at the socioeconomic and academic level that I lived in the stigma associated with what the doctor proposed was an undeniable risk. However, I was sure that there were no other options. It was either this or definite disaster, maybe even my death.

I was open to the idea despite the social stigma that was sure to follow and the blow to my independence that such a move entailed. I had never depended on anyone or anything. I always felt like a hawk, strong and vigorous, but now I was a sparrow, mangy, malnourished, and missing feathers. I nodded. I wasn't convinced it was the best idea but I was resigned to it.

The die was cast. I had to go to a rehab clinic. I had no idea what fate had in store for me there. I'd never been to any place in the least bit similar. I hadn't even seen one from the outside.

"Alright, doctor, if that's what you think is best, we'll go with it," replied Graciela.

"Good. You need to be there tonight at 9:00 p. m. This is the address. I'll see you there. Take clothes and personal hygiene products, and they'll give you more information once you get there. Have faith; Daniel will get better. We'll do everything we can," said the doctor to Graciela. She handed her a folded sheet of paper with the address and a few handwritten notes.

"Thank you, doctor. You have no idea how much this means to us. We're at the end of our rope. He's extremely important to us. Our children and I have had a hard time watching him deteriorate like this. It's been so hard for our family."

We were at the address given to us at 9:00 p. m. on the dot. It was a large building, similar to an old colonial estate house. The small exterior windows must have limited the amount of sunlight that could get in during the day.

The doctor arrived before us so that she could give the night-shift nurses and paramedics their instructions.

"Everyone, this is Daniel and Graciela, his wife. Here, these are the medicines he needs to take and at what times. His diagnosis is severe stress with signs of depression. Please keep me up to date with his progress. You can use the established methods of communication. He's in a bad way but I'm sure you'll do your best to help him," said the worried doctor.

"We'll start on this right away," replied the charge nurse. He received the paper that the doctor had written the prescription on.

"Good. We'll leave Daniel in your hands." Then she turned and spoke to me. "Daniel don't worry. We'll get you through this."

The charge nurse read every line of the prescription and started to prepare the insipid cocktail of pills I had to take. In a few moments, he handed me a glass of water so I could take the first dose of medication. The doctor's final orders had been given.

"You'll start to feel better with this. Now say your goodbyes and we can show you to your room," instructed the nurse.

Obeying the young man like a child left at daycare would, I kissed my wife and said my goodbyes before leaving them behind. Both women watched me for a moment and then turned to leave.

As soon as they had gone, the nurse spoke again. "Alright, follow me. I'll show you to your new home."

With my duffel bag in hand, we walked down a long corridor with several doorways that led to different rooms in the old house. The silence was oppressive. The only minor sounds that interrupted the silence of the corridor were caused by patients, who I could only see in silhouette, timidly moving about in their rooms.

We soon reached the room I had been assigned to. It was a cozy room with wooden floors. The temperature was pleasant as well. A tall wooden door opened into the room from the outside hallway. In it sat a twin-sized bed with a night table to one side and an old, brown fabric armchair on the other. There was a dresser against one wall with a small TV set on top of it. Further from the bed was an old, free-standing wooden wardrobe made up of three sections.

A skylight in the middle of the roof about 9 feet off the ground caught my attention. I didn't recall ever having seen a room designed like that before.

On the farthest wall, two doors with windows and a curtain led to an improvised emergency access. The nurse moved the curtain a bit to check the locks on the doors. When he did, I saw what looked to be metal lockers on the other side of the doors.

"This is the paramedic's locker room. They change there, and sometimes talk and laugh there, so don't worry if you hear noise coming from behind the door," informed the nurse.

I took my time to lay down on the bed while the nurse put things away on the furniture. He gave me some last indications as he did so.

"We already know that your health is the top priority. Curfew is at 10:00 p. m. and breakfast is at 8:00," he explained. I didn't say a word. I didn't feel like trying to put words together. The medication had started to take effect, and my mind was starting to wind down. It was a pleasant feeling.

"The bathroom is through here, just across from your room. Alright, I'll leave you alone so you can rest. I'll see you in the morning. Please, try to go to sleep early." He walked out of the room and closed the door with care.

After he left I stripped down to my underwear. I put on the pajamas that Graciela had packed for me. The bed had white sheets and a gray comforter on it. I lay down on my back and covered myself with them, then stared at the ceiling.

There wasn't a single thought in my head. It felt like my brain had been emptied out, memories included. Nothing remained, in particular nothing that would make me abandon the calm state I had entered, so pleasant and far removed from the stress of my job or my life in general, agitated, cannibalistic, wretched, and insensible as it was. That life had made me a slave, and I knew it was time to escape.

Slavery has always existed, but that doesn't mean that we shouldn't criticize it, much less give up on breaking its chains. In a world where few inherit privileges and, in consequence, suppress others, it's difficult to eliminate the succession since it's the slaves who betray their peers.

I lay there, silent and with my eyes unfocused. Some minutes had passed since the nurse had left. Without warning, I started to hear small steps moving over the wooden floor. They walked toward the end of the bed, coming from the old and imposing wardrobe a few feet away.

I didn't move. I lay still. I didn't even bother to lift my head to see what was the matter. I stayed in the same position I had taken when I first lay down on the bed. I continued to look at the ceiling, and as I did, I decided to begin a retrospection on my life.

I started to go over every milestone in my life, like it's said happens before death. I was on board with what would happen. After all, I was convinced that I wouldn't make it out of that problem alive. I was resigned to the idea that I would never see my loved ones again.

The sound of the steps made me think that they were made by a cat but, as the minutes went by, I asked myself what would a cat be doing in the room? This was supposed to be place where patients with complicated diagnoses of different manners were treated. It wasn't the most adequate place to have animals, though truth be told, if the sounds did belong to a cat, it would have made me happy. I had always had an affinity toward animals. But there was one unsettling detail: the dense, dry, and penetrating sound on the floor seemed more like it was made by some kind of footwear, not by bare feet or paws.

I remained concentrated on the nooks and crannies of the ceiling and on the slippery thoughts about the life I had lived. Just then, the feet that made the perturbing tapping on the floor jumped up onto the bed. I felt the pressure on the mattress with each step, pulling on the comforter in a subtle and intermittent manner just like when a small animal walks on the bed.

The delicate steps started to move up alongside my body until they reached my elbow. I looked over with just my eyes. I didn't move a single muscle of my face or neck. I was so relaxed and comfortable, and expected to see the silhouette of some domestic animal.

What would it look like? It has to be a chubby cat, one that always gets too many treats, I thought. I've seen felines that look like literal furballs but are always affectionate. Some are like that when their owners love and take care of them.

Before I could blink, two small people stood next to me. Yes, two small people about the size of a two-liter bottle of soda. One of them was thin, had a wide smile, prominent mustache and a thin, even pointy, nose. He was dressed with a brown shirt and black pants with suspenders. They'd both abandoned all caution and appeared without any shyness or insecurity in front of my surprised, though resigned, eyes. Who were they? What were they doing there? How was it possible that people this small could exist?

I felt perplexed for a moment, and then I convinced myself that it was a side effect of the drugs that I had taken moments before. After processing their presence, I studied them in great detail. I had nothing to lose and even less to be afraid of. I had reached the limits of rational thought and was convinced that I would never recover my normal mental state. I was sure I had already lost my marbles. If what I saw was real, I would have quite a tale to tell my skeptic acquaintances. If not, then the incredible scene would be relegated to a casual tale to be told to friends over a drink in some bar in downtown Santiago.

The other elf had a burly figure and was of a similar height. He had gray hair, a thick beard, wide nose, and large eyes. He wore old-fashioned glasses, like the ones used by the aristocracy during the colonial period. He wore a shirt with black stripes and pants that looked like jeans. I couldn't see their shoes because of the angle of my head on the pillow, but from the noise they made when walking, they seemed to be made of leather. I had no intention of proving the authenticity of these impressive characters. I thought that they would in all probability run at the first sight of any movement I might make, so I settled for what I could see.

It was strange that I didn't feel any fear, didn't give this surprising occurrence the importance or dramatism that I would have under other circumstances. Believing that you've gone insane allows a person to accept things that they would consider frightening to the extreme if they were in their right mind.

The unexpected visitors had their arms around their waists, as if they were the best of friends. They didn't once take their eyes off me, not even for an instant. Their tiny fingers pointed at my face and they chortled with laughter. From my perspective, I could just see the amusement on their faces. I couldn't hear their laughter at all. To me, it looked like they were making fun of my dismal situation.

I still believed that this was all a product of the drugs that I had been given. There was no way that this could be something other than a drug-induced hallucination. I remained calm and didn't question their continued presence. There was nothing else I could do.

After all, I had already hit rock bottom and, for all intents and purposes, it was like being in a harmless dream that I didn't want to wake up from. I had never seen anything like it, as I had never done any kind of drugs. In school we were taught that drugs would ruin our lives and be the end of us as people if we started using them. As an adult, I had taken the time to study their implications and risks when I volunteered at a safe house for drug addicts.

My suicidal thoughts weren't constant. There were moments within the fog of my depression when I would try without success to suppress them. I was also certain that, if faced with a moment where my life was in extreme danger, I wouldn't do anything to save it. My mood was in a never-ending downward spiral that I had no clue how to escape from. My consciousness was directed by something I couldn't control, clouding my judgement, making me crash into an invisible wall full of doors whose locks and puzzles were impossible to solve and open. The result is death, a suicidal wish, the essence of a voluntary end that in reality is involuntary as you depend on luck to survive.

In other words, I would be saved if a miracle happened at the moment I made the cruel decision to end my life by my own hands. Otherwise I'd be condemned to disappear from the face of the earth.

The tiny men stood there no longer than ten minutes, watching and laughing at me, not showing any remorse at all for their conduct. They then turned and retraced their steps, walking over the bed and jumping to the floor before walking back to where I believed they had come from, somewhere near the old wardrobe.

As they left, I turned my head again to look at the ceiling, just as I had been doing since my recent arrival at the facility. The overwhelming odor of alcohol started to emanate from somewhere in the room, though I couldn't figure out where the source was. I supposed that the tiny men might have overturned on accident a bottle of wine left forgotten in a corner by one of the previous tenants.

Moments later the air became thick with a heavy fog. It was so dense that I had trouble making out the furniture in the room. It was at that point when I adjusted the pillow so I could change the inclination of my head and observe the room around me in comfort. There was no way I could have imagined what would happen next, which I later came to call "the show."

If the drugs were the cause of this hallucinations, there was no way that I would refuse to enjoy their bounties, as well as everything that was about to be revealed.

I didn't show the smallest hint of surprise when I started to see the figures of several people from different ages walking through the door and into the room. My eyes had adapted to the darkness and the mist, and I could tell from the way they dressed they weren't from my time. They started a slow and subdued pilgrimage toward me. Some wore clothes from the colonial era. Others wore clothing styles popular in the sixties, seventies, and even eighties. Most of them had serious expressions, as if they were going to meet someone or something they needed to treat with care.

Convincing my mind that everything I saw was another hallucination was the best, though at the same time the worst, strategy that I could come up with. I managed to remain calm through it all, even forgetting at times why I was there. It was like watching a 3D movie in a theater where I was the single lucky spectator. On one hand, it appeared to be so real. On the other, in my mind I had convinced myself that it was an optic illusion projected by my brain under the influence of the blessed medications I had been given.

Something inside me told me that the figures wanted me to see them. But it didn't stop there. They wanted me to feel their energy and spirits. The following scene was a very common one: family and friends visiting a sick loved one in the hospital. In this case, I was the unfortunate patient that they had come to visit.

I felt with extreme clarity how two of the improbable visitors sat on the right side of the bed, almost touching my legs.

I sensed how the mattress bowed under their weight in each place where they sat. All of them stared at me, a group of men, women, and children standing around the bed. Each one waited their turn as the first one touched my face, head, or arms. It was a wonderful, indescribable, blessed experience.

At times I felt as if I were in a trance. They all made me feel more special than I ever had in my life. Never had I seen so many people worried about me, and I couldn't contain the happiness and gratitude I felt.

After watching me for an instant, the figure before me bent down to kiss my forehead with utmost tenderness. As they did, I could feel their energy: subtle electric currents that gave off small sparkles of light surrounding the contours of its body. They seemed to be in a different dimension but somehow existed side by side at the same time. Everything felt sort of like a ritual that I didn't want to miss.

Each kiss I received transformed into a shot of medicine to my soul, something that only a dying man could feel.

Even as I attributed the experience to the incredible effects of the medicine I had taken, I realized that it was difficult for me to believe such a religious experience could be true. I just let myself flow with it.

In my jumbled thoughts I tried to make sense of the show. However, I didn't make the slightest effort to try to understand what was going on. Each figure made an electric crackling sound as it kissed my forehead, similar to the sound made by high voltage wires or the persistent buzzing of bees hovering around flowers.

I then noticed something. Unlike the rest, one of the figures was ignoring me. Instead of moving with seeming free will as the others did, it made the same repetitive motion over and over. It was a young woman who wore a white apron. She would walk from the door to the dresser and look for something. I had no idea what it could be. Then she would search the nightstand on the right-hand side of the bed.

The loving kisses on my forehead didn't stop while I observed her actions. I was still surprised at how many people were there. I couldn't say a specific number; there were so many. It seemed like the night would end before they were all done. In the off chance that it was real, I wondered if these beings had been sent by a divine entity, or if they were a spontaneous expression guided by a celestial force. If so, who? Who would make the effort to send spirits to help me and why?

The most incredible part was yet to come. A beautiful young woman in her early twenties appeared among the host of people around me. She looked glamorous, dressed in a sparkling green tunic, and wore a large turban decorated with a gleaming medallion of the same color as her dress.

She took her time walking toward me before stopping a few short inches from my face. She watched me for a few moments that I wished would never end.

I was entranced by the penetrating color of her large, green eyes, her golden blond hair, and her skin white as milk. I felt even more out of it than I had been, almost as if I had left my body. I regained my will to live, but not in my dimension. I wanted to live where this glorious being did.

She kissed my forehead with supernatural tenderness, expressing the sweetest love I had ever felt. It was without malice or eroticism, just purity in its maximum expression. I had never seen anyone like her. Her smile was so sweet that still to this day I don't have the words to describe it. I wanted to break the silence and say so many things, but her gaze left me speechless. I heard her words of encouragement in my mind. She didn't move her lips as she spoke to me. "Don't worry, everything will be all right. You'll soon be out of here. Rest for now."

    I had never had a previous experience with telepathy, and this was extraordinary. Her siren's voice, heady and beautifully soft, made me feel as if I were in the halls of Olympus. It was an extraordinary gift. There aren't enough diamonds or gold on the planet to pay her back for that wonderful moment.

    If Heaven came down to earth, it would be in her presence. As I couldn't string any words together, I tried to reply with my mind. I managed to form a simple thought: "Thank you. Thank you and whoever sent you to me."

    She smiled and we continued to gaze at each other. Her hand caressed my cheek and I wondered what kind of blessing this was, that so many people were here, worried about me, and helping me to climb out of the hole I had fallen into? Did it have anything to do with the clinic, where so many people went in search of elusive healing?

    How was it possible that I deserved this gift, if my spiritual malnourishment was such that I was for all intents and purposes at death's door? After I had been a superficial, materialistic, individualistic, and critical person for so long? Someone empty, lacking in celestial awareness, who had lived his life as if it were the only one that existed? No, I couldn't understand it.

    Each being who kissed my forehead would leave a few minutes later, walking through the wall behind the headboard. She, however, stayed with me far longer than I believed I was worthy of. I didn't want to see her go. The peace she had given me was something I had never experienced in all my time on earth. However, deep inside, I was sure that I would never see her again. Beauty isn't eternal, and the gift of her presence was nothing more than a fortuitous event for me.

    After kissing my forehead a second time, she ran her hand through my hair. I felt the effects of the electric field around her all over my skull. I couldn't tear my gaze away from her large, deep green eyes. The humming from her body didn't stop, becoming louder and more intense the closer she came.

    For a few moments I felt as if I were levitating. I almost believed that I was one of them. I have no doubt that the experience was the closest I would ever come to paradise. Before leaving, she looked at me one last time. I could smell her perfume, see the purity in her kind face, and was left blind and breathless from the sight.

In an instant, my love for her was total and complete. After one last sigh, she left along with the rest, moving through the wall behind the bed and disappearing from my sight.

I wasn't sure, but I felt that the visitors weren't there just for me but had come to see all the patients in the clinic. Exhausted in both mind and body, I lost the fight and moments later fell into a deep sleep.

At eight a. m. sharp the next morning there was a knock on the door. I opened my sleepy eyes, still groggy from the drugs.

"Good morning, Daniel. Time to wake up and have breakfast," said a feminine voice from the other side of the door. I woke up with my spirits low, so I didn't reply or open the door.

"Sorry, can I come in? I have your medication with me and it's time for you to take it." Without waiting for me to say a word, a woman wasted no time in entering the room. She had a glass of water in one hand and a disposable paper cup with an assortment of pills in the other. She sat on the bed and started to talk to me.

"Come now, you can't stay in bed all day. You have to get up. There are some people outside waiting for you to talk to them," she insisted with an authoritative voice.

"Leave me alone. I don't want to talk to anyone. You don't know what I'm going through, and you never will. Just go!" I raised my voice in anger. It had been a long time since I had spoken to anyone like that.

She stood up, put her hands on her hips and said, "Stop looking at me like that, trying to act so tough. Get dressed and go have breakfast. We don't tolerate problematic patients here."

With great reluctance I got up and got dressed in front of her, obeying her terse commands. Then I headed to the bathroom, where I splashed my face with water. I looked at my reflection in the mirror, and I saw a man whose expression reflected unguarded sadness. I felt intense pain in my throat, not caused by a disease, but rather from a tense knot of accumulated anguish. My swollen eyes and droopy lids exacerbated the gloomy countenance I saw.

Never had I seen myself looking like that. It wasn't me in the mirror. An involuntary tear slid down my cheek. I dried it with a bit of toilet paper and then walked out to see what awaited me in the spirit's clinic.

The bothersome woman who had gone to wake me up still waited for me in my room. When she saw me, she took me by the arm and guided me down the corridor to the dining hall, located about sixty feet from my room.

My total lack of interest in meeting the other patients was more than clear. In any event, I still looked around, taking in a spacious dining area where several people sat and ate their breakfast. Plates were piled high with food, including bread, jam, cheese, and eggs. The tablecloths were bright and spotless, and the cloth napkins had elegant, embroidered edges.

The bothersome woman next to me smiled at the people there and hurried to introduce me. "Hi everyone, how are you? This is Daniel. He arrived last night and is going to have breakfast with us." Some of the men and women of differing ages paid attention to her; others reacted with total indifference.

"Daniel, come sit by Fernando and Marcela. He's a doctor and she's a psychologist. Daniel is an engineer. I'm sure you'll find a lot of things to talk about. You make a pretty interesting multidisciplinary group," she commented with a permanent smile. Then she left and headed toward the garden.

I sat down with subtle shyness and an unfocused gaze. Marcela, the psychologist, tried to talk to me. Fernando drank his coffee, his expression pensive.

"What are you here for?" Marcela inquired. She was a young woman, in her mid-twenties, with light brown hair, fair skin, large, honey-colored eyes, and full lips. She had an athletic build and was almost as tall as I was, just shy of five feet ten inches. Her delicate and educated tone of voice caught my attention. She seemed to be calm, from which I deduced that her stay would in all probability be over soon.

Her gaze settled on me. My eyes were still heavy from sleep. At times I tried to smile at her, though in vain, and at others my attention wandered to the design of the room. It took a few minutes for me to reply.

"I'm here because I've been diagnosed with depression and couldn't follow the treatment at home." I lowered my arms to rest them on my lap, lacing my fingers together. I didn't want to eat, so I ignored the cup of milk and the fresh baked bread on the table. On top of the persistent melancholy, everything that had happened that night weighed heavy on my mind both due to how unbelievable it was and the flurry of questions that cropped up in my thoughts like weeds.

"Are you married?" she asked in a calm tone. Her face was beautiful. It was apparent that she took care of her skin. Her youth made her seem angelic but her mischievous smile gave her an air of malice.

Before replying, I adjusted the wooden chair I sat in. Though I was somewhat uncomfortable with the question, I answered it anyway. "Yes, I have three young children and an exceptional wife waiting for me at home." The question seemed to be somewhat invasive.

"Are you in love with her?"

That phrase was enough for me to know that there was something wrong with Marcela. My sensitivity was cranked up to the maximum. It seemed that there was an ulterior motive behind the question. In my present emotional state I had no intention of being politically correct as I would have been during normal circumstances. "Why do you ask? As far as I know, I'm not your patient, or am I?"

She lowered her gaze and thought for a few seconds. "I like to ask things that might be complicated for others to answer, in particular when they can't give a convincing answer," she said. Her white teeth flashed in a fleeting, mocking smile.

"I don't feel like answering that. I want to be left alone, don't you?" I let my annoyance show. I wasn't prepared for her answer.

"Alright, don't get mad. It's just a question. We're getting to know each other and I don't want to be your enemy." She lowered her head, her smile disappearing like a UFO behind the clouds.

Marcela knew that her question struck a nerve. I ate little of the food that was on the table. I took a few sips of water to dispel the dry mouth the medication caused.

The young woman looked at me. It felt like she still wanted to ask another question. Meanwhile, Fernando, the doctor, looked at us from the corner of his eye and didn't say a word. Silence took over as none of us spoke.

I felt that the nosey psychologist's conversation had been unpleasant enough that I was happy with its abrupt end. We had met a few moments ago and, according to me, she has tried to pry into personal matters.

In an emotional state like mine, sensitivity becomes more pronounced and communication becomes a complex process that can break down fast when one of the participants feels offended or uncomfortable.

I don't know if it was an effect of the medication or because of my depression, most of the time couldn't focus on anything. My mind was blank, and my physical aspect was that of someone stripped of the will to take care of myself, unmotivated and gloomy.

After a period of silence, my mind wandered from the table that I shared with my fellow patients. I was lost in thought when the bothersome woman came back and pulled me back to reality.

"Daniel, are you ready? Did you finish your breakfast? How was it? Let's go outside. The garden is a stunning place. Would you like to see it? Did you know that there's a pool you can swim in when it gets too hot? You'll see."

We walked to the garden together, leaving through the front door. The garden was an oasis: spacious, brimming with vibrant flowers, well-cared-for trees, and manicured lawns where relaxing was a luxury.

Wooden benches were scattered throughout the garden. There, patients could sit and listen to the birds singing. Further ahead, a trellis covered in red and white grapes created shade for a gaming table used for the patient's entertainment.

We stopped in front of a tree. Next to it there was a large clay pot with giant elephant ear plants and red geraniums. The annoying woman looked at me with her ever-present smile.

"I bet you've never been in a place as relaxing as this. What do you think about the pot in front of you? It's one of the clinic's treasures. It's said that it was brought from the town of Pomaire."

I didn't reply. I was lucky to have had the strength to get up and have breakfast and answer a few of Marcela's questions before walking there. I didn't have any energy left over to engage in a conversation. I felt numb.

"It's fine if you don't want to talk to me. I understand. I'll do the talking so buckle up, because I'm a talker," she affirmed, all the while smiling. She was a dark-skinned, thin woman with curly black hair and brown eyes. Her face was rounded and she had a curvaceous figure. I didn't want to listen to her anymore but, in a strange way, her presence calmed my anxiety. At this point I was sure that the drugs had altered my already unstable nervous system.

At times I would get muscle spasms. My body would shake from head to toe and an overpowering urge to run away would take hold. She noticed and held me until the shaking subsided. The sensation of her body against mine helped me regain my composure. I needed that contact with urgency, no matter how fleeting it was.

"Are you alright, Daniel? Do you want to go back to your room?"

"Yes. I don't want to be here anymore. I need to lie down and rest," I replied, my voice shaky.

"Ok, let's go back. That's enough for today, but tomorrow you need to spend more time out here. You can't stay cooped up in your room all the time. It's not good for you," the bothersome woman said. That was my official nickname for her. I didn't have the energy to ask her for her name. She'd soon let me know anyway.

We got back to my room and I sat on the bed. The bothersome woman sat next to me. Once more, for no apparent reason, tears started to fall from my swollen eyes. Depression is an incomprehensible and uncontrollable physiological state. It's not just feeling down. It's also a generalized physical malaise where even the smallest use of energy is an extraordinary effort, like living in a body the size of an elephant's but with the spirit of a human. Just moving a finger is enough to leave you exhausted.

"There, there, it's alright. Don't worry, you're with us now. Everything will work out," she comforted, holding me again and letting me rest my head on her shoulder.

Far from seeing any signs of recuperating, all I saw were signs that, to me, indicated that my stay there would be far longer than expected.

Suicide was still an ever-present thought. My mind seemed to become more and more disconnected from my body. I felt awful.

While the bothersome woman tried to comfort me, I remembered what I had seen last night. I thought about telling her but decided against it. There was no way she would believe me. I was sure that she's think I'd gone off the deep end, or at least, that she would see me as a small child who had suffered hallucination and needed to be taken care of, instead of the young adult and father that I was.

My energy levels went up and down as if they were attached to a light switch that someone kept flicking on and off, causing me mood swings. During one of the few moments where I felt stable, I managed to have a short conversation with her.

"Can I ask what's your name?"

"Oh, sure! I forgot. Really, I didn't tell you my name, Daniel? It's Carla and I'm a therapist specializing in helping people with depression."

"What kind of patients does the clinic receive?"

"We get people with depression, alcoholism, drug addiction, or people with slight mental disorders." From her response, I surmised that none of the patients there was in a better condition than I was. It wouldn't be easy to converse with them because of my deplorable condition and because they were in all likelihood as bad off or worse than I was.

I spent the rest of the day in my room. I slept a couple of hours, convinced that I could counter the unending sadness in some degree. However, each time I woke up, I wished I hadn't. Each time I woke up was a disappointment, in part because I didn't feel like doing anything and to top it off, the worrisome idea of suicide wandered through my mind like a ghost. Try as I might to get rid of it, at times it grew more intense and overwhelming. I thought that it was a matter of time before I made the final decision.

What drives a depressed person to go through with suicide? Having lived through a close situation, I can talk with surety about my particular frame of mind. I faced an existential and critical dilemma about humankind and its hypocritical society.

Psychologists say that our personalities are the masks we project to the world. In other words, we're not genuine or honest with those around us. In addition, some scientists say that each person tells at least three lies every ten minutes. That leads to the conclusion that humans are deceitful by nature. No one tells the truth. Even though these conclusions may be logical, for a person with depression, it's enough to make them want to disappear.

While depressed, a person can see these lies. For someone who is depressed, this very human behavior becomes a trap, an irreconcilable loss of hope for the world. The patient can't conceive such a degree of cynicism and hypocrisy in their loved ones and, in that condition, life loses total and absolute sense.

No one wants to live in a constant lie, much less those who are depressed. They analyze, just like true scientists, the smallest detail of their life and the people who are a part of it.

At times it may seem contradictory because they'd like to be spoken to with complete transparency. However, if they were spoken to that way, their suffering would be more painful as cruel reality is confirmed through the mouths of those around them.

In addition to a persistent physical malaise, a person with depression cannot find a way out of their situation. Then they observe their surroundings and think, "Well, even if I wanted to, I don't have the energy or the will to continue acting in this low-budget movie. No one can help me since they're lying actors who participate in the crude farse that I no longer want to be a part of. Besides, the set where everything happens means nothing to me. I don't even want to be here. If the world is a lie, what's the point of continuing to act in it?" For sure, there is no effective solution to the problem that doesn't consider medication.

Night fell, and with it came my now familiar cocktail of medication. A woman with a white apron came in at the specified schedule. She had a glass of water and a paper cup with several pills.

"How are you, Daniel? Here you are. Drink up and take them all," said the nurse on duty.

As I looked at her, I had no doubt that she was the same figure as the hologram that kept repeating last night. My jaw dropped. I tried to make sense out of the information that I had received so that I could analyze it and try to understand - at least in part - the jumbled-up puzzle that appeared before me.

"Why are you looking at me like that? I know I'm pretty, but it's not that surprising," she laughed. She appeared to be a cordial person who loved her job.

"How long have you worked here?" I asked after drinking the last drop of water to wash down one of the various pills. She smiled and looked up, placing her hand on her chin. She looked to be trying to remember events long past.

"It's got to be on about ten years," she said before getting back to the work she had to do.

"What's your usual routine in the patients' rooms? In this one, for example?" I continued. She was hard at work but again paused and looked at me from where she was standing.

"This is starting to feel like an interrogation. Do you by any chance work for a private security company or for the police?" she chuckled. After a sigh, she started to explain her job.

"My duties include making sure that the patients' medication is ready for them. I also check that the correct supplies are available in their rooms." I then understood why her hologram or energy field walked to and fro in the room, following her usual path.

I didn't want to talk to her about the show and the holograms. She wouldn't understand, so I decided to keep the unbelievable and strange tale to myself for another time.

I stayed quiet for a few seconds, not looking at anything in particular. She continued to clean and fix things on top of the dresser. After taking care of the night table, she turned to look at me.

"Had this ever happened to you before?" she asked. I came back to the present and replied.

"No. I never thought that I'd end up like this. I want to disappear and forget about everyone and everything."

My anguish provoked feelings of sympathy in her. She sat down next to me and took my hand.

"I understand more than you know. I lost my father due to depression. I miss him very much. He was the pilar of my family and part of my heart. You need to be strong and not give up if you want to live."

Sadness engulfed me. Tears flowed and we cried together. Then she went on. "Don't think that you're alone. We're here to look after you and help you. Let us do it before you take make any rash decisions. Don't go about thinking nonsense, and don't do anything drastic. Life is meant to be lived, with all the good and bad it has to offer. You still have a long way to go." She stayed with me for a couple of minutes, dried her tears, and then said goodbye. She had shared her words with me from the bottom of her heart. It was one of the most sincere conversations I'd had in a long time.

I got undressed and threw myself on the bed. The heat was unbearable, which is why I didn't cover myself with the sheets. A couple of hours went by until the clock showed ten p. m. I wasn't sure if last night's show would have a repeat performance. To be honest, my apathy was larger than any interest I might have had to be part of a new paranormal experience, no matter how entertaining or surprising it might be.

At ten thirty, just before the arrival of the holograms, I started to smell the repulsive aroma of alcohol. It was the same as the night before. I lay on my back on the bed. The room was dark. What little light there was came from the skylight in the roof.

Mist started to fill the room, repeating the same actions as the night before. However, one big difference was the absence of the little people. There was nothing to show they even existed. Some say that elves are servants of other spirits and are sent out as a decoy to test the waters. In my case, I supposed they had appeared to make sure that the spectator was able to withstand the great emotional burden of seeing the spirits in all their splendor.

A few minutes later the holograms showed themselves among the dense mist that filled the room.

Despite the large number of people, I saw that they weren't the same characters as the night before. There was no doubt, though, that they had the same intention of showing affection and kissing me on the forehead. They followed the same script. Some sat on the edge of the bed, making the mattress sag, as if they were flesh and blood people.

I was again surprised. I never imagined that the blessed event would happen twice.. I was happy it had as I had a second chance to observe the impressive and wondrous spectacle with more attention to detail.

A few minutes later, an old man with no legs appeared on my left. He had thin, white hear, a sharp nose, and large eyes. He looked at me with relative indifference. As a hologram, he floated above me, looked at me for a few seconds as if trying to recognize me. I wasn't the person he was looking for, and after making sure, he left the room without kissing me on the forehead. He floated through the wall behind the headboard just like the others had done.

I kept watching the show, growing more and more fascinated. I looked toward my right. After feeling a couple of people kiss my forehead, two of them, a man and a woman, caught my attention. They stood next to the bed, at about arm height.

They had their hands on the shoulders of a boy and a girl who looked to be siblings. They appeared to be between six and eight years old. The four of them looked to be posing for a beautiful, traditional family portrait from the colonial period based on the clothes they wore.

They watched me until the hologram of a young man entered the room. He must have been around twenty, more or less. His blond hair was his most eye-catching feature. He had light-colored eyes, dark skin, and a wiry build. He wore a white shirt, dark blue jeans, and white sneakers with black stripes and laces.. I could see him with total clarity. He came towards the bed but walked away from the family, stopping near my left foot. He looked confused, but as the minutes went by he seemed to accept the situation. I studied him as he stood there. He looked like he was trying to talk to me, but I couldn't hear him.

He made gestures at me, inviting me to stand up. I ignored him but he was so insistent that in the end I got up to see what he wanted.

It was hard for me to get up. The potent medications somewhat impaired my motor control. When I at last made it to my feet and walked over to him, he started to move his hands with inordinate speed. His lips moved without him making a sound. It was clear that he wanted to tell me something of importance but for some reason I couldn't hear him at all.

After watching his gestures for several minutes, I had an idea. It was the simplest form of communication I could think of.

"I'm sorry, but all I can do is see you. I can't hear a word you say even though I know you want to talk. Since I can see your eyes with crystal clarity, let's do this. I'll ask you some questions. If you close both eyes once, that means yes. If you do it twice in a row, that's no. Do you understand?" The young hologram closed his eyes once in affirmation. We'd found a simple way to communicate.

"Are you dead?" I asked without hesitation. His eyes closed once. He was conscious that his life wasn't part of this plane. He lifted his index finger and ran in across his throat, signaling death. With his right hand he pointed north, towards the garden of the huge house that had been converted into the clinic. He repeated the gesture three times to make sure that there was no doubt about what he was trying to convey. Even so, I still had questions. What did he mean by using the gestures for death and pointing to the garden?

"Did you die here, in this place?" His eyes closed once more, confirming that he had indeed died in the garden of the spirits' clinic.

At times he looked frustrated, wishing for a more efficient form of communication. However, that was almost impossible since I couldn't think of a more dynamic way to converse when I couldn't hear him.

Several minutes went by since we had agreed upon the simple protocol for communication between us. At one point he came closer to me and the summer heat contained in the room was diminished by the cold air that surrounded his hologram.

Everything was so unbelievable that at times I wasn't sure if what I was living was reality or a dream.

All of a sudden he interrupted our dialogue to float about three feet in the air. When he reached that height, he turned around to show me something on his narrow back. He used both thumbs to point to the design printed on the back of his shirt.

It was hard to see the black design in the darkness of the room, so it wasn't easy for me to figure out what it was. I think it might have been an eagle, but I wasn't sure. I gave him a thumbs up in approval.

"The design is beautiful. Congrats!" I exclaimed. He came back down to the floor and closed his eyes once. Though I wasn't surprised by these events, I was still incredulous. I still wondered if maybe the medications I was taking for my depression could be responsible for the hallucinations I experienced.

After asking him several questions, in my ignorance I thought of a question that I believed someone in his condition could answer. "Can I ask you a question that most humans wonder about?" The hologram looked at me with a quizzical expression on his face but still closed his eyes once to show he agreed. "Alright. I want you to answer me with honesty. Does God exist?" It was a simple question, but a profound one.

In an instant his eyes grew wide before he began a flurry of blinking, doing so at a rate that I hadn't seen during our entire conversation. It looked like he had something in his eyes and was trying to get it out. I don't know if he didn't want to reply or if something or someone wouldn't let him. I had once heard a cleric say that evil spirits will not answer questions about God. In this case, I didn't judge these spirits. If they were there it was because they had a mission to help heal others. I never saw a different intent. As an agnostic, I tried to find an explanation for everything based on what I knew about religion and its precepts. What else could I do? I didn't insist on getting an answer. It was obvious that I wouldn't get one from him, but why?

Both of us sat down on the floor near the bed. I asked him several more questions, none of which I remember well. The medications did their work and little by little I started to fall asleep. The conversation with the young spirit didn't change much so I decided to bring it to a close and go back to bed.

"Can we continue the conversation tomorrow? I'm sleepy and I want to go to bed," I said, rubbing my tired eyes. He blinked at me once. I think that he had also had enough.

I had hoped to see the young woman in the green tunic again, but she never showed up.

I went back to bed and covered myself with the blankets. I looked around the room one more time in case I had missed anything. I didn't know if more people would parade by my bed, waiting to kiss my forehead. I never found out if the show continued straight through the night until morning. I fell asleep before I knew it.

At eight a. m. sharp there was a knock on my door. It was Carla, the bothersome woman, with my morning dose of medication. We followed the same routine as before.

"Come on, Daniel, get up! Go take a shower and hurry up so you can go have breakfast. Marcela and Fernando are waiting for you in the cafeteria." The young therapist was in a good mood.

"If there's something I detest, it's falling into a routine," I muttered under my breath as I walked to the bathroom.

"I know, but that's what discipline is about. Besides, I need to tell you a secret. Ever since she met you, Marcela hasn't stopped asking about you. If you weren't married, I'm sure you'd have many more admirers confessing their undying love. What have you done to these women, ladies' man?" I heard her chuckle as I washed my hands. I didn't pay much attention to what she said. Maybe the bothersome woman thought that using the "heartbreaker" strategy would improve my mood and my self-esteem. It backfired though since I didn't even feel like taking a shower.

Soon we were in the dining hall. Just like the day before, I sat next to Marcela and Fernando. The day's menu was almost the same every day: cheese, butter, jam, eggs, and milk for breakfast, and legumes, spinach, and carrots, among other vegetables, for lunch.

My energy level also hadn't varied much. I didn't want to talk to anyone. I just wanted to be left alone, in silence and in peace.

This time Fernando was the talkative one. Marcela sat in silence with her elbows on the table and her hands holding her face. She wouldn't stop looking at me while I tried to ignore her.

I have to admit that her beauty made me nervous. Her big eyes observing me without wavering seemed like a gift to me. The day had dawned sunny, and high temperatures were expected.

"Did you sleep well, Daniel? Everything alright? I slept like a log," commented Fernando with a smile I hadn't seen before. Despite his enthusiasm, I didn't respond. Instead, I tried to process what had happened during the night. What could I do to find out if it was real or if I was hallucinating? It was an intriguing enigma, a complex problem I needed to resolve.

I wanted to figure it out even though I was otherwise disinterested in life. I was obsessed with finding out what it was about. Just knowing that it happened had been beautiful and incredible at the same time.

The young man with the eagle print had been the most communicative of the holograms. In my mind, that fact alone was enough to consider that he needed to be studied by itself. Who was he? What did he want from me?

"Do you know if anyone has died in this clinic?" I asked Fernando without preamble. The seasoned doctor, a former civil servant of the urgent primary care hospitals (SAPU, from its name in Spanish) in Santiago, opened his eyes wide in astonishment.

"I have no idea. Maybe the receiving nurse at the front desk could answer that question for you. Why do you ask?" he inquired.

I thought for a few moments before I replied. "No reason in particular. I was just curious. Sometimes life isn't as pretty as everyone says it is."

Fernando didn't hesitate to speak his mind. I saw that my question had discomfited him. "Don't tell me that you're thinking about taking your life. That would be the most illogical thing I've seen in all of my fifty years. A young man like yourself, with a successful career, a wife, and children. Your entire life is waiting for you. I'm sure I wouldn't understand it. I'd be a more probable candidate, but I'm not that dumb."

I got up and went to the reception area without saying a word. It was about ninety feet from where we sat in the dining hall. All this happened under the watchful gaze of Carla, the bothersome woman. She made a subtle attempt to stop me but thought better of it. Marcela tried to follow me but Fernando took hold of her arm and asked her to sit back down.

I walked with a decided pace to the front entryway. There I found myself face to face with the nurse on duty who was walking in the opposite direction. He was a thin man of medium height. His brown hair and fair skin hid his forty-something years well. I stopped him by placing my hand on his arm. He looked surprised but stopped and smiled, showing large, asymmetrical teeth. He seemed to be trained in how to act cordial and empathetic with the patients that had chosen the clinic to recover.

"Hi, how are you? I'm Daniel. Can I ask you a question?"

"Sure. What would you like to know?" the nurse replied with a commendable attitude of customer service.

I scratched the top of my head a bit. I had to think of the best way to phrase my question. I didn't want to look like I was crazy or I ran the risk of being forced to stay there longer than I should for a diagnosis like mine. I saw Carla spying on us from the end of the corridor. I knew that she wouldn't let me out of her sight for any reason. With some trepidation I took a deep breath and started to ask the confused and expectant nurse.

"In the history of this clinic, has anyone ever died here? Don't worry. I'm here because of severe clinical depression but I'm not planning on taking my life. It's not related to the question at all. Well, at least not at the moment."

He looked at me with a confused and curious expression. I saw worry reflected in his face. He mulled his answer over for a few moments before he decided to talk. "I don't know. I've worked here for ten years and I've never heard of a death. But I know who might be able to give you an answer. Ask Carmen, the cook. She's been here for more than thirty years."

After I heard his answer and thanked him for his help, I started the walk back down the same corridor I had taken to get there. Carla waited for me a few paces ahead. I had seen her walk towards me. As soon as I caught up with her she started to ask me about the improvised interrogation I had given the nurse.

"Why so inquisitive? You need to rest and not stress yourself. Now I know why you're in this state," she recriminated.

"I want to know where Carmen, the cook, is." I was determined to get my questions answered that same day. Who knew if later I would forget everything as a side effect of the drugs.

"Easy, she's cooking right now, making lunch, by the way. I don't think you should bother her. Why don't we go to the garden?" she suggested. I heard her but weaseled my way toward the kitchen. There were five people there, all of them wearing aprons and white caps. They all looked started by my unexpected entrance into a restricted area.

"Hey! I want to talk to Carmen, the cook who's been here the longest. Please, help me!"

They all looked at each other. Some of them shrugged at me. One of them, after seeing how determined I was, tried to calm me down.

"Carmen is changing in the bathroom. What do you want with her?" He was a young man of medium height, light colored eyes, and a little on the chubby side. He had a well-groomed beard, coffee-colored skin, and small hands.

"I need to find her. She's the one person who can help me to answer an important question. It's a matter of life or death."

"Alright, sir, don't worry. Just please wait for her outside. You shouldn't be in here. We do food prep here and you don't have the necessary sanitary requirements to be allowed in.

I saw Carla communicating with the young man behind my back. They were using signs. For the first time I felt like a patient in a mental institution. Some time ago I had seen some videos online where at critical moments nurses communicated among themselves with signs while they went along with the patients' demands until they were able to subdue them following necessary protocol. Most of the time the patient ended up strapped to a bed with a straight jacket, knocked out by tranquilizers until so that the nursing staff could get them under control.

Being surrounded by people who thought you were crazy, whether intentional or not, while you tried your hardest to show you weren't, has to be one of the worst nightmares a person can face. But how would someone deal with that? I reached the conclusion that it was impossible to prove your sanity. Either you died fighting or you gave in to what others thought of you. How many fortunes or inheritances had been stolen from their rightful owners, including by family, on this pretext?

To my great fortune, none of that happened. Just then, the woman I was looking for showed up just a few feet away. She was short, robust, had an ample smile and gray hair covered by the white nylon cap that prevented any stray hair from falling into the vats of food. She introduced herself in an unassuming manner.

"Hello, son. I'm Carmen. I was told that you were looking for me. Tell me, what can I do for you?" She walked up to me and took my right hand in hers. She started to stroke it with kindness as she waited for me to reply.

"Nice to meet you, Carmen. The receiving nurse told me that you might be able to answer a couple of questions I have." I don't know what expression she saw on my face, but in that second she squeezed my hand and we walked over to a nook on one side of the extensive kitchen. The small area felt like a confessional in a church.

"Tell me, son. If I can, I'll be happy to answer your questions" she said without hesitation. I looked her in the eyes, feeling sheepish, and I started talk.

"How long have you worked here at the clinic?"

"Ah, is that it? You had me worried. How can you ask me that? Can't you see that it would give away how old I am?" she laughed in a much more relaxed manner, showing the charisma of a happy and optimistic woman. "Well, I think it's been around thirty years, more or less. Why do you ask?" Carmen didn't suspect the real reason behind my question at all. In my paranoia, I thought that I needed to be extra cautious in each of my interactions with clinic staff, as the slightest indication of incoherence in my thinking might work against me, extending my stay there until who knows when.

"In all that time, have you seen or do you know of anyone who has died here?" I knew the question was a tricky one for her, but I was determined to get an answer.

"Oh, Lord, why do you want to know? I shouldn't answer that. No one wants anyone to die, let alone here." I realized that getting a straight answer from here wasn't going to be easy. I needed to take drastic measures. I changed my strategy and decided to take the plunge. I looked all around to see if anyone else was listening in on us. Once I was convinced we were alone, I spoke.

"You know, I have a secret I'd like to tell you, but if you don't help me, I can't share it. Listen, I just need to know if anyone died here. Please, I promise it's not because of anything bad. Besides, I'm here so that I can follow the recommended medication schedule to the letter, as I can't at home with three small children, all with ADHD. It was impossible."

She looked me in the eyes for a moment. After some thought, she replied.

"Well, yes, it has happened. Two people have died here. Please, don't let any of the other patients know. All of you have a tendency towards suicide."

"Was one of them a young man, around twenty, thin, with olive-skin and light-colored hair and eyes? Was he wearing a white shirt with an eagle printed on the back, jeans, and white sneakers with black stripes?"

As she heard my description her jaw dropped and she lifted her hands to cover her mouth. Her eyes looked like they were going to pop out of her head. She couldn't hide her surprise. I think that she might have thought that she was standing in front of a psychic or something like that.

"Claudio! Oh, my God, how can you know that? Who told you?

You've been here two days, and I've never seen you before in my life!" she exclaimed. She squeezed my hand again, this time harder than before. I couldn't believe that she knew who I was talking about.

"Claudio? Was that his name? He was in my room last night. He tried to talk to me but I couldn't hear him, just see him. He pointed toward the garden and swiped his finger across his throat, signaling his death" I related. The woman put a hand on her waist and the other on her head. She had a clear expression of bemusement on her face.

"Son, I can't believe that Claudio visited you. He came here because he was addicted to drugs. He was in a bad way. He pointed toward the garden because that's where he died. He hanged himself from the tree next to the Pomaire planter with the Elephant's ears and red geraniums."

In that moment, I remembered the large pot that Carmen was talking about. I had seen it the day before on my walk with Carla, the bothersome woman. She had pointed it out to me.

The humble and down-to-earth woman called Carmen hugged me and cried on my shoulder. Some of the cooks continued with their chores but looked at us out of the corners of their eyes. They didn't understand why she was upset. I tried to calm her down a bit.

"It's alright. You don't know how much you've helped me with this information. I want you to know that, at least for now, I'm not thinking about taking my life." However, deep down in my heart I was still considering the option.

I left the kitchen in a different mood. Far from appeasing my need to know more, the questions multiplied.

For the most part I had confirmed my theories, though I didn't understand why the medication I was taking for my depression had opened what in metaphysics is referred to as the third eye. I had heard that it was an immense privilege reserved for a select few and that it was a gift from God. But why me? I always thought of myself as someone average. I never thought I had any special characteristics that would be worth rewarding with such a magnificent gift. Who was I to deserve it? I was just a guy, superficial, ignorant, and ingenuous, and to top it off, agnostic by essence. What could motivate God to reward me with something like this?

After the conversation with Carmen, the news spread through the clinic like wildfire. The nurses looked at me funny when I walked past them. I came to believe that they thought I was crazier than I was. I didn't think that Carmen had been the one to spread the story. I guess everyone had found out after listening to our conversation. As my grandfather used to say, even the walls have ears and the trees are always listening.

Consumed by my questions, one night I started to think about how I could continue to prove my theories based on all the events that I had witnessed. Carmen's confirmation had been fundamental in making sense in my investigation. Claudio's hologram was, to me, irrefutable proof of the existence of another dimension, the grandiosity that I had heard preachers and psychics, people tied to miracles and esotericism in general, talk about all my life. There is a plane that is different from ours and it's not in Heaven, but here on Earth.

I had always been convinced that several movies that seemed to be fiction were in reality truths that someone for some reason didn't want to express in an explicit manner. Far beyond conspiracy theories, maybe they weren't allowed to and used signs, symbols, and metaphors to express their ideas, seen as complex puzzles by normal people. A small portion of people dedicated to interpreting secrets and reading between the lines could solve them and then publish their findings. These, with time, for the most part turn out to be true, as if movies and their themes were crystal balls.

On the third night, close to ten p. m., I was getting ready for bed. I had a feeling that the show was about to start so I hurried up. Just as I had before, I lay on the bed facing up. I waited for the smell of alcohol that preceded the arrival of the holograms in my room to fill the air before the accustomed ritual began.

Once more, at ten p. m. sharp I felt the unpleasant odor. Thick fog started to fill the room not long after. It had become something habitual. Everything repeated at the same time, with the same effects, and the same setting. Only the actors changed.

I had learned the script by heart. The figures showed up and started to stand in line to wait their turn to kiss me on the forehead, a marvelous blessing. I couldn't figure out where so many people came from or why they acted like they did. I wasn't sure that I would ever know.

This time convinced that nothing that I had seen up to now had been a hallucination, I wanted to see if in effect I was the protagonist of the story. Maybe I had become a simple and transitory involuntary spectator. Were the holograms kissing me? Or was there an invisible person laying on the bed, someone like them or even more so? Were these visions an energy recording of something that had happened decades ago? Was the person lying on the bed one of them? Whatever the case, I was about to find out.

Everything was going according to plan. The night nurse walked in without warning, making me jump. He turned on the light as soon as he walked in. He was a pale man with a beard. "Life" in the "divine dimension" continued on its normal course but he didn't seem to notice.

"Why are you still awake? You know the instructions are clear. You need to go to sleep early. How else are you supposed to regain your health so you can go home?" the young and spindly nurse asked. This was my chance.

"I'm sorry. I'll have to ask my doctor to review the dose she prescribed. I don't feel like they're having the desired effect on me. What's your name?" I asked. He looked at me out of the corner of his eye as he tidied up the things on the dresser.

"My name is Juan. Can I get you anything? Water? Something to eat?"

"No. I do want to ask you a favor but I don't know how to say it without you thinking that I'm crazy. I suppose that you know that I'm here because of severe depression and not because of any other mental illness," I commented.

"Yes, I know. What favor do you need? It has to be something quick because I need to get back to the other patients" he replied as he continued to tidy up.

"I know you won't believe me and you'll think that I've flown over the cuckoo's nest, but I'll risk it. I can't handle not knowing anymore. I'd like you to take a seat on the chair next to the bed, and when the lights are off, I want you to look at the bed and its surroundings. Then please tell me what you see. Just that. Can you help me?"

He turned to look at me, not finding a valid reason for denying my request. My mind kept telling me that he was in all probability convinced that I was crazy, just one more mentally ill patient among several at the clinic, a lunatic asking him to participate in one of my mental breaks. Even so, he agreed and took a seat in the old armchair I had mentioned.

"Are you ready, Juan? I'm going to turn off the light. Try to see what the dark will show you. If you get scared, don't run away. They're harmless," I instructed in a calm voice. I turned off the light and went to lay back down on the bed. I lay on my back and started to look around me while the young nurse stayed seated in the dark, unmoving.

The holograms continued their routine without interruption, one after the other. They would stop when they reached my forearm, then bend down and kiss my forehead. Then they'd stand up and continue on their way through the wall to the next room.

"Do you see people next to the bed? Do you? A lot of people? Can you see them as they kiss me on the forehead? Please, tell me what you see," I asked, full of hope.

"No, I can't see anything in the dark since you turned off the light," he stated with some contempt in his voice. I'm sure he thought that I was pulling his leg.

I didn't insist. I got up and, feeling dejected, turned on the light. Everything was crystal clear for me, but for the young man with the beard it was all a huge waste of time spent with a man with a huge imagination.

I thanked him for his time and apologized for the inconvenience. Then I said goodbye. "I'm sorry for taking up your time. Maybe what I think I see is no more than a figment of my imagination. The drugs are making me see things."

"Yes, that's probable. Don't worry. It's normal that some medications can cause hallucinations in patients. We see it happen all the time. Lay down and rest; tomorrow you'll feel better. He walked to the door and turned off the light. Then he left with no further comments. I'm sure he left thinking that I was another perturbed patient who believed in ghosts. Thinking about that was so funny that it made me laugh way too much after so long without laughing. If he had heard me, he would have been even more convinced that I was crazy.

The failed experiment wouldn't make me give up. I decided that I needed to try something different, though it was unfortunate that I wouldn't have any witnesses. At times I felt discouraged, thinking that my efforts to investigate the events were stupid and a waste of time. Buy why not? After all, I had a lot of time on my hands.

I planned on following this strategy: I'd start in my usual place on the bed, then I'd get up fast and sit on the old armchair, before my luminous visitors had the chance to react. After observing them a few days, I knew that their movements were slower than those of someone with a physical body, which gave me a slight margin to act in.

This idea would answer a simple question. If when I got up the holograms would turn towards me, that meant that the attention that I had received during the last few days was meant for me. If not, then that meant that the attention was directed at another hologram who, just like me, lay on the bed in a similar fashion. I thought that maybe the other being was similar to them but I wasn't able to see it for some reason, even though I had tried several times. In all, it was a strange and confusing situation.

Judging from the number of spirits parading through the room, for sure it was someone of importance who might have had a terminal illness. It might have been his or her deathbed sometime in the past. However, there was a flaw in my thinking. Why did the spirits wear clothes from different decades, even different centuries? In any event, I thought that my theory was feasible and I decided to put it to the test.

I lay down for a few minutes, and then I got up in a hurry and sat on the armchair. One of the holograms was about to kiss the forehead of whoever was laying on the bed while the others waited for their turn. To my complete surprise, the strange visitors froze. The first one in line looked disconcerted when he noticed that I wasn't where I was supposed to be.

None of them looked around to see where I had gone. The long line stopped its forward movement. Sitting on the armchair, I observed the scene a few moments, just in case it was something circumstantial. From the way he first hologram reacted, it appeared that their radius of sight was limited to about four feet around him. How was it then that Claudio, the suicide victim's hologram, could see me and try to catch my attention when he was about twelve feet away? I reached the conclusion that having made a rapid and abrupt change in my position the holograms lost sight of me for a moment.

I then decided to go back. I walked back to the bed and lay down in the usual position. In an instant, the holograms started up their ritual again, recovering from the interruption.

When the first one in line saw me again, he came closer and kissed my forehead, then walked through the wall into the other room. Everything else continued the same as it had the previous nights, following their well-rehearsed script.

My suspicions had been confirmed by that simple test. The holograms were there to contribute to my healing. I was impressed. It was so surreal that on more than one occasion I doubted my own existence. I wasn't sure I was alive since what I saw I had heard several times was reserved for the dead or people with special gifts.

Up to that moment, I had taken great strides in determining the truth behind the supernatural occurrences, dismissing in part the possibility that they were hallucinations. However, I knew that it was the tip of the iceberg.

Now that I was even more motivated, I knew that I needed witnesses. The test with the night nurse had been a failure but that didn't rule out other efforts to collect empiric proof.

I believed it was reasonable to continue investigating. Some being from the other side, I don't know who, had shown me this incredible dimension. I called it the divine dimension, and I thought that it was worth it to understand everything related to it. Besides, I had always enjoyed researching things. I would continue to look for answers, though some seemed to be impossible to obtain.

I talked to Graciela one day when she came to visit. I asked her to stay late as I wanted to find out if the show was real or not. The path was clear. I needed to start the long road of investigation to find a reasonable explanation for the paranormal phenomena that I was experiencing in the spirits' clinic.

I told her everything that had happened to me since my arrival. Knowing her as I did, it was very probable that she wouldn't believe me at all. When I saw her initial reaction, it was obvious that I hadn't been wrong. She didn't believe a word I said. I didn't blame her. In her shoes, I wouldn't have believed me either. I told her that they could be mere hallucinations which she would help me either confirm or deny. In my erratic thoughts lived the possibility that they could be an optical illusion caused by the drugs I was taking, while at other times I was convinced that they were real.

Graciela arrived around nine thirty that night, half an hour before the show. The motivation that her presence caused in me, giving me the chance to verify things with a witness, was greater than my depressive indifference. The medication also helped in improving my mood at times.

"Thanks for being on time. It's very important to me because it will clear up a lot of questions that could forever change my way of seeing life," I commented with an abundance of enthusiasm.

"How have you been feeling?" After looking over the room, she observed my expression. Her eyes shone with satisfaction at what she saw.

"I've been alright."

"I see you're in a better place than before. Let's get your answers. What do you need me to do?" Graciela asked. Facing the difficult circumstances of my illness alone must have been a huge emotional challenge for the young mother of three.

Before the hologram's arrival, I asked her to lay down on the bed next to me. I didn't share any of the details of what was to come. That way I avoided contaminating her thoughts or associating her experience to something like, for example, the intense aroma of alcohol or when the holograms sat on the edge of the bed and caused the mattress to sink next to you.

We spent several minutes talking about domestic matters until the clock struck ten. I got up to turn the light off and then went back to lie down.

"Do you really have to turn the light off? You know I'm a afraid of the dark!" she exclaimed.

"Don't worry, it'll just be for a few minutes. Long enough to know the truth. I need you to relax and set aside your fear for a bit."

The intense smell of alcohol started to fill the room at the usual time, as it had every night during my stay there. Graciela had her eyes on the ceiling, her body relaxed next to me. I think that she believed that it would turn out to be hallucinations and therefore there was nothing to be scared of.

"Do you smell anything weird?" I inquired, hoping for a positive answer. She took a deep breath.

"No, I don't smell anything. Should I smell a specific odor?" she asked. She didn't show any surprise at all. She had always had a better sense of smell than me.

"Please take another breath, as deep as you can. Do you smell anything different from when you walked into the room?" I insisted. She breathed in again, deeper and more intense than before.

"No, I still can't smell anything. I think that you're hallucinating. Have your medications affected your sense of smell as well as your sight? Is the dose too strong?" she said, not smelling the pungent odor of alcohol. Seconds after saying those words and just before I was about to stand up, frustrated with her response, she exclaimed, "Daniel! Why does is smell like alcohol? I didn't smell it when I got here. I'm starting to get scared!"

An indescribable feeling of happiness welled up in me. The incredible had happened. A few minutes later, she gave a start and clutched the bedspread with her fists. "What's happening? Someone sat on the bed next to my feet!" she exclaimed. Her face showed how close she was to panicking. "Please, tell them to leave me alone and go away! Please, you know how frightened I get, and this is terrible! Why is this happening?" She gripped my arm with both hands, holding on for dear life.

"Take it easy. You're hurting my arm. I'm going to stand up and try to communicate with them. Though you can't see them, there are several people here. Maybe you can ask them questions. Trust me!"

"Please, don't leave me alone. I'm so scared!" She couldn't get over the fear she felt. Her eyes were wide, alert for any sign of danger that would cause her to run away.

I stood up and walked to the foot of the bed. I could see with total clarity the holograms that sat there, next to Graciela's feet.

There were two people, one on each side of the bed. The one on the left was a burly man with a youthful face. He wore a brown shirt and black pants. Next to him sat a young man with a red shirt and blue pants. Both of them sat impassable at the foot of the bed while the line of spirits continued its nightly routine. However, to my amazement, the spirit would reach Graciela's elbow and, when they saw that it was another person, they ignored her and continued on to walk through the wall and into the next room.

This behavior made it even more obvious that the holograms were there to help someone sick, not someone healthy. After her operation in 2004 for her pancreatic cancer Graciela had complained about certain ailments in her abdomen, so I wanted to consult with the spirits in case they could help her. With my wife looking on in incredulity, I stopped the first spirit that I came across and I asked them. I used the same protocol that I had used to communicate with Claudio, the boy who had visited me the second night.

"Hi! Listen, I wanted to know if you could help me, please." The hologram, an older man, ignored me. He looked like he was there with a mission and I had interrupted him. When he saw that there wasn't anyone sick on the bed, he continued on his way and through the wall. After a bit I was able to catch the attention of one of them, who stopped to converse.

He was a robust man with a thick beard. He wore a red shirt and dark blue jeans. The first thing he did was to hug me as if he had known me all my life. When he did, I felt the inevitable flow of cold air that emanated from all the holograms all over my body.

"My wife is here, and she may be sick. Could you please check if everything is alright with her abdomen?" Graciela observed the air, waiting for a response from someone that she couldn't see.

The old hologram nodded and went to check her abdomen. She remained on the bed. The generous man bent down, put one knee on the floor, and set his ear on his improvised patient's stomach. He stayed there for a few seconds.

"I feel cold air on my stomach, Daniel. What is it?" Graciela asked.

"Easy, their temperature is lower than the temperature around us," I replied. "Be patient. One of them is checking your stomach right now."

The man took a few moments. Then he stood up, looked at me and was able to indicate through gestures that we needed to keep an eye on her stomach.

"Did one of your spirits say anything about my stomach, Daniel?" she asked with anxiety.

"Yes. One of them says that we need to keep an eye on it, but didn't specify why," I explained.

After his inspection, the hologram shook my hand to say goodbye, like a true gentleman. He then walked through the wall and left.

When I saw him disappear, I decided not to try to ask anyone else so as to not disturb them from their mission. I was happy with what I had managed to discover up to that point.

The experience was extraordinary for both of us. More and more, the simple questions I had were dissipating, but at the same time new, more complex ones were forming. The presence of a witness gave me another piece of the puzzle, but I still lacked definitive proof. I was sure that I would never know the absolute truth, but I insisted on getting as close to it as possible.

I spent several nights reflecting on everything that had happened. Despite my mood improving and me feeling happier with what had happened, I was still worried because I didn't have a coherent explanation, and worse, I couldn't share it with others without being labeled as insane. The implacable cultural mark printed on the core of my being made me fear the prejudice of others more than I feared the holograms and their actions.

In some way I was convinced that the radical change of my life's perspective would bring unforeseen consequences in the future. In my state of scarce lucidity, I wasn't able to think things through as I would in normal circumstances. Questions came and went in my mind. What would I do with this revelation? Who could help me? Who would believe me? I asked myself these things over and over. I'd have to consult with a psychic or expert in energy work or someone skilled at so many other esoteric alternatives that I had never believed in.

So the days passed in the Spirits' clinic. Truth be told I didn't want to leave. Go back to the whirlwind of excessive work, full of nonsense problems? No, I didn't want to face that again. After all, my lifestyle and the problems inherent with the reigning societal model and its culture had been the reason why I was in the dark hole I found myself in.

I decided that once I got out everything would be different. The mental architecture that I had been programmed with since my youth had crumbled in a spectacular fashion. My life was now on another path, one much more spiritual and removed from the materialism that I had not chosen but had accepted, believing that it was the road to happiness for my loved ones and me.

One cloudy day I got to the cafeteria to have breakfast. Marcela was there, the young psychologist that Carla had introduced me to. She was at the clinic seeking treatment for clinical depression, same as me. However, she had violent episodes that, when compared to mine, made me think that maybe her diagnosis was somewhat more complex.

As I got closer to the table, I saw on her face an expression that was different from her normal self. She looked more withdrawn and her damp eyes emanated profound melancholy.

"Hi, Marcela. How are you feeling? Can I join you? I'm a bit better than yesterday, but not too much better." She took a few moments to reply. Anything outside the perimeter of our conversation seemed to distract her with ease.

"I'm sad, Daniel. I'm upset because I can't believe in love."

"What happened? Did you have a falling out with a significant other?" We had all the time in the world so I tried to draw the conversation out as long as I could. After all, she and Fernando were the two people who were willing to have a conversation that lasted more than five minutes. I wanted to know if I could help her with anything.

"Not quite. I fell in love with a married man and that has me tied up in knots," she replied, folding her hands on her lap.

"Well, you're not the only person it's happened to. Many people fall in love with someone who they can't be with due to prior commitments." She studied me for several instants with her large eyes and then continued speaking.

"Would you like to know who the married man I fell in love with is?"

This made me feel uncomfortable. Who was I to know her secrets? Besides, I asked myself, why did I go and get involved in something that wasn't my business? "I don't think it's relevant but go ahead and tell me if you want."

"No, I don't think I should. I don't think you're ready to hear it. I'll let you know next time," she said. She got up and walked at a brisk pace toward the garden. I lost sight of her among the bushes. I stayed seated at the table, drinking milk and coffee, and eating a piece of bread with some of the delicious cheese the kitchen staff had left on the table.

After my breakdown there were several occasions when I felt the unpleasant sensation inside my head as if part of my brain and my cerebral cortex had separated. This made me lose interest in everything and decreased my energy and mood until I reached a point of total apathy.

Two days went by. After lunch, I sat on the bed in my darkened room, lost in thought, as had become my habit. I heard the door open, which I didn't expect at all. Hurried footsteps came towards me, and from the shadows someone threw themselves at me, took my face in their hands, and kissed me with tremendous passion. I was so taken off guard that I couldn't react.

I had no idea who it was as it was dark. The person's long hair and curvaceous body let me know that they were a woman. Even if I had wanted it, in my current state of apathy I had no desire to hug, much less kiss, someone. My libido had gone extinct, thanks to the anti-depressive medication I was taking. I went from feeling surprised to fear. I didn't know if it was a flesh-and-blood human or if it was one of the many holograms that I saw every night. It was possible that one of them had materialized for some reason. There were so many unexpected things that happened in the clinic that nothing seemed implausible.

I fell backward onto the bed, feeling the woman's weight on me. I knew in that second that it wasn't a hologram. I struggled against her for a few seconds to dislodge her even though her lips had captured mine and I couldn't get away. At last I broke the kiss and sat up. In that moment I saw her face, blurry but recognizable in the dark.

"Marcela! What are you doing here? Are you crazy? What's wrong with you?" I blurted. I couldn't believe it. My lungs heaved from the effort of pushing her off. I had no idea what the impetuous psychologist was thinking.

"You know that I like you. You're my impossible love. I knew it from the first day I saw you," she replied, agitated.

"How did you get into the men's corridor? If someone sees you here, they'll jump to the wrong conclusion. I'm a married man, remember? I don't know if anyone will believe that we're depressed if they see us like this." I was angry at the situation and moved away. She gathered her composure and sat next to me. Her head drooped. Then she looked up and turned toward me.

"I'm serious. I'm in love with you. I know you're married. I don't know what came over me. I can't explain it. Do you not like me at all? I'm young, pretty, and have blonde hair most men like. I have a nice body. I'm being sincere. Please believe me. When we get out of here, come live with me in Chillán. I'll make you the happiest man on Earth. I've got everything you could need: a large house, cars, and a sizeable bank account. You won't want for anything, my love. My parents will be more than happy to have a son-in-law like you."

The entire scene felt surreal. She spoke with total confidence, though some of her phrases were incoherent and others seemed to be nonsense. She stated them with such confidence and persuasion that it made me sad that I couldn't reciprocate her feelings. I let my head fall forward as a sign of empathy. I had to say something to calm her down and make her understand.

"Listen, you're a beautiful and charming woman. I recognize that. Maybe, if we had met in different circumstances, I wouldn't have hesitated to take you up on your offer. But now I have a family that I need to take care of. If I'm lucky, I'll get better and I'll be able to do that. I'm sick. I wouldn't be worth a single cent to you. You deserve someone better, a young, healthy man closer to your age."

She remained quiet for a minute before speaking. "We're here because we've got a health problem, but that doesn't mean that I don't have feelings. I want to share the rest of my life with you. Depression doesn't last forever and we can get out of it together," she said with tears in her eyes.

A couple of minutes went bey before the charge nurse came into the room. "Marcela! What are you doing here, in Daniel's room? You know you can't be in the men's corridor. Come with me, please." She took her by the arm and pulled her up from the bed. After looking at me one last time, Marcela walked out of the room with the nurse. I sat there pensive as I wiped the lipstick from my mouth. I hadn't seen her wear makeup before. She was beautiful. However, our destinies were already set, or at least that's what I thought.

It didn't take long for Graciela to find out. She was furious when she asked to have the safety measures reinforced. She didn't believe the excuses that the nurses gave her. It had been a case of the people in charge being careless and complacent.

Days later, at lunch, Fernando told me that Marcela had been having episodes starting a few weeks back. Her doctor, Maria Luisa Cordero, who was my doctor as well, was having a hard time getting her under control.

Fernando was a general medicine doctor who had severe schizophrenia. He did have lucid moments where you could see that he was a great person. During these moments he would give me advice that overflowed with knowledge.

We'd spend entire afternoons talking and playing chess until out of the blue he would change our conversation to something nonsensical, demonstrating his illness. We became close friends and spent most of our time playing together. I got used to how he communicated his ideas, and he said that he thought of me as his son.

Carla, the bothersome woman, would often sit with me in my long hours of silence. She had become my guide. I came to see her as the sister I never had. I felt protected by her presence, and at times I was content and secure.

"How are you feeling? You know, this will all pass and I'm sure that once you leave, you'll never come back again. I don't know of anyone who has been here twice. It's like a nest where the baby birds grow up and fly away from once they're ready and don't come back," she observed with an angelic smile.

"No, I promise that I'll be the exception. I'll be the first one to come back after I get better. I'd like to help the people who stay here." I was convinced that this would be the case.

Day twenty rolled around. My children came to visit me along with Ximena, my niece who was my sisters-in-law's oldest daughter, and Graciela.

Ximena was an introverted nine-year-old girl. She loved me and never missed the opportunity to show her respect and affection toward me. Her parents had made me her godfather, and she visited our house often, staying for days at a time.

"Uncle, I've missed you. When are you coming home? I want you to get out of here soon," the skinny little girl said to me with childish innocence.

"Patience, your uncle needs to recuperate before going home. We all want to see him get better as soon as possible," Graciela intervened. I was thankful I didn't have to explain things to her.

The three children sat on the bed, watching TV. They were in the same spot where all the strange events that changed my life had occurred. Graciela sat on the old armchair, reading a magazine that she had brought with her to pass the time. I stood in the doorframe of the closed door, looking melancholic. From there, I could watch my children in their splendor and look at their young, innocent, and smiling faces.

I wondered what the future would bring for them. What did they think when they saw me here, confused, helpless and out of it, after they had seen me as a kind of superman with everything in my life under control? I had been someone who solved complex problems, gave my friends advice, and who had received respect in return.

The thirty-five-year-old man, the father that I had tried to be, had succumbed to the cruel demands of the political, economic, and social constraints in place in our society. He was a victim of neoliberal policies that were determined to crush suppressed, gullible, and credulous minds like mine had been through lies hidden under the guise of "progress" and "making someone of yourself" in life.

The man I had been had wanted, through work, sweat, and tears, to achieve the goal of social mobility, the same idea that the conservative political world boasts of in their role of staunch defendant of a desensitized socio-economic model.

The prize offered for hard work was an illusion. The ideology of the whip and carrot represented in the triparty transfer caused my former self to live in the poor encampment on Mapocho street in the community of Cerro Navia during the seventies. Then, in the eighties, he lived through his short childhood in Pudahuel, among drugs, crime, and prostitution, before at last reaching Maipu, where he lived a multi-faceted adulthood as a father.

He was an uncultured man, though an avid seeker of elusive hidden answers off limits to the social class of intellectual poverty. This class is condemned to suffer the submission and treason of their own children because, through no other sin but ignorance, they have given their masters total control, which is then used to exploit and control their poor and defenseless lives.

The awakening of this unfortunate flesh and blood individual made me realize that everything that I had been taught amounted to nothing. On the contrary, it promoted my invisible, slow, and inevitable self-destruction, just like cancer. The mental algorithm that I had been programmed with made me see things backwards and give an absurd and excessive value to the superfluous elements offered by a system in crisis and even sicker than I was. A person has to be insane to accept living while ruled by a neoliberal societal model. If you don't think you are, sooner or later society will make sure that you reach that point.

All this ran through my mind as I observed my children. Out of the blue, I saw a hologram of a thin man of medium height sitting between them. He wore glasses and had a beard. He wore a white shirt and light green pants. I realized that for the first time I could seem a hologram in the full light of day. My immediate thought was, "This means they're always here. They don't descend from Heaven at night. Their presence doesn't depend on the mist or the smell of alcohol."

I didn't give any explanations. Rather, I came right out and asked the hologram a couple of questions. "Who are you? What are you doing next to my kids? Come here; let's talk."

The other people in the room looked at each other without saying a word. They didn't understand my illogical actions. I think that they thought that my mental health had deteriorated instead of improving. They were seeing their father, uncle, husband talk to himself. All the while, the hologram looked at me and stood up. He walked toward me, just under the doorframe of the wooden door, painted with a dark, coffee-colored varnish. My shadow looked solid on it, thanks to the brightness that percolated through the skylight in the room's ceiling.

When he reached my side, I started to talk to him just like I would with any other person. At the same time, the hologram tried to answer my questions, moving his hands up to his face with great speed. He followed an identical pattern of conduct as Claudio, the boy who had committed suicide in the old house and who had visited me to tell me about it, had.

"Let me introduce you to my family. These are my children Gabriel, Miguel, and Ignacio. She's my wife and she's my niece, Ximena. I hope that you like them. It seems so. I saw you enjoying TV show with them."

As I spoke, I also noted that he also cast a shadow on the varnished door. I tried to get him to come as close to me as possible so that the shadow would be obvious and leave no doubt that someone was with me.

"Are you a guardian angel? Are you here to protect us?" I continued with my apparent monologue.

In a trembling voice full of surprise, my niece exclaimed, "Uncle, who are you talking to? I see a person's shadow on the door!"

"Yeah! Who is it?" my children yelled after they noticed it too.

"Easy now. It's a spirit, but I don't know who. Don't worry. He won't harm you," I said in a relaxed tone. Graciela put down her magazine to try to see what Ximena had mentioned. The little girl's hands covered her mouth, showing her amazement.

After talking, though I didn't know what the hologram tried to say, I ended the conversation that had been more of a monologue than anything else. I thanked him for the opportunity to obtain new evidence about the reality of his existence. I was getting used to their presence.

"I don't know what's going on, but I'm confused and worried. I need to know. What can we do about it?" asked Graciela with deep worry in her voice. The kids had lost interest in their TV show and were watching their mom with intensity and surprise.

"Do spirits exist for real, Dad?" my oldest son asked, waiting for a convincing answer.

"Son, I'm not so sure, but I hope to find out with time." I had no idea how this would end. I was confused and didn't have a clear vision of how to continue investigating until I could find a concrete answer. I sat down next to them. The hologram of the bearded man with glasses had evaporated. The bright light had made it much more difficult to distinguish his eyes, which in turn had made using the same method I had used with Claudio almost impossible.

A week later, my mom and her sister-in-law (my Uncle Miguel's wife) came to visit. She was from Punta Arenas. I met her as a young adult when by coincidence we visited my grandfather's house in Los Angeles at the same time. On that occasion, she was there with my Uncle Miguel and their daughters, my cousins. They had talked to me a lot about her. She was a short, plump woman with wavy hair, large eyes, and fair skin.

I remember that on our first meeting, we spent the time laughing with her daughters. My simple and sometimes silly sense of humor and joking attitude caused a good impression. They were the first and only people in my life who enjoyed my jokes. We had a great time together.

When we saw each other again in the spirits' clinic hallway, she hugged me in a tender fashion. Her eyes looked at me with sadness and emotion, filling with tears which she dried with a white embroidered handkerchief that she carried in her purse.

Maybe she was expecting to see the happy, smiling, and funny young man she had met some years before, who she had seen dance and clap along to the rhythm of Greek and Spanish music. However, a different man stood before her. This man was sad, dejected, depressed, and defeated. She took my hands and placed a light, brown-colored package in them. It looked like a gift. I held it and thanked her with a kiss on the cheek.

"Here, son, take this. I brought you something that I know you've wanted since you were twelve. We've been praying for you, for your quick recovery, because we love you," said the short woman, giving me a fierce hug.

"Aunt, what a surprise. Thank you very much. You shouldn't have. I have no idea what it could be." My eyes filled with tears as well.

"Open it and find out. I know you'll like it."

I tore off the paper and opened it. I pulled out a framed picture. The picture was old, and I didn't know who it was. The image showed a woman dressed in a style popular in the forties, wearing winter clothes. A long coat and black patent leather shoes stood out in the picture. Her dark hair, light-colored eyes and skin, as well as her medium height indicated a woman of Chilean nationality.

"Who is it?"

"It's your grandmother, your mother's mother, the wife of your grandfather Ismael. I was told that when you were around twelve you wanted to know what she was like. Well, now you have her picture," she said with a shaky voice before pressing her lips together to stave off fresh tears.

I never dreamed of receiving a present like that. A picture of my maternal grandmother. I had wanted and hoped for one since I was twelve, and now, at age thirty-five, I at long last had it with me, just like I had always imagined. I was shocked into silence for a few moments, looking at and memorizing each detail shown by the black and white print, a graphic testimony of my grandmother at that age. I hugged the picture to my chest for several seconds.

"Grandma, I've waited so long to see and meet you. I've missed you," I whispered between silent tears.

"I'm sure that if she had met you, she would be very proud of you, Daniel."

"I'm all choked up. You have no idea how much I appreciate and am thankful for this gift."

That afternoon, we took a walk through the garden with my mother and the others who had accompanied her to visit me. Sitting on the steps, I watched them talk. Depression has an element of autism in it where you get bored with people and their mannerisms, no matter how important they may have been to you in your "normal" life.

I asked the bothersome woman if she could let them know that visiting hours were over. I didn't want to see anyone else, and if possible, I wanted them all to leave. I went to my room without saying goodbye and didn't come out until the next day.

CHAPTER IV: CHRISTMAS

It was December. I was soon coming up on a month of being at the spirits' clinic when Graciela, my ex-wife, had the idea of asking Dr. Cordero for special permission so I could spend Christmas and New Year with my family.

I didn't have the mental faculty to oppose the decision. I did as I was told.

Permission was granted and soon it was time for me to be picked up. I was a little better, though at times I suffered muscle spasms, product of the antidepressants I was taking. We were still calibrating the dose based on the feedback I gave the doctor. Sometimes things were good, but at others the medication caused the opposite of the intended effect.

My children and Graciela were happy. We'd be able to spend time together despite my long absence. I tried my hardest to be alright, but deep down inside I knew that the intense treatment was still in the preliminary phase. According to several experts, depression takes no less than four years to be cured, no matter how effective the treatment may be.

Christmas Eve brought about a change of plans. We spent it at my in-law's house, who were happy to see us. They knew that my mental health affected the wellbeing of their daughter and grandchildren. I went with the idea that the holograms were limited to the spirits' clinic, so I didn't make any effort to see or meet any of them in the old house. My objective was to rest and enjoy different surroundings for a while. Though they were somewhat dense, their company was easier to bear than being confined at the clinic.

The stories from the "devil's house" (that's what I called my in-law's house) hadn't been my best experiences. When I was younger, when Graciela and I were still dating, some sad and unpleasant things for both of us had happened there.

I always felt that the house, a typical low-income house built in the eighties in the Pudahuel community, harbored bad energy. As such, it would in all probability produce extreme thoughts that in my manifest depression I didn't want to experience.

I wasn't wrong since as soon as I walked through the door, with my heightened sensitivity, I felt a great weight on my shoulders and dense air that emanated from all the corners of the house. I sensed the deepest, most hidden emotions and feelings of the people who lived there.

"Daniel, come in. How are you? You look lost in thought, like your mind is a million miles away. You need to be strong, son, so that you can get better soon," my mother-in-law tried to encourage.

I didn't reply. I kept quiet though her words resounded in my ears like church bells. In a flash I felt saturated. I didn't want to hear anyone talk, and even less if what they had to say made no sense to me.

How could I explain, unbelievable as it may seem, that I could intercept thoughts and even see the place's amplified energy field. Some manifestations surprised me. I had never seen them before, not even in the spirits' clinic.

The weary woman invited me to take a seat under the watchful eye of my father-in-law. He was a tall, thin man with a furrowed brow and large hands. He didn't understand much of what was going on with me.

I had never been a favorite of my in-laws, though it didn't matter. They were both difficult people to get along with and at times curt with those around them. Their history as a couple had recurrent episodes of family violence. I never intervened because, though they affected the emotional stability of their daughters, including Graciela, it wasn't my place to say anything.

"Francisco, as you know, Daniel is being treated for depression. Don't ask him a lot of questions because he won't answer them," she told the thin man. Her voice had a sharp, authoritarian tone in it. Years of torment had passed between them until their relationship had reached a modicum of stability. I figure that it's something common in old chauvinist marriages of every social class.

"That's fine. I'll take it that he's crazy then," he replied in an ironic fashion.

The Christmas celebration lasted until the wee hours of the morning, though for me, due to medical recommendations, bedtime came early. Without saying goodnight, I walked up the stairs to the second floor where the bedrooms were located. The floor had three rooms. The master bedroom was the largest. The second room, the one in the middle, was smaller than the other two. You had to go through it to reach the third room, which was a wooden add-on they called "the coop." In it were two beds, one of which had been assigned to me.

Ever since I was young, when I first met Graciela, her family had told stories about the second floor of the devil's house, in particular about the coop. They said they could hear steps, small feet playing on the wooden floor. Something similar happened at my mother's house a few blocks away.

I'll never forget one summer around the mid-eighties. As a teenager I listened to music on an old cassette player that we shared at home. I could spend entire days recording popular music on it. My mom still had her Julio Iglesias cassette tapes, her favorite singer, who kept her company during the long hours she put in, repairing clothing for people who hired her services as a seamstress. Woe to the person who recorded over one of her tapes. It was best if you avoided her after that.

One Sunday, I had been recording music all morning, so I left one of the cassettes in the player. After lunch, my mother took us out to Santa Lucía in downtown Santiago. The house was empty, or so that's what we thought.

When we got back that night, I took the cassette recorder to my room on the second floor, as usual. After I lay down, I plugged it in and pressed play to hear the music that I had recorded earlier. I was perplexed when I heard two songs playing at the same time. The main song was by Bill Haley & His Comets, and in the background I heard a song by Julio Iglesias. I had never heard that effect created con an old cassette recorder like that despite years of experience recording with one. I took out the cassette to make sure that it wasn't some error on my part. I almost fainted when I realized that it was one of my mom's favorite tapes. How was I going to explain to her that I wasn't the one responsible for ruining her cassette? I fast forwarded through the tape to see how long it lasted. Ninety interminable minutes later I determined that the same phenomenon was present on both sides of the tape. It faded out just before the end of the second side, but then I was taken aback when I heard a low, guttural voice. It sounded like a demon from a horror movie saying, "I did it. I did it. One more time!"

The next day the entire neighborhood had listened to or heard of the tape. No one could understand or quite believe what they heard in the satanic recording. This time my mom wasn't able to hide her fear and asked me to get rid of the macabre finding at once.

Several times during the same decade our neighbors would complain about noise coming from my mother's house. According to them, they could hear the sound of children laughing and playing with marbles at all hours of the night coming from the second floor. No one could ever come up with a logical explanation to this since there were no young children in the house at the time and, besides, we always went to bed early.

Now it was my in-law's house. I walked up the stairs in silence until I reached the top floor. I walked through the small room until I saw an almost imperceptible and strange glow on the floor six feet in front of me. It was less intense than the light of a gas lantern. I rubbed my eyes to see better and was shocked to see two small beings walking without worry towards the coop. Both were about four inches tall and two inches wide. They looked like glowing cylinders. They didn't have a human form, just invisible feet that they used to move from one place to another.

Some conspiracy theorists say that true infrared technology isn't available to the public because what can be seen with it would surprise us so much that we'd forever change our concept of the planet and life on it. At times like this during my illness I thought that my eyes had started to function like infrared goggles. What was happening to me was crazy indeed.

The cylinders ran away in terror when they noticed me. This time and contrary to my reaction to the elves in the spirits' clinic, I decided to not lose the opportunity to chase after them and touch them with my own hands.

The green cylinders moved toward the coop, moving as if the devil himself were chasing them. They jumped onto the bed and stopped there, waiting. I soon caught up to them but before I could grab one, they threw themselves off the other side and under the bed.

I got up as fast as I could and moved the lightweight cot to try to see them. It was obvious that they wouldn't let me touch them no matter what.

I saw them once more, but after I reached out to touch one they ran again, scurrying over the wooden floor. They escaped toward the same place where I had first seen them. I persisted in my intent and chased after them. As soon as I did, I lost sight. I had no idea where they went.

After a few moments I went back toward the bed: I sat on the edge so I could get undressed. As I did, I looked up and at one of the windows between the two rooms. In the glass's reflection I saw the energetic hologram of my sister-in-law, Patricia. She was a thin woman, white as milk, with black hair and large eyes. Her hologram had her back toward me. It was like an energetic movie where she took off and put on a black blouse over and over. Because of the repetitive nature of the hologram's movement I was convinced that the tall, thin woman was alive. The repetitive and routine image was similar to the nurse I had seen in the spirits' clinic, the hard-working woman who checked and gave the patients their medication.

I fell asleep, again sure that everything was a side-effect of the medication I was taking. The realism of the visions was unsettling. A battle raged in my mind, with my rational thinking on one side and the spiritual doubts I now had on the other.

The next day I woke up in a different mood. As if normalcy had returned to my life, we went to play soccer with my children and some friends near the Pudahuel airport, about two miles from the devil's house. Out of ignorance, no one could have imagined the consequences of that unfortunate decision.

We got back in the afternoon. Just before entering my in-law's house I started to suffer intense spasms throughout my body. As the minutes ticked by, they became stronger and stronger. Having exerted myself playing sports in the state I was in had been a terrible idea. I had the strongest breakdown I lived through during the entire process of my recovery.

They were quick to move me to the coop. Once there, the scene turned tragic. My body jumped all over out of control, as if in an exorcism gone wrong. I saw the room moving in different directions. My pupils wouldn't keep still. Everyone present in the room tried in vain to help me. My eyes rolled back and my arms and legs cramped up with strong contractions.

The convulsions got stronger and wouldn't stop. I thought I was going to die. I managed to eke out the request that no children be allowed to enter the room. I didn't want them to see me like that, afraid that they might be traumatized by being present in a scene that, even to me, was horrific.

I don't know how much time passed until someone decided to call an ambulance. Thank Heaven that the paramedics didn't take long to get there. After giving me first aid, they took my pulse and got me into the vehicle and took me to the closest emergency department.

I stayed at the hospital the rest of the afternoon. To my good fortune, after several medical procedures they were able to stabilize me.

At first the doctors thought that they were treating a drug addict. Graciela soon set them straight.

"We've ruled out that it's a heart problem. It seems to be caused by an imbalance produced by the antidepressant medications that he's being treated with," said the physician on duty. I was released from the hospital later that afternoon.

It felt so strange that I went from convulsing on the bed as if possessed to being back to normal in little more than an hour. Though far-fetched, I believed that it had all been caused by the green cylinders as payback for having chased them the night before. I didn't know what to make of it.

Days later, when the leave had ended, they took me back to the spirits' clinic. I needed to continue with my established routine. I had been in the clinic for a month. It was my second home.

On the way back, the thought that my full recovery was a long way away tormented me. My recurring feelings of having lost my mind didn't do anything else but make me lose hope, leaving me more and more dejected each time.

One day after I had returned to the spirits' clinic and as I walked down the corridor, one of the male nurses spoke to me.

"Hi Daniel, how are you? How do you feel? Marcela has asked about you a lot. She missed you. She's head over heels for you. How did you do it? Can you share your secret?"

I didn't reply. I just kept walking. What a misguided comment! Off in the corner of the dining hall I saw Fernando, and Marcela was with him. This time I decided not to sit with them. The incident a couple of weeks ago had left me bewildered and gave me no reason to want to interact with her again. Besides, I had no idea how she'd react when she saw me.

I was given a glass of milk and a cheese sandwich. The colorful napkins on the table made me go back in time and remember the decorations in an elegant hotel I had visited during my years of traveling.

I thought about some of the business trips that I had taken out of the country: the USA, Mexico, Peru, and Argentina. We stayed in luxury hotels where in each of the rooms' exquisite designs overflowed with refined details. The high-end hotels felt like palaces. And to think that there are people who live in places like those, as if they were another home.

My table was a few feet from the inseparable friends. Once or twice they glanced towards where I sat. They didn't say a word, just looked at me. Marcela looked at me with indifference. Minutes later, I saw a pair of nurses walking toward the table to get the pretty psychologist. They passed in front of me and took her to her room. She avoided my gaze as she left. I got up from my chair and sat down with Fernando. I wanted to know what had happened to her.

"How are you? Can I ask what's up with Marcela? Is she alright?" I asked with a tinge of anxiety in my voice.

"What? I thought that you had a problem with us. Otherwise, I don't know why you'd sit at a different table. Didn't you know? She's been having new episodes. She'd been alright but something happened in the last few days. I'll be honest with you. I know what's going on. She told me that she's in love with you and can't get you out of her mind, and that now you won't even talk to her," said the former SAPU physician. I remained silent for a few moments.

"Yeah. Last week she snuck into my room and threw herself at me. She kissed me and we struggled, but that was it. I don't have anything against her. You need to understand my position too. This is a very uncomfortable situation for me. As her friend, I'm sure she must have told you about it."

"Yes, she told me all about it. She said that it was the sweetest kiss of her life even though you didn't return it. I think that she's suffering in silence and that isn't helping her recovery one bit. She likes you a lot, but I understand your position. Ah! I had a friend who was a rich freemason. He had lots of influence over top-ranking politicians."

That's where I stopped the conversation. I stood up to go to my room and left without saying another word. Fernando had started to show the effects of his schizophrenia, mixing unrelated topics into the conversation. There was no point in continuing to listen to him.

I was full of guilt, and in my hypersensitive condition, my feelings were multiplied three-fold. It was still early. Most of the other patients were in the cafeteria or in the clinic's garden. I got back to my room and lay down on the bed. In an instant, uncontrollable tears started to flow down my face. I was heavyhearted. Under normal circumstances, I would have felt bad for Marcela's situation, but now I felt that my heart would break in two.

I felt no joy on learning that another person has suffered an aggravation of their mental illness due to my indifference. My chauvinist upbringing formed by a conservative family had established an implicit rule. "It's important to make the woman happy because you're the prince and she's the princess."

My mother, a small woman with black hair, almond-shaped eyes, and a medium build, was very strict and disciplined. The people who knew her remembered her as always being ill-tempered. Why wouldn't she have been? She worked from sunup to sundown every day, struggling to make ends meet for her and her two children.

The poor, exhausted woman would toil for days and nights at a time over her old sewing machine.

In the lower classes of the seventies and eighties, getting enough money to buy food was a very complicated mission. The Minimum Employment Project (PEM, from its initials in Spanish) and the Head of Households Occupation Project (POJH from its initials in Spanish) became extreme alternatives for many Chilean men and women. It was during the world-wide recession at the beginning of the eighties that the banks in Chile went bankrupt. Like other families, ours went through hardships. It was a miracle we made it through. My mother's sewing skills provided little income; enough to not starve.

I fell asleep for a few minutes. In my unconscious state, I felt cold air and the electric current from a hand stroking my face. I woke up, rubbed my eyes, and opened them. Then I sat up and looked around. I couldn't see anyone at first, but when I paid more attention, I saw a hologram. It was a tall woman, around seventy years old, with gray hair and a solid build. She stroked my cheek again and her eyes shined with tenderness. She wore a radiant white dress with remarkable embroidered designs that I couldn't make out what they were.

I saw that the parade of "transparent people" continued even during the day. My holographic vision was improving, and now I could see them at any time.

After receiving her blessing, the old woman started to talk to me using telepathy, just like the young woman with the green tunic had.

"You've been suffering your loneliness in solitude."

"Who are you? What do you want?"

"I'm not allowed to say more than what you're willing to hear."

"I just want to know if I'm going to get through this. If not, I think I may end my life."

"Hush. It's not wise to silence your own voice. You must not refuse to live the most essential experience a spirit can have. You'll rob yourself of another chance and will live without recourse, tormented through eternity. Hold on because you and others like you will contribute to the hope and happiness of your people."

"Please, answer my questions. Who sent you and for what purpose?"

"The faith of men and women has brought us here. Do not fear. Hold on to your faith with all your strength and you will be able to overcome anything."

Her words were precise. She wasn't going to say anything more than what she had been allowed to. But who set the limits?

The old woman passed through the wall and left, the same as the rest of the holograms I had seen during my stay. I looked at the ceiling for a while, then I got up and walked to the garden. When I got there, a nurse walked over to talk to me.

"Hot today, isn't it, Daniel? You should take a swim in the pool. Marcela won't come to see you because her parents took her home. She'll be back next week."

It was then that I knew that what happened between Marcela and me in my room wasn't a secret!

I walked back to my room to change clothes. I put on my swimming trunks and went back to the garden to enjoy the pool. The water reached up to my waist. Afterward, I lay in the sun and had the most relaxing sunbath that I had had in a long time. I almost fell asleep.

While I enjoyed the water, I took the time to reflect on my situation once more. What did the future hold for me? Everything was still a mystery. As I loved to analyze things, I knew that after my health had recovered, I'd spend a large part of my time researching the matter in depth. A door of abundant knowledge had opened before me and I was going to study it in all its dimensions.

Everything pointed toward the existence of life after death. The unavoidable questions were what was that life like and was it able to reach that state without dying?

The first thing that came to mind was to try to understand the relationship between different religious ideals: the bible, God, Jesus, existence, paradise, and the holograms. How could I make everything I had seen fit with the premises I had been taught since I was little? There is a huge amount of literature where each event I had gone through was explained, but it was very different to live through it in person and have the fascinating opportunity to write a first-hand account.

If everything I had lived through was nothing but hallucinations, the problem was solved. And if not, then there was something very interesting that needed to be explained. I took the stance that everything had been real. This also helped to keep at bay the rudimentary and ordinary thoughts typical of slaves to the societal model. The answers would also shed light on the reason why we lived as we did.

In a certain way, the supposed great revelation that had been given to me left me in a similar place as when in Pudahuel, with my neighborhood friends in the mid-eighties, we were witnesses to a UFO sighting. We thought we had dreamt it, but the story came out in the news the next day in all the news outlets of that era.

This was my first experience with a close encounter of the third kind. The second, much less spectacular, happened when I was an adult and I visited a friend in the city of Curacaví.

Even with witnesses we didn't have a logical explanation for the presence of the incredible and hypnotic flying objects that flew over us with colorful lights and quick turns.

The major difference between the two, the UFOs and the holograms, was how long the sightings lasted. The UFOs were visible just a couple of minutes while the holograms had been with me for over a month. In both cases, I had no evidence other than a fantastic story with a couple of incidental witnesses.

Far beyond the comparison and their size, what I experimented with the holograms was more intangible than a UFO, where existential questions started to flow to the surface like water from a spring.

I wanted to study the biblical perspective in a scientific manner so as to not discard the theological aspect out of hand. Was God like He is described in the bible? Why does the bible talk about first, second, and third-class beings? Did classism exist in the divine dimension?

Jesus was Jewish. I remember having seen a video online where someone of the Jewish faith tried to explain to an outsider how God saw all people where are not Jewish.

"You, everyone not Jewish, are an impure race, who we call Goyim. We are the chosen ones of God, so says the Torah. Each one of us, in divinity, could have up to two thousand slaves of our choosing. As such, if you're lucky, we can save you by choosing you as one of them, if and when we want to. If not, you will disappear like miniscule particles of star dust in the vast universe, defined by insignificance."

The derogatory tone of the person's voice directed at everyone else, everyone who didn't think the same, made me nauseous and sad at the same time. Maybe it was a bad joke. I know other Jewish people who are good people.

Is there a God more powerful than Jehovah? Do the vices of our dimension also exist in the other? If so, are there universal sacred scriptures that are of a higher order than the bible and that contain the truths that govern the laws of eternity?

As an aside, during part of my teenage years I dedicated a large part of my time investigating different religions. I went to several meetings where they all in turn assured their believers that they are the true religion, the one chosen by God. In all of them the common denominator was the persistent and unrestrained praising of a supreme being, based on the instructions of their holy book. The prize? Eternal life. The punishment? Eternal punishment. In between, purgatory. A special collection of subjects for slaves, assigned with love until the end of time.

Could the apple have been the fruit that the serpent used to open Adam and Eve's eyes, thinking that it could free their consciousness from supposed slavery? In other words, was the serpent a pure activist of the revolution, one that ended up being just what God wanted it to be?

In premeditating his journey to sacrifice, did Jesus emulate the Father? If so, did God know from the beginning that the serpent would entice Eve to bite the apple and that her fall into the trap was inevitable? Was everything written that way?

"Are you comfortable, Daniel? You seem to be lost in thought. I think you were missing out on something big by not coming out to enjoy the pool. It's magical. Relaxing in the sun-warmed water makes ideas clearer. I hope you enjoy it," the nurse said. In the meantime, I had gotten lost in the bubbles of my thoughts. The mental hurricane was taking me to the edge of insanity. However, I didn't feel unfortunate. I thought that I was reaching a peak existential moment in my life.

My irregular mood did nothing more than isolate me for long periods from the other patients and staff that worked in the spirits' clinic. If someone spoke to me, they had to understand that it was most probable that I wouldn't respond. The thing was that nothing they said or thought was important to me. Though most of the time the ambiance at the clinic was agreeable, the sensation of being where you don't want to be and, on top of everything, have people talk to you is very uncomfortable.

At times, the depression provoked contradictory feelings in me which were very difficult to explain. It made me lose the will to do anything, leaving me in a state of brutal apathy. In that condition, my feeling was that life had nothing that would justify my presence on Earth, much less the wearing down of fragile human integrity, run down by everyday acts that seem insignificant in the sad, indifferent, and tired eyes of someone with depression.

After experiencing paranormal episodes and having a couple of witnesses to them, I gathered my courage to tell all to Maria Luisa, the renowned doctor of psychiatry.

In my mental bubble, I had one great fear: that after I told her of all my experiences, she would say that I was crazy and would extend my stay at the clinic or diagnose me with a more serious illness, along with all its corresponding consequences.

The day of my follow-up appointment came and a couple of specialists arrived at my room with the purpose of taking me to the doctor.

"Daniel, please come with us. Today is your appointment with the doctor, and she's waiting for you. We'll take you to her. Are you ready?" one of them asked.

"I guess it wouldn't do any good if I refuse."

When I got to her office, I went in. It was a room at the end of the garden. The doctor was writing something down in an old notebook. Her glasses were perched halfway down her nose as she looked me up and down, as if analyzing the situation. Her face showed her approval.

"Daniel, how marvelous. You look much better. How have you felt with the medication?"

I needed to put on a good front if I wanted to get out of there soon. "I'm alright, doctor. I think I'm getting better. Can I take a seat?"

"Of course. Let's talk. How has everyone treated you here?" she asked.

"They've been great. Despite the reason why I was brought here, it's been a great stay. I've got a lot of things to tell you," I commented.

"All positive things, I hope. You look much better. Your face even has more color." The doctor knew that her treatment was working. What she didn't know were the collateral effects that it had caused in mi. Could the dose of medications transform in a detonator for other problems? I wanted to get to the point as soon as possible.

"You know, I don't know how to say this so that you don't think that I've gone off the deep end and decide to leave me here longer. Maybe forever. I know that it can all be a product of the medication you prescribed, but I'd like you to either confirm or deny it is."

After listening to my words and without taking her eyes off of me, she lifted her right hand to lower her glasses to the tip of her nose. She stared at me in a thoughtful manner. Her expression made me wonder if it was a good idea or not to tell her about the holograms and the other incredible paranormal events I had decided to share with her.

"Come, Daniel, tell me everything. I'm your doctor and I need to know what's going on with you. It is necessary so that you get the proper medication."

She seemed willing to listen to me, so I tried to summarize everything in the most precise manner I could. I started to narrate the strange experiences. After listening to the intriguing tale, she stood up and walked to the window before opening the curtain. She observed the lush, green garden for a few seconds before turning back to me and speaking.

"Daniel let's agree that what you just told me is incredible. Do you want me to tell you something?"

Several seconds of tense silence transpired and I felt immense dread. I should have kept quiet. Fernando had taught me a wise saying during our long talks: "You'll never regret having not spoken." I should have applied that in this situation.

"I believe everything you've told me. Relax. What you experienced isn't a figment of your imagination, nor is it hallucinations caused by the medication. It's something very feasible, so you can rest easy. I won't recommend that your stay be extended, so don't worry about that. You're close to the point where you can follow the treatment at home," she stated. Her words made me feel like I could breathe again. I gave a small sigh of relief.

"Thank you, doctor. That makes me feel better, though I can't say I'm not surprised at your reaction to what I told you. Your easy acceptance gives me goosebumps."

She sat down before speaking again. "Listen to me. On day, I saw a certain patient. His expression was desolate, and I thought that he looked like he was about to die. After talking to him for over two hours, I diagnosed him with severe depression. I prescribed medication similar to what you take now. When the session finished for the day, we got up and shook hands. As he walked to the door, I glanced up at his head. A few centimeters above it I saw a floating black mass that accompanied him. I felt so scared I couldn't say a word. I'd never seen anything like it in my life. I asked him to come back in two weeks, but he never showed up. I asked my secretary about it, and she said that she'd been informed that he passed away. I have several other stories like this, either my own or told to me by my colleagues or other patients."

The doctor was a famous TV and radio personality because of her brash and acerbic commentary on current events. Her persona was very polemic and irreverent, which had created a large income stream but also an equally large number of problems, or so she said. We would talk like we'd known each other for years. She was a health professional who took the health of her patients to heart.

"You have no idea how it makes me feel knowing that I can trust you. It hasn't been easy." I never knew if her story was a ruse to calm me down, showing empathy with me, or if it had been something real. In any event, the experienced doctor had won my complete trust. Her devotion to her job was indisputable.

"You're welcome, Daniel. Don't forget that we need you to make a complete recovery. Your family is waiting for you. This is a fifty-fifty process. Half of it is up to you and the other half is the treatment."

We said our goodbyes. I went back to my room feeling lighter. I was content knowing that I had been as honest as possible. At times, when I felt fleeting reasons to live, I held on to the small hope that I would soon get out of the mental hell I had fallen into. The question was whether it would be walking or in a coffin.

After a month and thirteen days in the spirits' clinic, it was time to go home. The doctor said that my condition had improved enough that the treatment could continue at home.

That day I got up early, earlier than usual. I spent most of the morning thanking the holograms that had gathered to send me off. I tried to do it with as much discretion as possible since I didn't want the nurses to hear me as they changed in the locker room next to my room.

I'm not going to deny that at times I felt self-conscious, in all appearances talking to myself. Mental illness has no modesty or shame. The holograms were there, in front of me, looking at me as if I owed them something. I still couldn't believe everything that had happened. I never thought that the other dimension existed, the mirror image of ours.

"Dear friends, from the bottom of my heart I want to thank you for having been with me all this time. I arrived here thinking that my life was useless. I was convinced that I didn't want to go on living, but you, with your expressions of love, changed my mind. I owe you all my life. I hope that you can continue to help the other patients here. As for me, I will also try to help others with the secret that you have confided in me. Don't worry about me. I'll be fine, I promise. I want you to know that I will remember you all forever. Thank you."

Some of the holograms hugged me after my speech. I felt the cold air around them. Others applauded and several were teary eyed, just like I was. I felt that we had developed a mutual feeling of affection for each other. Later on I started to say my goodbyes to the spirits' clinic's staff and the other patients that I had interacted with.

"Daniel, I hope that you do well in life and that you remember that you have friends who care about you here. You have a gift. I'm sure of that. Use it to help others, those who need urgent spiritual help," requested Carmen, the cook who had been there for years. We hugged and said goodbye.

"I know that you'll be fine. You're a good man. You have a guardian angel the likes I've not seen more than a few times. Take care of yourself and your beautiful family," said Carla, the bothersome woman, as she dried her eyes with a handkerchief.

"My friend, I hope that you can come and visit us after you've recovered. We'll miss you. I'm sorry that Marcela isn't here to say goodbye, but I'm sure she'll miss you too. Maybe you'll meet again in a future life where things will be different. By the way, my freemason friend struck it rich by gambling in a casino," said Fernando with damp eyes. He couldn't hide the usual phrases out of context that were a sign of his disease. I hugged him like the best of friends.

"Please tell Marcela that there's nothing to be sorry about. I hope to see her again and that when I do, her depression will be a distant memory."

Graciela arrived at noon. A nurse helped to get my bag into the car.

"That's everything, right?" Graciela asked, her hands on the steering wheel.

"I think so." At times, the strong medication accelerated my reactions while at others I wasn't as quick to reply. Graciela started the car and soon we left the parking lot. We headed down the main road towards the west, heading home.

"Do you feel better?" Graciela asked with a relaxed tone of voice.

"Yes, I think that being there was a good thing for me."

"The children are waiting for you."

"I hope that they've been behaving while I was away. I missed them."

"Rambunctious as always, but they're fine. By the way, how did your friends take you leaving?"

"What friends?"

"The holograms that you talked to me about and that we felt that night. Did you feel the smell of alcohol again?"

"Yes. I spent most of the morning saying goodbye to them. I owe them a lot."

"The day you decide to say something about it, no one's going to believe you."

"It doesn't matter. I think that if someone had told me something like this a year ago, I wouldn't have believed it either.

Every so often I would glance at the back seat through the rearview mirror. Something told me that we weren't alone in the car. On one of those glances, I saw a hologram. I rubbed my eyes more than once to make sure that I wasn't seeing things. After a couple of minutes my jaw dropped like the hatch of an amphibious assault ship. I couldn't believe what I saw.

The same hologram that I had seen weeks before together with my children and who's shadow my niece saw on the door of the room I stayed in was riding with us in one of the back seats.

"You're not going to believe this."

"What? Don't tell me you forgot something."

"We're not alone. One of the holograms is with us and he's sitting in the back seat."

"I don't believe it! Please, tell him to get out of the car. I don't want holograms at home. Spirits bring money problems. Either you tell him, or I will!" Graciela exclaimed when she heard the news.

It was a nonsensical conversation, talking about something that didn't exist. I thought for a few moments before I replied. "Let him be. What if someone asked him to watch over us? I don't want him to go. Maybe he's not even a hologram but rather the energy of a living person who spent a lot of time there. It depends on his movements."

"What do you mean it depends on his movements?"

"If they're repetitive, then it's the energy of someone who's alive. If not, then we're in the presence of a spirit."

"Daniel, I'm scared. We don't know what their real intentions are. Are the good or bad? Who can say?" she asked with worry in her voice.

"I don't know. We'll find out once we're at home and I can observe their new routine away from the spirits' clinic. Right now I can see only one, the guy with glasses and a beard. I think I'll call him Glasses.

I was one hundred percent sure that Glasses was a spirit. I had been observing him and his actions were those of someone watching over something. I wondered about the reasons behind such care. Maybe he had always been by my side, like a guardian angel I had never been able to see before. He could also have been watching over Graciela. I'd soon find out.

The analytical process of looking for answers to everything related to the holograms left me exhausted. There were times when I didn't want to know anything else about spirits and dedicate myself to living a normal life. In other words, I wanted to let my soul do what it wanted to do, relegate the spirit to the back burner and let it act on its own.

CHAPTER V: "GLASSES," BACK HOME

I had been home from the spirits' clinic for a few days and Glasses was right at home in our house. He would sit at the table with us as a family. He watched us all the time, sometimes with his arms crossed on the table, as if he were waiting for someone to bring him a plate as well.

After checking all the corners of the house and sitting in various places (the bathroom, bedrooms, and the garden), I reached the conclusion that he was the only hologram there. But why had he followed me to home and stayed there like an shameless surprise tenant?

Some days I couldn't find him. I'd look for him everywhere until I'd find him at last. The bearded man could spend entire days walking around the house, observing each and every detail. He was always interested in everything, acting like a new member of the family.

One day when I was at home by myself, I went to my son's room and sat at his desk in front of the computer. Behind me, my dog was asleep on the bed. He was a cocker spaniel-fox terrier mix. The loyal canine had decided to stay with me. Without warning and for no apparent reason, he stood up and started to bark. At first I didn't think much of it, but his barking became louder and more insistent. I decided to scold him.

"Quiet, Micky! If you don't stop, I'll have to send you outside!" I was surprised when he ignored me and, on the contrary, started barking even louder. I could tell he was nervous. I turned to look at him to see what was causing his reaction. His eyes were fixed on something above my head and his barking became more and more intense. I got up fast and moved to the bed next to him, at about his height and position, as he continued his enthusiastic protest. I looked in the same direction he did and bingo! Micky was barking at Glasses, the hologram. I could see him standing with his arms placed on the chair's backrest. He took his time to react and turn around to look at us. When he did, Micky ran out of the room toward the front door. He continued barking from there but didn't come back into the room. I sat down in front of the computer again.

"How about you let me read the news and try not to scare my dog?" I asked, trying to be patient. Glasses was always interested in what I did on the computer. I was glad at the situation because, without meaning to, Micky had become the first animal witness, joining the ranks of the human witnesses so far.

As time when on after Glasses' arrival, more unexplainable situations started to happen around the house. They were things that had never happened before and that were, little by little, starting to overwhelm my family and me.

Without a doubt something that at first I had thought was a miraculous revelation, knowing that a large number of deceased people moved around with us on a daily basis, no longer amazed me. Though their presence made me feel special, the presence of specific meddling holograms became less welcome as the days and months went by.

It may seem tragicomic, but Glasses would move about the house without any regard for our privacy. Each time I spoke to him using the language I'd defined to communicate with them (as most holograms couldn't communicate using telepathy), he would ignore me. That irritated me to no end. How was it possible that this unwanted guest could ignore me in my own home? Even our dog had gotten used to his presence. I could see Glasses next to him and he didn't bark like he did the first time. Now Micky would even wag his tail each time he saw Glasses.

Overall, things started to flow, but not for long. The first horrific event was about to happen that would make us question the permanence of this intruder who had made his way into our home without any warning.

One night I was brushing my teeth in the bathroom. Everyone else had gone to sleep. When I got out, I walked toward the master bedroom where I slept with Graciela. She was getting ready for bed as well. I stopped in the doorway before going in so I could turn off the light outside. On the wall, just above the light switch, was a black-and-white picture of my youngest son, who was five years old at the time. His childish face glowed with happiness in a shy, spontaneous smile. He was wearing a Colonial-style painter's cap.

I turned off the light but something about the picture caught my eye. To my amazement, the angelic face of my son started to deform until it became an indescribable, almost demonic, image. It was like looking at the Mona Lisa melting in the sun, the paint running together and forming random colors. The eyes in the picture grew out of proportion. His smile turned malevolent, terrifying. I was stunned.

I couldn't believe what I saw. I rubbed my eyes over and over to make sure it wasn't some kind of optical illusion. His eyes kept growing and his smile mutated into something diabolical. I heard a noise behind me, something shaking in a frenzy. When I turned to see what it was, I was horrified to see that it was a potted plant, about three feet tall, shaking and moving as if it were alive. I questioned my sanity. I was losing my mind.

I turned the light back on as fast as I could. When I did, the picture started to revert to its original form. At the same time, the plant stopped moving. I wasn't sure of what I had seen, so I turned the light off again. That was enough to start up the new and dramatic antics again.

Bit by bit the picture began to deform and the plant started its agitated dance. There seemed to be two dimensions present, one visible when the lights were on and another when the lights were off. One dimension was full of logic and the other defied the elemental laws of physics with no remorse.

This behavior was something very difficult to believe and had no rational explanation. I was overwhelmed knowing that I was the only person who could see it. I had no idea if I was having a hallucination exacerbated by the dark or if it was reality. It was mortifying to think that my mind could be short-circuiting in such a spectacular fashion.

I tried to react as fast as I could and I called Graciela to have her see the unimaginable: a normal picture moving and the enthusiastic dance of a potted plant. It was crazy. What a pain!

"Graciela, please come quick! I need you to see something! Hurry up before it goes away!" I exclaimed. I started to think of ways to make her impression as unbiased as possible. By no means did I want Graciela to see something I had described without having first seen it for herself. I needed to be very cautious with the questions I asked her.

"I'm half asleep. I don't want to get up, and even less if it's about your holograms. I'm fed up with them," she replied in a tired voice. I was convinced that I couldn't let this opportunity slide. I insisted.

"Please, help me. I promise that it'll be the last time that I ask you for something like this."

She got up from the bed and came toward the door where I stood. Her slow steps were evidence of her fatigue.

When she reached me, I gave her instructions that I thought would be the most appropriate to get the answer I was looking for.

"Listen to me. When I turn off the light, I want you to look at Gabriel's picture and tell me what you see. Then I want you to look at the plant in the living room and do the same. Are you ready?"

"Yes. I don't know what you want me to see, but I'm already scared."

I could see Graciela's worried face in the light. Her pale face with dark circles under her eyes looked at me, willing to help. I turned off the light. Was it all real or was it a hallucination? I'd soon find out. It didn't take long for me to get an answer.

"Daniel, what's happening? Gabriel's picture looks deformed!

Look at those eyes! Why does his face look like that? It's not possible! Tell me what's going on!" Her expression was terrified. She lifted her hands to cover her horrified expression. She turned to hug me tight, unable to get over her surprise.

"Please, look at the plant. What do you see?"

"It's moving! What's making it move like that? The windows are closed and there's no wind!" she exclaimed in fright. I turned the lights back on. Graciela couldn't stop shivering and pressing against me, her face burrowing into my chest. She was consumed by fear.

"It's okay. That's all I wanted to know. We're done. Let's go to bed." I took her by the hand and we went into our room. There, we talked for hours, looking for a reasonable explanation for what we'd seen. There was no way for logic to explain an event like that. Graciela suggested we sell the house. She thought that it was haunted.

"Your spirit friends have lost all sense of respect and decorum. What else are you waiting for? What will happen next? Will there be plates, glasses, and chairs flying around like in Poltergeist?"

We continued talking about the situation the next day during breakfast. We were both incredulous and had plenty of questions. Something supernatural, incredible, and unexplainable had happened in front of us. This fueled my urgent and untiring need to find answers, starting a long scientific journey toward the truth that no one up to now has found.

But where should I begin? Who could I ask for help? There were people on TV who claimed to be mediums or have extrasensory powers allowing them to see things beyond what normal people could. Even so, I needed to consider that several of them had been accused of fraud. They took advantage of unsuspecting people, of which there is a large amount in this appearance-based world.

I spent days thinking about how to string together answers that could help me understand what was going on. I had been away from work for three months due to medical leave. From time to time the office would call, asking how I was doing. Graciela always gave the same reply: "He's making progress but still isn't ready to go back."

One summer night, I was lying on the bed in the master bedroom with Graciela and my youngest son, trying to fall asleep. It was a large room with its own bathroom and closet. Gabriel, still awake, had decided to go to sleep between us. Light from the streetlamps outside filtered in through the thin curtains covering the windows, somewhat dissipating the relative darkness.

Before I noticed, I was deep in my thoughts. I lay on my back, looking at a fixed point on the ceiling. Out of nowhere the hologram of a young man dressed in black appeared levitating above us. I had seen something similar in the spirits' clinic with the indifferent old man, but this was the first time it happened in my home.

I had talked to my family so many times about the apparitions that my first reaction was to tell Graciela what I saw. In the next instant I decided against it. I had saturated them with so many stories that I was sure they didn't want to hear any more. Besides, I wasn't even sure if that young hologram was something real.

I kept quiet and watched him, believing that my companions were asleep. The young man moved his hands in a quick and erratic manner, as if trying to get my attention. I was used to these repetitive gestures so I ignored him. Some of the holograms in the spirits' clinic had done the same when they caught my eye.

My son, who had been lying on his side facing his mother, turned until he too lay on his back, looking up at the ceiling. He looked up for a few moments, not noticing that I was still awake. After a couple of seconds he exclaimed, "Mom, what's that man doing floating up there?"

"Oh, my God," I thought to myself, "my son can see them too!" I turned to him, a large lump forming in my throat.

"Gabriel, what did you say?" I asked, feeling like I was choking on my emotions. He looked at me in surprise at seeing me awake.

"Dad, who's that man with the huge wings flying over us?" Graciela turned to look at me, her expression showing her confusion.

"Gabriel can see the same things I do! It's real! A child wouldn't lie about this, much less him. Either we're both crazy, or there's no reason to believe they're hallucinations," I pronounced. My son's generalized development disorder wouldn't allow him to concentrate on anything long enough to ask him for a detailed description of something. The times that I had tried it was like talking to a wall. The desire to communicate had to come from him. His comments now were an extraordinary instance of unusual and spontaneous eloquence.

"I don't see a thing," Graciela commented.

Starting the next day, Graciela began a pilgrimage through various places, looking for recommendations to find someone who would give us the help that we needed.

At this point my depression mattered little. What mattered most was understanding the reasons behind the change in my brain that had unwittingly revealed a great secret to a common and ingenuous man like me.

Seeing beyond what's visible to others was making me more ill than the depression was. I couldn't understand how I had ended up like this. At one point I thought that I might have schizophrenia, but this was put to rest after consulting with several specialists. I was even seen by neurologists who subjected me to different scans in order to discard the possibility of a brain tumor.

Judging by the type of problem, help was unlikely to come from the rational medical world. Therefore, we reached out to the spiritual world.

We went to the Votive Temple of Maipu, looking for a priest to guide me and help me find a modicum of the peace that had been taken from me more than a year ago. I didn't know what would put me over the edge first, whether the spiritual or the material world.

When I entered the imposing building, I was overwhelmed by a feeling of intense anguish I had not experienced since the day of my breakdown. I saw few physical people. On the other hand, the holograms were innumerable. It looked like a jam-packed stadium before a high-profile concert. Women, men, and children walked, ran, and jumped everywhere. There were so many making such a fuss that their energy intermingled with the physical people who in all likelihood visited the temple to practice their faith, in total ignorance of the monumental show going on around them.

It was disconcerting. There were times when I couldn't distinguish between physical people and spirits, another fact that made me question the specialists' opinion that I didn't suffer from schizophrenia.

Just like in the spirits' clinic, the holograms in the Votive Temple wore clothes from different decades, made from varied materials and colors. In contrast to the rehabilitation center, they all behaved with indifference towards me. None of them paid me any attention. They didn't show the slightest bit of curiosity. It might have been possible that in the midst of such a whirlwind of energy and chaos that they didn't notice I could see them.

My tolerance level was low. I couldn't stand for very long the chaos that flowed there, so I asked to leave the place at once before I was overcome by a panic attack or something similar. Never again would I, in the state I was in, get close to the great architectural colossus of Maipu. I wouldn't even come close to the entrance.

It would soon be time for me to go back to work. The treatment had managed to stabilize my mood, which, however, was far from reaching a state of emotional equilibrium appropriate my job's demands. At times I felt a severe lack of energy that affected me at the least opportune moments. I had been in the same situation for a while, so I had gotten used to the idea that I would never overcome my depression.

A few days before the end of my medical leave, Graciela came home happy. She thought she had found a satisfactory answer with solid arguments to explain what was going on with me.

"Come on, let's sit and talk. I have an idea that might explain what's going on with all this," she commented full of optimism. I was more cautious. I didn't trust a hasty conclusion, but my despair made me willing to hear any ideas that she wanted to share with me.

"I went to a numerologist. She told me everything. She's very skilled in her craft. Someone recommended her. She says that you and our three children are indigo. That means that you have a special spiritual condition. You can see things that others can't. You possess spiritual intelligence and special sensibility. To say it another way, you've been touched by magic. You were sent to Earth to carry out a mission to guide others to achieve peace."

"What?" I couldn't hide a sarcastic smile when I heard her. It appeared on my face in a spontaneous manner. I couldn't hold it back. All those esoteric definitions were all the rage, though I hadn't paid them any attention until that moment. My empiric rationality didn't think it was worthy of my attention. In a world where everything was suspect, it's difficult to reconcile so much information without bias or skepticism.

"You're telling me that we're some kind of alien sent to Earth with a special mission? Please, I thought that you had something serious to say." I was blinded by my disbelief. I couldn't take in anything that I had heard, so I got up and went to the bedroom feeling disappointed. Without a doubt I was grateful for Graciela's effort and worry, but I wasn't about to listen to an explanation that, at least to me, was a vague and baseless assertion.

I started to look online for people who practiced clairvoyancy or associated disciplines. I wasn't going to accept an answer like the one Graciela had found. I encountered several people who claimed they saw deceased people, discerning the dimension beyond ours in its entirety.

I went to as many meetings with mediums as possible. I hoped to find people who had experiences similar to mine, but I found egocentric men and women who talked a lot but had little or nothing to say. Most of their speech was made up of refined sentences with hints of charlatanism that made it impossible to take their words to heart.

"Hi! I have a serious paranormal problem. I know it sounds strange, but I'm at my wit's end. I see spirits. I want to know if you can help me to figure this out. Apart from seeing it as something novel at the beginning, I can't see it as anything useful or that makes sense. I want to get rid of this spell or whatever it's called."

"You need to give thanks to the Lord. He has blessed you with a gift by showing you something that very few have seen. You're a special person on Earth, a chosen one sent to protect the weak. You need to use this gift to help those in need" said one of the many mediums I went to.

"But if what you say is true, why was it revealed to me now that I'm thirty-five? Why can I see them but not hear them?" I asked each medium over and over.

"Jesus received his calling at the age of thirty and carried out his work during the three years after. You can't hear them because you refuse to accept the blessing that you've been given. Accept it and let the divine gift that God gave you guide you to help others." They repeated this reply again and again until I got fed up with trying to investigate.

Convinced that there was no way to get a straight answer, I fell into a state of lethargy. I was about to give up on everything and start to act with absolute indifference whenever a hologram would show itself to me. If they weren't able to tell me what the reason behind their presence was, I wasn't going to wear myself down trying to figure it out. After all, I hadn't been the one who asked to see what many others would consider another dimension: the divine dimension, or the dimension of the others, the dead.

One night I came home from an appointment with a numerologist. His answers had been along the lines of what I had heard before. I was tired and couldn't take it anymore. I knew that my patience would soon run out. The young, bearded hologram that had followed me home from the spirits' clinic who I called Glasses saw that I was sad. I sat down on the edge of my oldest son's bed, trying in vain to analyze the situation. I was overwhelmed to a distressing degree. Without any hesitation, Glasses came and sat next to me, maybe trying to console me.

When the young, bearded man sat on the bed, I felt it sink, just like it happened at the spirits' clinic when one of the holograms that often visited me would sit on my bed there.

Rage welled up in me as I saw him sitting there. He had become the symbol of my self-diagnosed schizophrenia. He didn't speak, but his impertinence was astounding, trying to fit in where no one had asked him to be.

At that moment, he was the number one being responsible for the spiritual confusion in my head. He was a living portrait of a time when I was ridiculed in the eyes of many. People who before had shown me profound respect now said I was crazy with little to no emotional stability when I talked about paranormal things from a supposed other dimension. I felt like my life was over and I couldn't change a thing. Where had my professional reputation and socio-economic pride gone? It had taken me so much effort to achieve it, rising from misery like a phoenix. It was all gone. That was my narrow-minded thinking at the time, individualistic and materialistic, capitalist and neoliberal, that I had naively and shamefully accepted for most of my life, like a sheep or a servile slave. It was the product of a cowardly upbringing that was in line with the established system.

Though the decision had been taken, I still reflected on the tireless mental struggle between being part of a collective or another individualist among many. I reached the conclusion that the societal model and its competitive and predatory culture had forced me to create a persona with artificial status through which I was able to interact with other rich, intellectual, and well-educated people in general. It made me feel important and hid the fact that when we gathered together I would always be the only one who didn't belong. Glasses, the hologram, was with me during the definitive collapse of the paradigm scorched into my brain. I saw him as responsible for the mental deconstruction of each and every one of the most essential values and principles that I had assimilated as a child. He was the executioner of my past, but at the same time held the keys to my new future.

What did I have to gain by telling everyone everything that I had seen of the divine dimension? After all the supernatural occurrences, it was probable that no one would believe a single one of the experiences I had lived. Even so, in my ingenuousness, I held on to the small hope of being understood and not labeled as insane, which was the obvious result.

"Go to hell! I don't want to see you anymore! Get out of my sight! Go, I said! Go now!" I yelled and threw a half-full glass of water at the wall. The poor spirit looked at me in fear, got up and ran toward the front door. When he got there, half of his body was hidden and all I could see was his head and torso. He seemed to be waiting for something, giving me time to change my mind. Maybe he believed that I was playing a bad joke on him.

"Don't you understand, you goddamn ignorant? Go! Don't ever come back! No one asked you to come here in the first place! Leave now and get out of my life!" Some people say that the best way to get rid of a spirit is to hurl insults at it. In this case, I didn't need to say more. He left. I didn't see him for a long time. There were nights when I looked for him so that I could apologize for my rude behavior, but he never showed up again at my house.

There were several times when I thought I was going crazy. Who wouldn't if they were in my shoes? I had told my closest friends about what was going on. Seeing the disbelief and subtle skeptical expressions was enough for me to know that they didn't believe a word that I said. To be honest, if I were in their shoes, I wouldn't have listened to all the things I had to say. Only someone insane would recount stories full of atypical, almost movie-like, descriptions and events of a parallel world.

Yes, I think that I understood them to perfection as in my youth I had also heard stories of people who claimed to see paranormal things. I thought then that they were crazy, liars, or had overactive imaginations. Time would make sure to rub this lesson in my face: for with the measure you use, it will be measured to you.

CHAPTER VI: HOSTILE HOLOGRAM

I went back to work after six months of medical leave. I stopped seeing Dr. Maria Luisa Cordero for follow-up appointments. She had proven herself to be a great person, a capable professional, and someone unmatched in her field.

From time to time she would send messages through others, inviting me back to her clinic to make sure that the healing process had finished. I didn't think that it was necessary because I was better, or so I thought. In any event, for a time I still followed her indications and kept up with the prescription. I know it was irresponsible of me, but no one could expect anything else considering my mental state.

At the time, my job was located in a building at 333 Teatinos street, on the fifth floor, next to Huérfanos street in the middle of Santiago. It was a building that had been constructed some years ago and housed several companies, both public and private. The company I worked for had rented a full floor for the IT department that I worked in. There were a little over twenty workstations, separated by movable panels.

A rudimentary lighting system illuminated the old office space. Looking back on it, we should have done something to fix it.

Turning off the lights for the floor before heading out for the night wasn't a simple routine. A series of steps had to be followed, including pressing several buttons on a run-down electric board located in the reception area at the entrance of the office.

Most of the lights depended on the energy provided by the old condenser. Just the bathroom lights were on an independent electric circuit and needed to be turned off manually by using the switches in the bathroom.

If the main lights were turned off first by accident, the entire process had to be carried out in reverse to turn them on again. The other choice was to walk to the bathroom in the dark. It was more efficient to do the latter but at the same time it was the less amenable option because of how gloomy it was.

It had been about a week since I had started work again. I was in the middle of the process of adapting to my new life and the new installations. I still felt down from time to time, though the periods when I felt this way weren't as intense as to impede me completing my every-day assignments.

The medication caused me to feel slow and shrouded my mind in a mental fog. This made me run late in turning some tasks in on time. In order to make up for it, I decided to work longer hours. The workaholic in me almost came back as I never felt comfortable leaving work unfinished.

Countless times my sense of responsibility made me do everything in my power to finish my assignments on time. I think that the disciplined upbringing I received thanks to my mother was the source of my diligent, strict, and square work ethic. I needed to finish what I started and to have everything ready according to the deadlines I agreed to. I didn't allow mistakes, nor foul language, nor did I want to be seen as someone unjust, sloppy, or lacking in judgement, though in more than one occasion I know that I may have been these things.

My paternal grandmother had married a navy officer. Things were done in a very rigorous manner in their home in Llolleo (fifth region). My grandmother, a short, big-boned woman with wavy, dark-brown hair, was a good woman. She usually wore plain outfits, nothing ostentatious. I never saw her go out with anything fancy, much less sexy. Maybe it was because the old sailor had always been the conservative type, as I imagine is the case with most military men. In all probability he didn't like to see his wife dressed in anything daring.

The house in Llolleo was stuck on a mountain a few miles from the sea. It had a large garden where my grandfather had planted fruit trees and rose bushes of diverse types and colors. Breakfast was at nine and lunch at one on the dot. Meals were impeccable. Luxurious ornaments adorned the place mats on the wide and elegant table. It looked like a party taking place at an important castle.

My grandmother would serve three courses plus dessert. This contrasted in every way with the reality we lived in at home. At our home in the Villa El Sauce camp, now known as Cerro Navia in Santiago, the menu usually consisted of only one course, but thanks to my mother's sacrifice, we never did without.

After an intense day of work, I stayed at the office until I was alone. It was the first time I had seen the space without any people. It was dark and created in me a strange and uneasy sensation. In any event, I didn't want to concentrate on it and fall into the temptation of trying to see more than met the eye like I did when I looked for Glasses, the thin, bearded hologram, at home.

When I decided it was time to go home, I started to carry out the lengthy process to turn the lights off, but I got the sequence mixed up. I left the bathroom lights on. The worst-case scenario had happened. I chose not to go through the entire tedious procedure again and instead walked the sixty feet to the bathroom in perturbing darkness.

I could see the dim lights from the bathroom at the end of the corridor. A disagreeable walk through the shadows awaited me. Visibility was low and coming back it would be down to almost nothing once all the lights were off. I remembered the time at my grandfather's house when we left the rustic kitchen at night with my cousin Patricia so we could go to bed. It had been a horror-filled night when my grandmother's spirit had manifested, drowning my anguished scream.

I preferred living through that again rather than repeating the damn sequence to turn the lights on and run the risk of making another mistake and wasting time in the process.

I got to the bathroom, more or less feeling my way there along the corridor. I turned the lights off and a shiver ran down my spine. I started to walk back toward the exit at once. A cold mist ran down my back. My instinct told me that it signaled the presence of something. Half-way down the hallway I turned to my right. Though I had no intention of seeing anything in particular, two holograms were visible. They walked at a brisk pace towards the south. They were two men. One had dark skin, was medium height, and had a full moustache. He wore a white shirt and brown pants. The other one was a tall forty-something-year-old with pale skin. He wore a black jacket and blue pants with white splotches. They walked with confidence away from me, not more than twenty feet from where I stood. I stopped for a few moments to avoid being seen. My decision, however, came too late. Right then they noticed my presence.

The light-skinned man continued walking without changing his direction, but the dark-skinned man stopped in his tracks. He stood still a few seconds and then turned his head to observe me. I could feel the malice in his penetrating and intimidating gaze. His body took on a defiant posture, and he raised his fists. I was sure that he didn't have any good intentions towards me. For no apparent reason, he started to run in my direction. I froze, not knowing what to do. There were less than twenty feet between us.

I had never encountered this type of situation with any other hologram. I was scared out of my wits but I didn't move. I wanted to run but I couldn't. It was like I had been hit with some kind of gas that paralyzed me. Once more I remembered the time when I was twelve and my grandmother's spirit appeared, leaving me speechless and terrified, unable to scream for help. A similar feeling took over, but this time I wasn't a child.

I saw him approaching me at a full run. Everything pointed to him not stopping at all. With less than nine feet to go, he sped up and ran even faster, throwing himself at me like someone throwing themselves into a pool. His cold presence enveloped me like ice. He went through my body and my skin became covered in goosebumps. My hair stood on end, buffeted by a gust of intense wind produced by the energy from his frenzied dash. I turned around to look at him, but there was nothing. I thought that he may have disintegrated after crashing into me.

The next second I started to feel strange. After making sure that everything was all right, I took the elevator down and hurried out of the building. I drove home and tried to understand the hologram's violent and hostile attitude. Had he had even the slightest hope of taking over my body? This was one of several questions that I couldn't answer.

At home, I told Graciela what had happened. We went to bed after dinner, neither of us suspecting what effects the strange incident would have on me.

I woke up at dawn. Half of my body hurt. It felt like someone had thrown boiling hot water on my entire left side. My face felt burned and it hurt when I touched it, like needles being stuck in an ultra-sensitive area.

I don't know if what had happened was something positive or negative. The most value I got from the experience was the information and the data I obtained for analysis. There are holograms who you shouldn't look in the eye for any reason. They notice it and when they do, there is no way of knowing if they will react with good or bad intentions. The dark-skinned man decided to save time and skip any attempt of communicating with me. His aggressive reaction confused me.

The pain in my left side stayed for two weeks. Nothing on Earth would make me repeat the uncomfortable episode. From then on, I learned that I needed to be much more cautious when dealing with spirits. The parallel world was still so intriguing to me that my eyes refused to stop seeing it.

Some time had passed since I had left the spirits' clinic. After that, and much to my surprise, I never felt the need to go back and visit. The promise I had made Carla, the bothersome woman, had disappeared without mercy.

I continued with my unceasing search. I started to investigate online. I read many books about the supernatural, clairvoyance, and paranormal events. I consulted with acquaintances I thought could help guide me in some way.

Due to the lack of time and the enormous amount of available information I had to read and analyze, I didn't seem to be making any headway. It had turned into an uphill climb. Nothing I read matched with what, in my opinion, had turned into an emotional burden that I was in no condition to carry.

Around that time, Graciela's maternal grandmother was on her deathbed. She had been diagnosed with lung cancer. Before leaving this world, she took the time to visit as many relatives as possible one last time. One of the people she loved the most was her granddaughter, Graciela, so one day she showed up unannounced at our house, along with one of her daughters.

She and Graciela had a private conversation that I absented myself from. I didn't feel it was my place to intervene in the special and moving encounter between them. A few months passed after her visit before she passed away.

I always wondered about the sublime act of saying goodbye before dying. People resist death, hoping to say one last goodbye to their loved ones.

CHAPTER VII: UNCLE VICTOR

A short time later, while still recovering from my depression, I received the news of the death of someone special in my life. I traveled south to attend the wake and the funeral of someone who I considered a father figure. It was my Uncle Victor, my aunt Marta's husband.

He was a kind man who had given me advice full of wisdom as I grew from a child to a teenager and then into an adult. I respected him and loved him like no one else. There was always a reason to meet up and drink a glass of good wine and enjoy a delicious meal of grilled meat. He loved that. Unfortunately, most of the time when a serious illness finds us, there's no escape. Such diseases have no mercy. It was my uncle Victor's time. He was a victim of one of the cruelest illnesses.

He passed away due to cancer at the age of fifty-three. Even though the doctors had told his family early on that his chances of survival were low, the loss of the old farmer was a devastating blow to everyone.

I wore my sadness on my sleeve as I got on the bus to Los Angeles at the Santiago terminal, a six-hour trip. I couldn't miss his funeral, recent recovery notwithstanding. I needed to honor him as I would a good father, one who had been by his son's side without conditions at the time of his greatest need.

I arrived in the southern city with very little emotional strength. It's not easy to say goodbye for the last time to someone that is indeed loved. As soon as I got off the bus, I took a taxi to his house. Part of my maternal family was waiting there for me. I could see their expressions of grief all around me. My eyes were red and irritated both from lack of sleep and from the tears I shed when I gave my condolences to my cousins. Uncle Victor's inert body wasn't at home.

The need to talk to him one last time made me consider the possibility of using the optic ability I had developed at the spirits' clinic. I didn't mention a word of my supposed ability to any of the mourners present. I didn't think it was the right time to do so. I went ahead and tried to find his hologram somewhere in the house he had lived in. It was a small structure with three bedrooms, a kitchen, and a dining room plus a small patio. I searched the places where we would spend time together: the garden, his bedroom, or the table where the tasty meals he prepared were served. After a discreet but thorough walk-through, I didn't see him anywhere. His hologram was nowhere to be found.

"Are you looking for something?" my cousin Roberto asked, the oldest of my Uncle Victor's children. He was a young, charismatic man with dark skin just like his father. At the time, his hobby was rap music and he practiced often.

"What? No. I just wanted to walk through the places where I would spend time with your dad. By the way, where's the wake going to be?"

"At the catholic chapel, about ten minutes away. I'm heading there now, if you want to come with me," he replied.

My uncle's body had been taken to the chapel about a mile from his house. We got there around noon. I entered the area he had been assigned. People had come to pay their respects and bless him. Family and friends offered sincere prayers for his eternal rest.

I felt unsure as I walked up to his coffin and observed his face. He looked like he was asleep. I decided to look for his hologram. I hoped that I would find him there since I hadn't found him at home, but where? What section of the colonial chapel would he be in? A woman who loved all things esoteric once told me "Some spirits don't immediately travel to the other dimension. They wander around here because they haven't realized they're dead, or they have unfinished business here."

I gazed over the entire room. All those present had their heads bent in prayer. My mother, who had been his sister-in-law and best friend, prayed next to his coffin.

A few minutes went by before I could find him. He was closer to me than I thought. The silhouette of my uncle stood next to my mom, looking at himself lying in the coffin.

The dark, burly, six-foot man tried in vain to talk to his best friend. I could see that he was asking something at the same time that he looked around in confusion, his gaze wandering from time to time to the casket where his lifeless body lay. I tried to interpret his gestures. He seemed to be asking, "Maria, what are you doing? Why are all these people here? Why is my body in a coffin?"

Then the robust hologram moved on at a slow pace to look at everyone there, trying to recognize them and looking for someone who could explain things to him. I don't know how long he spent doing that. What was sure is that he still wasn't aware that he had passed away.

I didn't want to talk to him, as it would have looked weird to everyone else, carrying on a conversation by myself. No, thank you. Besides, a few months before dying, we had spent a long while talking about the possibility that his illness was terminal. No one had told him, not even less me, but I'm sure that he knew the end was near.

"Daniel, I know that this is serious, but no one wants to come out and say it because they think that it'll make me worse. If my time has come, I accept that. I know that I'll be able to go to a better place and rest. I'm sad for my family, but I'm so tired," he said with weary eyes.

"Uncle don't think about it. Things don't have to turn out that way."

"No, Daniel, I know who I am and what's waiting for me. They don't have to hide it from me. Besides, a person can tell when things aren't going right."

I left town without going to his funeral. I didn't have the strength to withstand such an emotional tsunami of sadness. I went back to Santiago on the first bus I could find, my spirits lower than dirt, but peaceful after having said goodbye to an important person in my life.

Time moved on in a flash. There were several moments when I tried to find a reasonable conclusion to explain the phenomena I experienced. All my efforts were in vain. I was as ignorant and confused as I was at the beginning, perhaps even more.

I tried to analyze how I had come to see the holograms. Why had this supposed gift never manifested itself before? What was different about the circumstances around how everything started? The only sure piece of data I had was that I had been drugged for prolonged periods of time due to my depression and to combat its potential deadly consequences. Dr. Maria Luisa and her treatment were my only benchmark in this regard.

When I was ten years old, I thought I saw strange things, like holy imagery, in the kitchen of the house we lived in at the time. The proof of those events was far from conclusive. Now, as an adult, I was faced with a dilemma: either I went ahead with my investigation and ran the risk of becoming a victim of prejudice and social scorn, or I lived my life as if nothing had happened.

Life as I had known it had transformed in its entirety. Each dark place that I went to was a potential universe of visualization. Diverse holograms appeared before my eyes, almost everywhere and at any time.

Sometimes I was invited out for drinks after work. I drank juice since I couldn't drink alcohol due to the medication I was taking. I could see holograms sitting or standing next to people, interacting with incredible naturalness. No one noticed their presence. They appeared to be eager to enjoy the same leisure activities as the living. They sang and celebrated, emulating the flesh and blood people, behaving like one more person among the crowd.

Countless times I saw them trying to act like flesh-and-blood people. That's when I understood something that has stayed with me until today and answers a permanent existential question. Maybe the conclusion that I reached isn't all true or decisive, but it's what I found after several years of profound and conscientious analysis.

Many of us during moments of pseudo-philosophical reflection have asked what the reason or objective of our existence is. Why are we here? Who hasn't asked themselves this? No one has the answer, though, just conjectures with no irrefutable evidence.

My conclusion is that everyone that exists came to this world or dimension to feel. Many people who engage in the esoteric arts affirm that the main reason behind our presence in this world is to experience things so we can gain enough knowledge to allow us to evolve. Maybe they're right, though I have no doubt that it's not the only reason.

Yes, it may be pretentious on my part, but as far as I can see, the essential purpose in life is to feel. This precise verb is what drives our behavior and makes us want to live each experience like we do. Then we digest them to learn, which in turn allows us to evolve supported by wisdom.

In an implicit manner the holograms had shared this idea on several occasions. In order to reach this definition, I had to interpret their behavior among the living. They were so joyful, so playful and so human in their spirituality.

The aggressive hologram at Teatinos 333 had tried to attack me and injured my left side. He also left a powerful message: "Here I am, in a dimension where I don't feel at ease, because I need to feel happiness, tears, pain, joy, and all the other emotions that can only be felt when you're flesh and blood. I want your dignity, even if just for a few minutes. After being lost in the fog for so long, at long last I'll be able to feel again."

CHAPTER VIII: GRACIELA'S GRANDMOTHER

One night, a few minutes before falling asleep, Graciela and I were in bed together. The light was off but the darkness wasn't total. The streetlights illuminated the room through the thin curtain on the windows, which we had changed not long ago with the arrival of summer.

I thought I saw small lights that looked like sparks come into the room through the doorway. They moved like whirlwinds, twirling non-stop and moving in a zig-zag fashion from one place to another. I didn't say anything until the concentrated luminous energy stopped in front of Graciela, who was still awake next to me. Then the unusual lights started to dissipate. As it did, I saw a new hologram appear, someone who looked familiar.

The visitor was intense. I realized that it was Graciela's maternal grandmother, who had passed away some time ago. The elderly woman looked sad, pensive, and wouldn't take her eyes off of her favorite granddaughter.

"You're not going to believe this. Your grandmother just sat next to you." Graciela turned her pale face to talk to me.

"Really? What is she doing?"

"She's watching you but isn't speaking. She hasn't even looked at me. It looks like she wants to warn you about something." The gray-haired woman continued to watch her for a few minutes. The scant twenty inches between them were insignificant next to the deep and penetrating gaze of the old woman. I continued to observe the situation. The grandmother seemed to be in a trance. Without warning she started to cry. I could see her watery eyes and the tears that fell down her cheeks. I began to worry. Something was wrong, and it wouldn't be an easy task to find out what.

"Your grandmother is crying. I don't know why." The old paranoia about Graciela's pancreatic cancer in an instant brought to mind thoughts of death. I started to think that the elderly lady wanted to warn us of something serious, maybe even give us unpleasant news about the health of the mother of my children.

"Is it related to your health? It's been a while since you did the exams to keep an eye on things because of your cancer." Worry oozed from each one of my pores.

"No, I don't think that's it. Maybe her tears are tears of happiness since we hadn't seen each other in such a long time."

"Stretch your hand out in front of your face about twenty inches." Graciela did as I instructed.

"It's incredible how the temperature changes in this area. The rest of the room is hot as blazes, but right here it's cold. Can you ask her something?"

"I don't know how long she's going to stay. It doesn't look like she's interested in talking to me, so I'm not going to force her."

We fell asleep early that night and I didn't notice when the old woman left.

I could have tried to ask her something, but I couldn't bring myself to do it. The incident involving the angry hologram's attack at Teatinos 333 had made me much more weary of them. Why should I stick my nose in their business? It's not like I could help them to resolve anything. No, my mind was made up. From then on, no more risky interactions.

The visits from her grandmother occurred three days in a row. On the third night, the scene was a carbon-copy of the first. The old lady appeared after the luminous energy whirlwind moved across the room in a zig-zag fashion. I thought that the situation was as far from logical as could be. I started to insist that Graciela should set up an appointment to get her exams done so that she could rule out a possible relapse.

I remembered what the hologram at the spirits' clinic had indicated after I asked him to check Graciela's abdomen. The spirit suggested that we needed to pay special attention to her, and I associated both events in my mind. The elderly lady waited, her face looking expectant.

Being insistent paid off at last. In the following days, Graciela talked to her doctor and did the exams necessary to detect eventual problems.

"Daniel, the results are normal. There's nothing to worry about. My grandmother must have been crying happy tears when she saw me after so long" she informed me.

I wasn't convinced. Something was off, but what? Never once during her three visits did the woman look at me. I didn't understand her indifference towards me, much less the reason for her tears.

Two days after her last visit, I as at work, sitting with my arms on my desk, and working on the computer. I started to perceive the presence of holograms though I hadn't consciously decided to look for them. The temperature in the room dropped and the pressure seemed to increase. I also felt like I was being watched. My intuition told me they were unequivocal signs that there were transparent visitors around.

I didn't think about it much. The cold relationship I had up until then with the divine dimension was unsustainable. I concentrated and focused my vision, even if it meant being attacked again by the angry hologram, the dark-skinned man that had attacked and injured me after hours at work a few months ago.

This time, however, it was Graciela's grandmother, the one who had visited us at home. She walked up to me with caution, up to the point of seeming shy. Her face was expressionless. She took a few steps and stopped about six feet away from me. I watched her from my chair, feeling perplexed. She lifted her hands to her face and started gesturing at a rapid pace, as if she were trying to communicate something. She had abandoned her apparent apathy towards me and was now engaging in extroverted behavior.

I was used to the expressive but undecipherable language the impetuous holograms used each time we shared the same time and space. As per usual with the rest of the holograms, the attempted communication with the large-eyed older woman was unsuccessful.

A random thought crossed my mind and took it over. I couldn't get it out of my head, not even for a second. Without realizing it, I took my cell phone out and called Graciela. At first I wasn't sure why I called her, but I felt a strange and imperious need to talk with her.

"Graciela! Do you have your Aunt Adelina's number? Your mom's older sister? I need to have it right now."

"But why? What's going on? I haven't talked to her in ages. Let me see if I can get it for you," she replied, feeling confused.

"Please! It's urgent! Your grandmother came to visit me and I think I finally know why."

"Incredible! I'll get it for you as soon as I can." A few minutes later I received a message with the phone number I was looking for. I called it at once, remembering the dark-skinned, petite woman with large eyes that I met at the end of the eighties at a New Year's party in her mother's house.

At the time, I was a young nineteen-year-old and was dating her niece. She didn't take long to answer the desperate call, almost as if she had been waiting for it.

She was married and had three daughters. She had always been a happy person, always smiling, but she was also extremely strict with her little ones. She had to endure the death of one of them under tragic circumstances. "Pain like this latches on to a person like an octopus latches on to a rock. It stays with your soul forever," she commented one day.

She never got over the death of her youngest daughter, and now she had to deal with the sorrow of her mother's death. She suffered in silence. Her siblings weren't aware of how painful and complicated her mother's death had been for her. She was smack in the middle of a bout of profound melancholy.

"Hello, Adelina? How are you? It's been a while since we've spoken," I said to start the conversation.

"Who is this? What do you want?" she replied with a quavering voice.

"It's Daniel, your niece Graciela's husband. I had a feeling that you're not doing well. Am I wrong?"

"Daniel? What a surprise! You have no idea how glad I am to hear from you. It's been so long." She hadn't finished the sentence when she started to cry inconsolable tears. I was sure that she needed urgent help. I heard her sobs and whimpers over the phone. Never before had I seen or heard her cry. She always presented a calm demeanor to those around her.

"Please let me know where you are right now. I need to talk to you. I have an important message for you."

"Sure, Daniel. I'll be waiting for you. Sometimes life tests us in ways that are too hard to bear." We were only five blocks away. Without wasting any time, I left my work unfinished on my desk and went to meet her. I remember running through the streets like an Olympic athlete, following Huérfanos street towards the east, convinced that Adelina was facing a life-or-death situation.

I soon arrived at the address she had indicated. I waited in the foyer of an old building on the corner of Paseo Estado and Alameda. Soon after my arrival, I say her walking toward me. Her face looked weary and worn. Her mascara had run down her cheeks due to fresh tears. She was pale, with dark circles under her eyes, and she looked apathetic in the extreme. She tried to smile when she saw me, but her tears started to flow again.

We hugged for a few minutes, neither of us saying a word. In that simple and straightforward human gesture where satisfaction fills the soul, deep breaths relax the heart, and eyes close, forgetting for a moment the world and all its problems, I came to see her as a mother figure. The people around us glanced at us out of the corner of their eyes. Despite the many years that had gone by without seeing each other, we seemed to share a closer bond than aunt- and nephew-in-law.

I didn't say a word. I stayed quiet for a few moments to give her time to get her evident sadness under control. She took out a white handkerchief from a black purse that she carried with her and dried her eyes. Then she looked up at me. I smiled to encourage her.

"Let's go for a walk. How about we go to the main square and talk?" I suggested. She nodded in agreement. She looked troubled. Inside me, a strange mental reset started to occur.

We began our walk among the crowd. At a slow pace we walked

to the main square in Santiago. As I spoke to her, I felt a weird sensation. It was like my mouth had been possessed by an invisible ventriloquist. Words came out on their own, straightforward and eloquent. I couldn't control what I said to the grieving woman. To this day, I remember little to nothing of the lengthy conversation we had.

We spent a long time talking as we sat on a varnished bench in the square. It was like someone had placed earplugs in my ears so I couldn't hear what I was saying. In a gradual manner and much to my surprise, her anguished expression underwent a metamorphosis and changed to timid happiness which occasionally allowed her to flash her white teeth when she smiled.

I never understood what happened that day. After about two hours of conversation, we stood up and walked to the Metro station. That's when I recovered my hearing and the ability to control my voice.

"Thank you, Daniel. You have no idea how much talking to you helped me. Everything you said was beautiful. It opened my eyes, and I can't explain what I feel after this conversation, but it's almost like I've been reborn. You're an angel who someone generous put in my path to help me out of my depression, if only for a few hours."

The small woman said several other complimentary things about me, to the point of making me feel embarrassed. I was a student getting the highest score on a test that I didn't take, a singer receiving a standing ovation for the playback of a song I didn't create. But how could I let her know without looking like I had lost my mind? How could I explain that it hadn't been me, but her own mother? I decided to smile and keep quiet while she showered me with all the praise she wanted to. The time to tell her the truth would come later.

We said our goodbyes with another hug and a kiss on the cheek. She would be all right. Her recovery was a matter of time and lots of love from her family.

Days later Aunt Adelina started to talk to my family with more frequency. Her daughters and husband said that she had taken a turn for the better after our meeting. She seemed to be a different person. Her mood underwent substantial improvement. She smiled in a way she hadn't done in years, said her astonished daughters.

Her deceased mother never visited us again. I suppose that she was saving her energy for another occasion when urgent need would merit her presence. A few years later I told Aunt Adelina about the circumstances that led me to contact her and have the fruitful and healing conversation with her. Then she recounted an incredible and unbeknownst to me story about her mother.

"It happened one day when I went to the cemetery. I bought a beautiful artificial rose and placed on her gravestone. The next time I went to visit her grave, the rose had disappeared. I thought it was strange as people usually respect things like that. I thought I would never see it again as maybe one of the cemetery workers might have thought it was trash and thrown it away.

"I was so wrong. During another one of my many visits, two teenage girls came up to me and handed me back the rose. They said, 'Ma'am, we're here to bring this rose back to your loved one, an elderly woman with gray hair and large eyes. She hasn't stopped bothering us since we took it. Please, ask her to forgive us and not show up at our house anymore. We haven't been able to sleep at all.'"

After I heard her story, I was convinced that María, her mother, was a hologram whose energetic abilities were above average. The whirling lights that I had seen at home during her visits were not a coincidence.

They say that spirits feed off of the energy that people provide by thinking of them or calling for their presence. In general, it's done without conscious intent. People hope that the spirits can help them to fulfil their wishes or solve problems. The most common example I can think of is the roadside shrines that people put up around Chile.

Aunt Adelina acknowledged that she had asked her mother for help to overcome her depression. She felt her mother's presence every day. Maybe her prayers, pleas, and petitions towards the elderly woman were enough for her soul to obtain the energy needed to look for help and, at the same time, demand the return of the rose that was a symbol of her eldest daughter's love.

CHAPTER IX: GUSTAVO CERATI'S CONCERT

Months later, my fascination with rock-pop music led me to go to a performance by Gustavo Cerati, the late singer and songwriter. The event was scheduled to take place in a stadium behind Edwards Portal, a building near Bascuñán Guerrero Street in Santiago.

I arrived excited to see my then favorite artist. It was the first time I went to a concert of that size. The crowd was enormous. The audio equipment's sound was deafening. I picked a spot a few feet from the stage so that I could better appreciate the show.

A little before ten P. M., Gustavo took the stage. Everybody danced to the rhythm of the forerunner of Argentinian rock and roll's songs.

I remember that we were stunned by the display and the artist's performance. Soon, people from the gallery started to scream louder and louder. I looked away from the stage and turned to see what was going on. Several people did the same. The disturbance has enough for several people to protest loudly against the people in front. I turned to look back at the stage when something on the roof caught my eye. Right there, in the presence of more than fifteen thousand people, I saw a different show. Not believing what I saw, I lost some of the enthusiasm I had for Gustavo Cerati's performance and kept my eyes on the roof.

Above the sea of people were thousands of holograms, all with disfigured faces that made them seem to be not quite human. Each one looked like a small cloud with flaming edges. Their faces were half-finished, and the suffering they expressed was eloquent.

Even with the spiritual knowledge that I had acquired up until that point, I couldn't tell if the distraught holograms were a product of the creative light effects, done on purpose as part of the show, or if they were the consequence of something supernatural. Maybe it was the energy of the people that had been present for so many recurring performances. I also came to think that they could belong to the souls of the dead. But why? What could have happened there to explain such a vast number? In any event, the striking holograms seemed to be interested in what was happening onstage.

I remained interested for several minutes, alternating between looking at the people around me to see if anyone else was as impressed with the surprising special effects as I was and observing the holograms. Nothing. Everyone around me seemed indifferent to the parallel spectacle that went on above us. It was possible that these small clouds with a human-like shape were another figment of my tricky imagination.

They remained above the crowd for the duration of the event. In my mind, I ruled out the possibility that they were an effect produced by the smoke and lights, created to impress the concert attendees. In my opinion, the most striking aspect was still the shape of their faces, expressing sadness and pain. I don't know if a producer would organize a show with special effects dedicated to sadness in a place where the atmosphere was supposed to transmit happiness within a festive framework.

As usual, I left the concert with lots of questions but no answers.

Next week at work, I told one of my coworkers about the concert. "I went to see Gustavo Cerati on Friday. It was great!" I said to Enrique, who immediately became interested. He loved rock music too.

"Really? Where did you see him?" he asked.

"A place behind Edwards Portal. Do you know what it's called?"

"Ah, the one on Bascuñán Guerrero Street. Are you talking about the Victor Jara stadium? It's the place were a bunch of people were tortured and killed in 1973."

I don't know what emotion my face conveyed, but my surprise was instantaneous. I had heard of the infamous Victor Jara stadium and the deaths that occurred there during the dictatorship, but at no point during the concert on Friday did I associate the stadium with that tragedy. Now the apparitions made sense. That explained the presence of the holograms and their pained expressions, didn't it? It was probable that they could have been the souls of all the people who had lost their lives there in such a cruel manner.

Enrique had taken on the role of my confidant in several aspects, in particular those dealing with spiritual matters and paranormal events. I'd tell him about all the supernatural things that happened to me every day. He always listened with care and never questioned what I told him. Maybe he didn't believe anything I said, but he was there.

Telling him about all these unexplainable events had become an indispensable process because it helped me to find inner peace at the times when I needed it the most.

CHAPTER X: BRIGHT LIGHT

The unending search for answers made me go to a group called "Bright Light" whose purpose was to teach people how to better manage their emotions, energy, and mindset through self-control and quantum healing workshops.

I was so desperate that I bought two tickets despite how expensive they were. One was for me and the other for Graciela who, I supposed, had started to believe in the strange and extraordinary world of the paranormal.

The things she lived through in the spirits' clinic when she saw the bed dip next to her plus the things that occurred at home with our youngest son's picture turning into something demonic and the potted plant dancing all over the place were sufficient evidence for her to feel the need to do something about it.

To tell the truth, I had already heard about energy manipulation, but skepticism was ingrained in my worldview so it took me a while to decide to sign up for and go to the workshops. At last we decided to go ahead and do it. We arrived at our first session on a weekend and sat down in the fifth row. There were about fifty people there, all waiting to find out what the instructor would say.

The leader of the workshop walked in at the appointed time. He was short, had thinning hair, a round face, and thick glasses. He seemed to be friendly and told us a bit about himself. He said his mom was from the USA and his dad was Russian.

"This guy thinks that knowing this is going to impress us and we'll believe everything he says," I whispered to Graciela. She smiled and got comfortable in her seat.

The talk began with the short man explaining how energy works and the essential technique needed to develop clairvoyance. He defined clairvoyance as the ability to perceive visual or paranormal realities that most people can't see, or the ability to see the future. He also talked about energy healing the mind and body.

As he spoke, he said that he believed that these same ideas had been used by Jesus himself when working his miracles. I was starting to feel like a fool for having paid for this absurd workshop. I still had enough patience, however, to stay seated for a while.

"Yeah, sure, and I'm Superman. This thing smells fishier all the time," I whispered as the guy kept talking.

He used several examples from the Bible, highlighting when Jesus had shown his ability to change reality in front of his perplexed apostles and the witnesses present at each one of his miracles.

According to the instructor, some of the clearest examples were when Lazarus was resuscitated or when Jesus walked on water or when he filled the fisherman's boat after they returned empty handed after a long day of work.

His theory stated that ninety-nine-point nine percent of an atom is made up of empty space and only zero-point zero one percent is energy. As such, concentrating on the physical or material made no sense. Jesus had this clear and that's why he developed his mental and spiritual control to such a degree. With this knowledge, he could have changed reality as many times as he wanted, bypassing the laws of physics established by Isaac Newton in 1665.

Then he started in on the concept of chakras, energy cones shaped like vortexes that are distributed throughout the body. They're invisible to most people but their existence has been scientifically proven. This was the first time I had ever heard of this. I was starting to get excited about the idea of changing reality through mind control. Just imagining having that ability was a fascinating thought.

The instructor told us that these cones captured and processed life energy, allowing it to flow in the proper manner through the body, especially through critical organs like the heart, brain, pancreas, liver, and kidneys.

He also talked about the seven most important chakras and how, through controlling them, it was possible to heal any illness a person might have, no matter how complex it was.

"We have incredible powers but they were blocked at birth. Every one of us has a powerful gland located in the center of our brains. It's a divine tool that was given to us by creation but few of us use." His conviction was profound.

"The only 'divine' thing here is this guy's imagination," I whispered.

"Scientists know of its existence and power but for some reason they don't want the general public to know how to use it. I'm talking about the pituitary gland, also known as the third eye," said the man with such conviction that it gave me chills.

All the rhetoric sounded like a scam and I was starting to get fed up with it. "I paid a lot of money to be here, and what I'm listening to doesn't live up to my expectations in the least."

I thought about leaving then, so I turned to Graciela to signal my intent. Her face, pained and pale, let me know that something was wrong.

"What's the matter? Aren't you feeling well?" I asked in a low voice.

"I don't know. My chest hurts a lot, I feel like I'm out of breath, I want to throw up, and I feel like I'm going to faint. Seriously, I don't feel well," she said, worried.

Despite the number of people in the room, the instructor noticed that something wasn't right.

"What's the matter?" he asked, looking me directly in the eyes.

"My wife is feeling unwell and doesn't know why." Everyone turned to look at her.

Without moving from his spot and talking in front of everyone he said, "Listen. I want you to pay attention to what I'm about to tell you to do. Lift your right index finger and point it at the sky, all right?" Everyone exchanged glances. None of us understood why he would ask her to do that. She obeyed and lifted her finger to point at the sky, though her face showed her uncertainty. "Now place that same finger on your chest, right where it hurts or you feel discomfort, okay? Then touch the tip of your nose." The instructor's expression was enigmatic. No one could have imagined what happened next. "Ready? How do you feel now?"

Graciela's eyes widened with surprise. We all waited on her words until she found her voice. "It's incredible! The pain and discomfort have disappeared! How did you do it?" she exclaimed. The room stayed silent for a few moments until a round of applause rang out. It was like being at a magic show.

We couldn't believe it. Even though I laughed along with the rest, I came to think that maybe Graciela was in on it with the instructor. She insisted that she didn't know anything. It was a strange and surprising experience for everyone present.

I was never a fan of courses that dealt with metaphysics because they were theories that lacked empiric proof. After witnessing this event experienced by someone in my inner circle, I decided to look deeper into it. In any event, I would hear out the rest of the enlightening workshop.

That's what I did. After it finished, I started to tackle what we had learned in an incisive manner. I practiced every morning, not resting a single day.

"The most important process of this technique is called 'energy flow.' It consists of assuming the existence of an aura, an energetic field that covers the body of every living thing. At the edges it contains attached representations of all of the experiences we've lived through," the instructor had said at one point.

"There are energy centers scattered throughout the body. They are cone shaped and behave like whirlpools and are known as chakras. Each one has unique characteristics and controls certain functions of our organic architecture. They need to be aligned. When an organ stops working properly, it means that one of the chakras associated with it has shifted. To get it back to its normal state of equilibrium, the energy flow technique needs to be used."

If I believed the instructor's theory, the chakra that controlled my brain wasn't aligned. Maybe all the strange events that I had lived through were related to this change. I needed to systematically follow the technique to confirm whether it was true or not.

Practicing it turned into something good for me. I understood many things about the brain, such as its ability to channel energy and the power that this has on our material reality. I needed to use and control it in an adequate manner to achieve the unimaginable.

"This workshop is one of many. This level is called 'healing.' Here you learn the basic concepts so you can acquire all its secrets. In higher levels, the knowledge and wisdom you receive will allow you to predict and change events, for example," he assured us.

Months later, after a hard and stressful day at work, I got on the bus to go home as I couldn't drive due to medical restrictions. Once on the bus and as had become my habit, I sat in the position that I learned in the workshop in order to practice the healing technique.

I sat there with my eyes closed when someone spoke to me softly, as if they didn't want to interrupt what I was doing. I opened my eyes and turned my head to the right, where I thought I heard the delicate, feminine voice come from.

"Hi, my name is Sara. What's yours? Can I ask you something?" A blonde, attractive woman in her forties sat next to me. Her face was round and she had almond-shaped eyes, thin lips, and a full face of makeup. She wore a black coat and a white scarf made out of lightweight material.

I tried to interpret her words while I sat there with my eyes half-open, trying to refocus my concentration.

The rest of the passengers continued with their lives as the woman placed her hand on my arm as if we were long time long-time acquaintances. I felt a little uncomfortable with the situation.

One time when I was much younger, a well-dressed woman of about the same age caught me by surprise and hugged me on the metro station stairway.

"Hey, can I ask you a favor? Can you lend a hundred pesos? I lost my wallet and I need to buy a ticket. No one else wants to help me." She had her arms wrapped around my waist and I couldn't get loose.

"Sure, I can," I said as I tried to get out of her suffocating embrace. "Let's go to the ticket counter, and I'll buy your ticket." After I bought it, I said goodbye and walked away, thinking that it was over. Out of the corner of my eye I saw her follow me, so I ran down the stairs to the platform. I don't know how she did it, but she managed to get on the same subway car I did, always staying a few feet behind me. I was scared at that point. I thought that I was the target of a coordinated mugging planned out by experienced criminals.

"I want to thank you for your generous help. My apartment is near the Los Heroes metro station. Let's go for a drink. What do you say?"

I looked at her with a blank expression. I couldn't believe what she had proposed. The entire situation was absurd. I was sure it was a hidden camera skit for a TV show or something.

"Um, I'm on my way to work, so I can't. Thanks anyway."

"Not showing up one day won't hurt. I'll pay you for it."

Two guys and a girl were talking a little further away from us. They heard our conversation and called me over to sit with them, pretending they were my friends. I walked over to them and started babbling about anything and everything. We needed to make the fortuitous meeting seem as believable as possible.

The blonde woman looked at us in confusion. Then she took a couple of steps back and sat down on one of the seats, leaving a couple of shopping bags on the floor next to her. At the same time, she lowered her head to look in the floor. From time to time she would look up at the ceiling, as if she were thinking about her actions. Without looking at me, she got off of the metro at the Los Heroes station. The people I was talking with, who had helped me get out of that uncomfortable situation, laughed.

"Did you have an enjoyable conversation with her? It's not the first time that I've seen her. Looks like she's in the habit of harassing young guys like you, someone who looks distracted and has a good boy vibe going," said the girl. I said goodbye to them at the Baquedano station where I needed to get off. I thanked them for the selfless help they gave to a complete stranger like me.

Now a very good-looking woman was talking to me. My instinct told me that her politeness was genuine so I decided to set my spiritual exercise aside and start up a conversation with her.

"Um, my name is Daniel. Nice to meet you. What did you want to know?"

"Are you practicing some kind of metaphysical technique?" She smiled, showing her white teeth in the weak light of an old bulb in the ancient bus's ceiling. Her teeth looked even whiter in contrast to the bright pink color of her lipstick.

"Yes, I'm using an energy flow technique that I learned a couple of months ago. How did you know?"

"Don't be so formal. It makes me feel old. I'm an instructor and I've taught several courses on reiki and healing. Have you heard of reiki? I can help you if you'd like. I love the metaphysical world and the fact that people are discovering this simple but very unknown power to help others."

We talked the rest of the way. It turned out that she lived only a couple of blocks from my house. She told me her life story, and that for several years she had lived with just her son and her granddaughter.

Metaphysics had started to interest me to a great degree, so I didn't hesitate to accept her invitation to get a cup of coffee the following week. I thought that I could learning everything she was of a mind to teach me.

Sara had lived through some unfortunate episodes in her life. Discovering metaphysics had been a lifeline for her. According to her, a friend had revealed the secrets of happiness to her.

"My friend taught me that there is grace in using the human mind's positive abilities. At the beginning, I was skeptical, but once I started practicing the techniques, my life changed forever." Her gaze was deep and full of wisdom.

"In my case, I'm just starting out. It's been a radical change, but I didn't have a choice."

"I bet that you had to live through something hard in your life that made you open your eyes."

"How did you know? You hit the nail on the head." She smiled and we continued to talk for another couple of hours.

As we talked, I realized the extent of her knowledge. She had several years of experience in the world of metaphysical studies. Several times she invited me to attend seminars discussing this topic, but I was never able to go with her.

I have to admit that despite all the evidence I had seen, the fear of social prejudice had become a huge obstacle that wouldn't let me set free my will to evolve.

Months went by after having met Sara, and the trust and friendship between us had grown. I decided to tell her my story.

One winter afternoon, as we sat at a centric café on the corner of Huerfanos and Teatinos Street, I took off all of my masks. She paid complete attention as she listened to my story. Her face didn't move a muscle and she didn't interrupt me a single time as she paid attention to what I said.

"Your story is incredible. Well, as we're being truthful here, I don't know if you'll believe me, but I know how to open portals to the other side to help disoriented spirits to move on to the other dimension where they need to go so they can rest. Many of them can't do it on their own and they stay trapped on Earth, wandering around for a long time. That's why, on occasion, people see them. They can show themselves to their family members in the places where they spent most of their time when they were alive."

"I'd always wondered why they seem so disoriented. Why do some leave forever and others insist on staying here? I have a couple of theories besides yours, but nothing concrete. I think I won't ever know the truth, since we've not evolved enough." I finally had someone I could talk with. Crazy or not, we understood each other.

"I don't see spirits like you do, but I can feel their presence. On a different note, in three weeks there's a seminar related to the change of consciousness that's coming. Humanity is going to make a one-eighty shift. It'll be an awakening on every level. It's going to be interesting but we need to prepare. I'd like to invite you to go so that you can learn more about it and be ready when it happens." It sounded interesting. However, my consciousness was trying to go back to its "rational" phase, and that seminar would be little to no use in achieving that objective. My new world had fallen into serious contradictions and material things were still heavy on my mind.

On one hand, I felt the need to evolve in a spiritual sense but on the other were all the obligations and pending tasks from my everyday life. Of course, I also had to deal with my fears, ghosts, and social pressure. It wasn't going to be easy to let go of my superficial and materialist tendencies. It was a "healthy" tick that had latched on to the largest dog.

Despite Sara's continued invitations to delve deeper into the spiritual and energetic world, I moved further away without noticing. I felt like I was sabotaging my opportunities to learn more. What was happening to me?

With all this going on, I continued to practice the energy flow technique. The empiric demonstration of Graciela's healing done by the instructor that day in the healing workshop had been enough motivation for me to continue and try to master it.

This objective had almost become an obsession. I wanted to reach a state of total control over my reality, something that seemed almost like a utopia. In theory, getting my thoughts to change my reality and making the intangible tangible seemed to be an impossible feat. What would life be like if I managed to do it?

Everything has a limit, however, and mine was about to arrive any day. Then the evidence would surprise me to such an extent that I would make a definite decision to abort the mission.

It happens that even something beautiful grows tedious, as would controlling everything that we see in this dimension. Life would be meaningless. Our capacity for wonder and amazement would be diminished to such an extreme measure that we wouldn't have a reason to live. In other words, it would be like living in a permanent state of self-induced depression.

Maybe, for someone who hasn't evolved much, having the power to make things happen however we want regarding time, cost, and form would be a wonderful dream come true. But, though at first it may not seem so, it's true madness. When we understand that we can say that we've taken a major step towards our real evolution.

CHAPTER XI: MENTAL POWER

The results appeared after practicing for a long time. I was able to alleviate any kind of pain I felt in about a minute, whether it was a headache, stomachache, joint pain, or others. I could make situations come true whenever I wanted, no matter how impossible they seemed. As I applied the technique in a more intense and disciplined manner, the events that I had foreseen happened faster and faster. Some of them bordered on the unbelievable.

I got on the subway one summer afternoon. There was a lot of people on the platform, so I got on the next-to-last car as it wasn't as full. A guy who was acting strange got on at the Padre Hurtado station. After careful observation, I saw that he was a pickpocket. No one else had noticed. He was very skilled.

I decided that I couldn't pass up the opportunity to do something. I concentrated and started to build my reality. I decided that a couple of police officers would get on two stations further ahead and they would catch him. The guy would fall to the floor where he'd try to get free, but it would be impossible. I built the vision in my mind with intricate detail, applying the technique that I had been taught and had practiced with rigorousness. The clearer the image of the eventual reality was, the higher the probability of it coming true.

At the Central metro station (exactly two stations later), two police officers got on. When they tried to apprehend the man, he threw himself on the floor, but his plan for escape failed. They cuffed him and took him off the subway car. Coincidence? The scene I saw was a ninety-nine percent match to the one I had imagined. I was speechless.

Far beyond the analysis to determine the probability of that happening, I was scared. If it was possible for me to make things happen how I wanted them to, what was the point? What about my ability to be surprised? It was like already knowing the end of the movie. Who would want to watch it?

Those who value material goods, money, and commodities would say, "It would be spectacular to get what we want. That's life." However, for a spiritual person o someone like me, the possibility of that happening was far from being a blessing.

The tests I did were quite simple, as simple or more than how to apply the technique. Nevertheless, the results could be complex but convincing enough to make even the most die-hard skeptic begin to doubt.

On occasion, framed by my superficial thoughts, I wanted to see my favorite soccer team win, or enjoy the victory of our amateur soccer club in games that in theory were impossible to win. The overwhelming success of our team in those matches defied logic. It made me doubt my presence in the real world. I had dreamed of this kind of total power since I was young, but when I thought I had it, the enthusiasm I might have felt dissipated little by little, like flesh melting off of a cadaver.

It was the same effect of a child with a new toy. You wait for something for so long that when you finally get it you're not interested in it anymore. Then it's left abandoned in the furthest and most hidden corner of the house.

When I wanted to obtain something, whatever it was, it came into my possession with improbable ease. For me, the technique had become a way of life, something infallible. As time went on and I gained more practice, it was easier and faster to obtain the desired effects.

After contemplating the success of several tests, I reached a simple conclusion: the essence of life isn't in controlling everything around us. It's not the ability to make our reality into what we want. No spiritual human being would want to exist knowing beforehand what would happen. Life is a voyage where we live and activate senses that allow us to perceive what our soul wishes to experience, without losing the capacity to be surprised.

It's probable that you can change some part of your destiny, but not all of it. Free will is the cornerstone to take the different paths that life opens up before us. However, there are situations that happen whether we want them to or not. We can postpone them, but it won't be for long. They are part of our story and need to be fulfilled no matter what. Because of that we need to keep in mind that tomorrow is today.

I started to remember some experiences in my life I could use to sketch some additional conclusions. For example, when I was seven years old, my mother took us to visit Aunt Victoria, one of her best friends. She was a short woman with round eyes and a slight frame. She was a social butterfly and was married to a man who worked as a paint and body mechanic. They had three children, the oldest of which was the same age as me. The other two were one and three years younger, respectively.

They were renting an old house with a large yard in the La Cisterna neighborhood in Santiago that doubled as an auto repair shop for a couple of partners in the business. The place was a veritable car graveyard covering a large part of the available yard. The site emanated the suffocating smell of gasoline mixed with burnt engine oil.

The "great truck," an imposing vehicle used in mining, dominated the northwest corner of the property after having been left to its fate there several years before.

The cabin of the old colossus was rusted. There were no windows or upholstery on the seat. In front of it there was a mechanical well about two meters deep, and it was the preferred play area for the children who visited there.

That week sometime in the mid-seventies, Aunt Victoria had organized a reunion for family and friends. Because of the curfew imposed during that time, get togethers usually ended in "malones" or house parties full of dancing and celebration. The house was full of people. The six kids went to play on the great truck. Among them were Aunt Victoria's three sons and three-year-old Paul, son of one of the guests. We reached the great mass of steel and walked up to the door where a rope dangled, just grazing the upper part of one of the tires.

"We need to climb the rope to get up into the cabin. I'll get a chair so we can reach it," said Jorge, the oldest brother and leader of that day's expedition.

"All right, but what are we going to do about Paul?" I asked, worried on seeing the toddler's enthusiastic expression at the chance of climbing the steep structure.

"I'll climb up first and you can hand him up to me. Then I'll pull him up. Don't underestimate him. Paul is a better climber than we are." In our innocence, we had no idea of the danger this represented.

"Are you sure?"

"Don't worry, Paul's done it before. The last time was just a couple of days ago." Jorge grabbed the rope and started to climb. He struggled to get up to the top. After several attempts, we got the toddler up into the cabin. He sat smiling in the interior. Seeing his happy face was like looking at an amateur mountain climber reaching the summit of Mount Everest.

The rest of us started to climb up as well, struggling all the way. Due to the height, the crude access, and our size, getting down from the mountain of steel wasn't going to be an easy task.

We made it up into the old rusty cabin. Once inside, we started to play. We jumped and moved around from one end to the other, up and over the colossus's steering wheel. The entire structure shook a little, which caused me enough unease to catch my attention. Something had me worried and on alert, but I didn't know what.

While the rest of the group jumped around and yelled with delight in the cabin, I looked out one of the glassless windows expecting to see a panoramic view of a beautiful sunny day. On instinct, I looked at the back end of the steel structure. There were two support hooks, one attached to the cabin and the other to the great truck's chassis. Both were held up by a thin wooden branch of a poplar tree which looked about to break. My brain went numb when I realized the grave danger we were in. Our destiny depended on the fragile branch that wouldn't withstand our weight along with the cabin's for much longer before it collapsed and let the heavy metallic structure fall to the ground with us in it. My pupils dilated and my heart began to race like a formula one race car.

"Jorge! We need to get down! The cabin is going to collapse!" I yelled with childish desperation. At first, no one paid attention to my warning. They continued playing and yelling and not paying any attention.

"We always play here and nothing ever happens. Stop being a worrywart and come have fun with us," Jorge replied with his high-pitched voice. I turned back to the window to check on the unstable branch's condition. What I saw was terrifying; the branch was breaking bit by bit. In a matter of minutes tragedy would strike. I started to cry and scream like crazy.

"We need to get down now! This thing is going to fall! We'll all end up crushed! See for yourselves! We're only held up by a tiny branch!"

When Jorge saw how upset I was, he poked his head out of the window to take a look. "Holy cow, he's right! We need to get down now!" the scared blond boy yelled when he realized how serious the situation was.

We started our desperate descent. In our haste, most of us grabbed the rope and jumped down as fast as we could. Some of us fell to the floor crying in fear and because of the pain from the impact. Paul and Jorge were the only ones who remained in the cabin. The branch was a couple of minutes away from breaking in half and letting the immense structure fall.

"I don't know how to get Paul down! He'll break something if I let him fall from up here!" Jorge yelled in a strained voice.

"Just toss him down to us, we'll catch him! Hurry up! The cabin is going to fall and you won't have time to get down!" I yelled back between sobs with tears in my eyes. The blond boy took Paul's hands and brought him to the door. The toddler felt that something was wrong and his eyes opened wide in fright. When he saw himself dangling from so high up, he started to cry.

"Come on, let him go!" I yelled. Jorge closed his eyes and dropped the toddler. In the same instant he grabbed the rope and jumped out of the cabin, crashing onto the ground. Not a second later the heavy cabin started to tilt to the front, it's encounter with the ground imminent.

"Ow, my legs!" exclaimed Jorge.

The toddler fell on me and on one of the blond boy's brothers, hitting his head not too hard against the dirt. Almost at once, as if it had just been waiting for us children to evacuate, the branch broke and with it the metallic heap came down like a building being demolished, hitting the ground with unprecedented violence, and tumbling end over end until it stopped in front of the well.

The violent impact created an infernal stentorian sound and lifted a cloud of dust that covered several feet around us. The deafening commotion made our families and several neighbors come running to see what had happened.

On seeing the disastrous scene, Aunt Victoria, my mother, and everyone else present cried out, fearing the worst. They walked around the great truck's body until they found us sitting next to it on the other side, dumbfounded at the terrifying scene. No one could believe it.

"Jorge, what happened, son? Is everyone all right? How did the truck's cabin end up like that?" Aunt Victoria asked with tears in her eyes.

"I don't know, Mom. I just know that we had a close call."

"Is everyone okay, Victoria? I heard the kids singing and playing and then a crash. Don't tell me the cabin fell off the old truck, did it?" asked a worried neighbor. Further behind was Juan, the mechanic in charge of the yard who, when he saw the structure on top of the well, grabbed his head in his hands.

"Yes, Pedro, thankfully everyone is fine," the small woman replied to the neighbor's question.

"Thank Heavens no one was hurt. If it had fallen on someone, we'd be in a panic right now," said the specialist mechanic.

"Uncle Pedro, we were in the cabin playing. We managed to jump out just before it fell," Jorge commented.

Juan understood the magnitude of what had happened and didn't hesitate to speak to everyone present. "I don't know how this happened or how the children managed to make it out without getting hurt. What I do know is that they avoided a catastrophe. God is great. Someone could have died here today."

There we were, under the attentive eyes of our families as they tried to understand what had happened. After the shock wore off, the six kids clasped our hands, made a circle, and started to chant, "We made it! We made it!" as we made a round. Our voices rang out as we laughed in joy. It didn't last long, though, as a month later Paul, the toddler, died in a tragic manner from pneumonia.

Was it coincidence? Was it written that Paul should have died in the accident and his voyage beyond was delayed because of me, an impertinent child?

Decades later I heard the story on the news about a police officer that had cheated death in a miraculous fashion. He had a metallic pen in one of his pockets that stopped a bullet from piercing his heart. A short time later, the uniformed officer died when for some unexplainable reason a pine tree fell without warning on top of his squad car.

In other words, renouncing absolute control of our reality could be seen as something absurd. Who wouldn't want complete control?

In my life, many times I heard the phrase "power is in the mind," but it always seemed to be a phrase without substance because I had never met anyone who could have made it materialize. See to believe was my motto.

I had made a decision, and it was to never use the treasure I had been taught. What was the point of using it? Could I learn something by changing the course of events or predicting my destiny? Of course not.

No. For me, the technique had made my life predictable. I decided to live my reality in a random manner, just like life had planned it for me. I had to accept whatever happened, whether pain or joy. The most important aspect was that I needed to feel.

Many holograms in the divine dimension want to come back and feel what we do. Some of them left believing that no other reality exists after this one. Maybe that's why so many of them could never take the necessary step to cross the portal toward eternity. They are trapped in limbo, in the cruel state of not knowing whether they're dead or alive.

CHAPTER XII: PORTAL TO THE AFTERLIFE

One day at work I saw Enrique looking worried. The poor man sat at his desk, holding his head between his hands. He had his laptop with him as he looked with tenderness at a picture of his wife and daughter.

"Hey Enrique, what's up? Is everything all right?"

"More or less. Now it's my turn. I need to tell you something that's been weighing on my mind for a while, but because it's a sensitive subject I haven't wanted to talk about it. Come on, we'll get some coffee."

"Go ahead and let it out. After all, you've listened to my stories of the paranormal without saying a word to anyone else. The least I can do is reciprocate."

"Well, you know that my brother committed suicide a few years ago. It still hurts, but he's given me several signs that he's still with me. I feel him near me all the time," he started to cry. I didn't hesitate to walk with him to the cafeteria to get some coffee and give him time to compose himself.

The eight years that I'd worked in the company, the same length of time that I'd known the dark-skinned programmer, had given me the opportunity to meet several of my colleagues' family members. One of them had been his brother. He was a very reserved person, as is common with people who have depression. He had a medium height and build with light colored eyes and straight, chestnut-colored hair. In contrast to Enrique, his skin was a lighter tone. He had fought a long and drawn-out war with depression, but in the end the disease took his life.

"I wanted to know if you know of someone who can help me get rid of the weight that I carry. I know my brother is with me wherever I go, and I also know that it's not good for him because he can't rest like he should."

"I'm sorry you feel that way. I think I can help. I have a friend who can open portals to the afterlife so that disoriented souls can move on to eternity in the divine dimension," I commented.

The strain around his eyes relaxed and he said, "Thank you so much. I'll do whatever you say, but please help me with this. I feel like it's draining my energy. You can come to my apartment and we can do whatever we need to there. I just want this constant state of worry I'm in to end."

As soon as I could I talked with Sara, my expert metaphysical friend. I explained the situation and at once she said she was willing to help.

"Of course I'll help your friend. It's something that those of us who know these things need to do for those around us."

I coordinated the meeting. I knew that Enrique was in a complicated situation because he had told me a very personal matter some time ago in confidence. He was taking medication to keep his diagnosed bipolar syndrome at bay.

"Listen. We need to do a ritual for your friend to open and close a portal to eternity. His brother needs to pass through it. I need to be honest, though. This is the second time I've done something like this. I'm not sure the first one worked, but we have an advantage now. If you're with me, you can guide me and keep an eye out for two things: one, if the portal opens, and two, if his brother goes through it," Sara explained.

I had more doubts than certainty of success but I was willing to help my friend and his deceased brother. "I'm ready. Let's get to it, Sara!"

We agreed to meet at Enrique's apartment at seven p.m. on a spring Thursday night after work. Sara and I arrived on time. Enrique was waiting for us with high hopes.

"Hey. Sara, this is Enrique; Enrique, this is Sara." Both smiled at each other. They both felt confident we would accomplish what we had set out to do. They talked for a few moments about his brother and his life. As they talked, I moved toward the balcony to observe the view. We were on the twenty-third floor, in front of the equestrian club. Soon the uneasy sensation of vertigo made me go back inside to where they were talking.

"Well, you know that I'm here more as an observer. Sara knows how to do this type of stuff. I'm more like her lowly apprentice," I said with a smile. Both of them laughed and Sara started to prepare some things that she had brought with her to start the ritual. The blonde woman looked through her bag and took out a book and some bunches of laurels.

"Ok, let's get everything prepared. Enrique, we need a room with low lighting and a bed where you can lay down," Sara informed him. He led us to a room that was a couple of feet from the kitchen. The apartment on Beauchef Street, near the University of Chile, smack in Santiago's downtown area, boasted of modern, cozy architecture and high-quality accessories.

"Perfect. Lie down here, close your eyes, and try to relax. I'll say a few words but try to keep your mind blank. Daniel, stand somewhere so you can see everything that happens around us. If it's possible, try to observe what happens here and in the other dimension. If you can make the effort to locate Enrique's brother, all the better. The idea is for you to tell me everything he does, as well as how he behaves," Sara instructed without hesitation. She looked and sounded empowered and dedicated to make sure the ritual's smallest detail came out right. Nothing could go wrong.

After some time, Sara started to pronounce a series of words that I couldn't understand. With the laurel in her hands, she moved them back and forth in the air and over Enrique's body. Minutes later, I decided to start looking for the presence of any holograms in the room. Up until then I hadn't seen any strange manifestations. I closed the curtains of the main window a little, thinking that there might be too much light.

"Do you see anything, Daniel?" Sara asked, showing a little impatience.

"No, I don't see anything yet. Maybe it's not my day."

"Sometimes that happens. Let me know if you see anything," she asked as she kept her eyes closed.

There I was, looking around like a periscope with a three-hundred-sixty-degree view, trying to find something that would corroborate the effectiveness of Sara's ritual. Out of nowhere I saw the silhouette of someone standing to Enrique's right, at about where his head was. I focused on it more, and there he was, Enrique's brother. The elusive hologram observed in surprised fascination everything that Sara did. His expression seemed to ask what the reasons behind the ritual were. "What are you doing to my brother?" seemed to be the precise question.

"Sara, I found him. It's Enrique's brother. He's on the right, near Enrique's head," I whispered.

"Unbelievable. Please, don't lose track of him. We need to open the portal as soon as possible," Sara said. She continued with her recital, following each step she had studied to the letter so that the divine portal could be opened.

It didn't take long for the hologram to feel me looking at him. When he did, he walked the few feet that separated us until he was in front of me.

"Sara, Enrique's brother is right in front of me."

"What's he doing? Let me know if you see the portal. I hope you can! It's the only way I'll know if the ritual worked or not," the blonde woman stated in a low voice. In the meantime, Enrique was still lying on the bed with his eyes closed and in silence, just like Sara had instructed.

The transparent man was still by my side. I saw that he tried to talk to me, but, as had been my experience with all other paranormal experiences, I couldn't hear a word. It looked like he was asking for an explanation, reiterating the question, "What is she doing to my brother? Tell me; I need to know." I ventured to talk to him to try to clear up his apparent doubts. Trying to fake ignorance would have been useless.

"She wants you to rest in peace, to go on to eternity. Your brother will be all right with us. Don't worry about it anymore. You just need to wait a couple of minutes until the celestial window opens and you can start your trip." He seemed to understand everything. His face had a peaceful expression when he turned to look at his brother once more.

After the strange prayer and with the laurel still in her hands, Sara drew a rectangular shape in the air near the main window. To me it looked like she had sketched a rectangular frame with smoky edges, though I never saw flames come from it. The smoke never got out of control either. A dense fog was visible within the framed area, similar to the one I had seen at the spirits' clinic. There it was. It was the much awaited and unknown portal to the afterlife which had been opened to take the disoriented hologram to its eternal rest. It was time for him to make his definitive voyage to the farthest reaches of the universe or, I don't know, to reuniting with his loved ones and an eventual supreme being.

"Daniel, do you see anything? The portal is supposed to be open." Sara waited for my answer.

"You're a genius, Sara. The portal is open. What do we do now?"

"Incredible! I'll never forget this. Tell him to walk toward it and to go through as it could close at any moment."

The hologram seemed to understand what was going on. I spoke to him in gentle tones and immediately the man looked at me. My words were soft but decisive.

"You need to go. Look! Right in front of the window there's a door to the other dimension. You need to go through it so you can have eternal rest. If you want, you can say goodbye to your brother before you do it, but then you have to go."

The entire situation was unbelievable. He extended his hand to shake mine and say goodbye. I shook his hand, feeling the cold air of his energy on my skin, confirming his presence.

He floated through the air back to his brother and bent down to kiss him on the forehead. As soon as he had, he started walking towards the smoky portal. When he reached it, he hesitated for a couple of seconds and turned back to look at each of us one last time. His eyes were full of tears but he was calm as he walked through the portal. A few moments later, he vanished in the thick fog of the mysterious door.

In a low but clear voice I did my best to narrate each of his actions so that neither Enrique nor Sara would miss the detailed effects of the amazing ceremony.

"Did he go through the portal?" Sara asked in an anxious tone.

"Yes, he did. I think you can close it now," I suggested.

"Right away. No one's going to believe this, but who cares? I'll take the memory to my grave." Once more she made some strange movements in the air with the laurel bunches, and I heard her say something akin to a prayer in a language I didn't know.

Not long after, the portal closed. The mist swirled around like a vortex and then dissipated. I never imagined I would see something so magical in my life, similar to the paranormal experiences described in movies or on TV. The experience I had just lived through was another element that would forever mark my concept of the world.

Death couldn't be so decisive as to decree the end of life and the eternal cessation of the soul and spirit.

No. Nothing ends with death. On the contrary, something starts from zero, or maybe moves forward. It's a rebirth in a different dimension. It's there, and it exists as much as the sun does. It's a reality that many people deny or react to with ingenuous indifference, influenced by traditional science.

Several days later, Enrique stopped me in one of the hallways of the office building where we worked.

"Daniel, I have to say that at the beginning I didn't believe a word of what you'd tell me. Today, I feel that it's changed my life. I don't know. I've felt lighter ever since your friend did that "machitún" or ritual or whatever you want to call it. You have no idea how thankful I am. I know my brother is in a much better place, and so am I. I hope that you can help more people. You two did a fantastic job," the dark-skinned man commented.

I'm sure that Enrique never suspected that not just his life changed that night. Mine had undergone a total transformation. From that day forward, my thoughts on the spiritual world and the divine would never be the same.

CHAPTER XIII: ENERGY OF THE LIVING

Several months went by. One day as I walked down the street after work, by coincidence I found a great friend of mine who I hadn't seen for some time. We went to grab some coffee at a café near Paseo Ahumada Street, close to the intersection with Huerfanos Street. We talked about a lot of things just to catch up on what had been happening in our lives.

"It's so good to see you after so long, Christian. How have you been?"

"Good, my friend, good. Trying to survive along with my small company. We moved out of the office and are no longer on Gran Avenida. We're in the downtown area now, not far from here, on Moneda Street and San Antonio." At the time, Christian was a man in his thirties and fairly tall. His hair was thin but he had large eyes, pale skin, and a robust build. We had met while working at Infocorp Limited, a company that provided commercial information about people and companies. He was a publicist and had always been sociable with a good personality and very correct in his actions.

"What about you? What have you been up to? Last time I saw you was when I visited you at the clinic, remember?" the expressive man said.

"Really? It's been a long time."

"Maybe you don't remember because you were out of it. I imagine you were high as a kite. You didn't look good at all. I was sure you'd be in there forever."

"I don't remember having seen you, but thanks for visiting. Lucky for me, I'm doing much better now, though I went through a really hard time with my health. It was so bad that I had to take a leave of absence for several months." The trust we had in each other forged through many years of friendship was still intact. I knew that I could talk to him about anything. After we spent a few hours talking, I worked up the courage to tell him everything that had happened in great detail. I really didn't remember his visit to the spirits' clinic. So many people had gone to see me that it's hard to remember everyone, especially as I was a patient taking psychoactive drugs at the time.

"I can't believe what you've told me. To tell the truth, I don't believe in metaphysics, spirits and all that esoteric stuff. I've always believed that they're a good mix of imagination and people's charlatanry. Maybe your depression was why you saw so many strange things," he replied with conviction.

As for me, I had no intention of convincing him to believe my story. However, Christian's curiosity was strong. As a challenge, he wanted to prove the veracity of the supposed powers I had hinted at in my story.

"Let me get this straight. You say you can see dead people in addition to the energy of living persons without them being present? I mean, if I show you an empty workstation at my company, would you be able to see who it belongs to? Stuff like that? That's crazy. If so, the only way to believe it is for you to show me in person. Let's see, what time is it? Ten thirty P. M. Why don't you come to my new office and you can show me your clairvoyant abilities and tell me who works there. Are you up for it or do you want to drop it and forget everything like a good fairytale?" he proposed, laughing as he drank the last sip of his fourth cup of coffee.

"I don't usually go for cheap tricks like that, but since you brought it up, let's go. People are blind. You have to show them something so they can believe it. They won't even believe in themselves even if they see their reflection in a mirror," I laughed.

"Don't be sarcastic. After all, we're the ones who move the world."

"I don't agree. The problem is the how much they need to pay for it and the miniscule return on investment. It's safe to say that it's a terrible deal, but they don't react even if they know it. We need to be off our rockers to continue feeding into this neoliberal Truman show."

"Now you're going to say that you're a communist?" Christian interjected with an ironic smile.

"Not in the least. You don't have to be a communist to understand that society as we know it is ephemeral. The worst part is that we're on a crash course and no one's doing anything about it.

"You're right. However, no one has come up with a better model. Would you have a solution, by any chance?"

"I'd like to say that I do, but that's a topic for another time. I just want to say that even anarchy would be less destructive," I chuckled.

We reached 814 Moneda Street, just before the intersection with San Antonio Street in downtown Santiago. The office was in an old building. We got on the elevator after Christian tucked in his shirt, looking at his reflection in the mirror in front of the elevator.

"What do you think about my shirt, huh? I got it a few days ago.

It was expensive. I need to keep up my appearance since I work in sales. Did you see my Rolex? Dress for success, they say. This country is very classist, so if you can't beat them, join them."

"Well, after having thought like you do for a long time, a lot of us have made do with the crumbs we get without questioning it at all. I paid a steep price for going along with that train of thought, you know. And now look at how I ended up, telling tales of spirits and trying to prove the existence of that kind of energy to a skeptical capitalist like you."

The bald thirty-something man barked out a laugh and put his hand on my shoulder, indicating that we had reached our destination.

We got out and walked a few steps before stopping in front of a brown door made of glass and wood. Christian pulled a keychain out of his pocket and selected a couple of keys that he used to open the locks on the door.

He turned on the lights as we stepped inside. I could see a medium-sized office divided into two sections. The first one was dominated by the meeting room. There other side had at least ten workstations, one next to the other. All of them had a computer and drawers to store supplies in.

We walked through the place. The lights from the cars passing by on Moneda Street towards the west reflected on the paintings hanging on the white wall, lighting it up with intermittent illumination.

"So what do you think? This is my base. Looks good, doesn't it?" said the large-eyed publicist.

"Congrats! The new office does look good. I'm sure you'll find the success you deserve, my friend," I said with sincerity as we continued our walk-through of the premises.

"Alright then, Mr. Psychic. How about we get this show on the road and you start telling me about the people who work here? By the way, everyone here is alive. No one has passed on yet, knock on wood," he commented with a smile, showing off the elegant fillings in his bright, white teeth.

"I need you to turn off the light and pick the workstation where you'd like to start."

"A-ha! So you're sure of yourself, are you? Alright. I'll turn the lights off. I want you to start here. Tell me, who works here?" he laughed without letting go of the cigarette he had lighted when we entered the building. I concentrated for a few seconds, concentrating on the desk. It didn't take long for a clear image of the person who owned the workspace to appear.

"I see a young woman, younger than thirty. Her hair is black and she has light-colored skin. She frequently uses a sky-blue blouse, slacks, and black shoes. For some reason she always looks for something in her purse. She picks it up and puts it back down on the floor often. She's looking for something."

As I described what I saw, Christian remained silent until he couldn't hold back any longer. "Paula! Yes, it's Paula! No, I think that what you said was just a coincidence. You've obviously come by here before." Still surprised, he ground out the cigarette in an old ashtray placed on top of a modern table. We continued on to the next workstation. "It was just luck. Okay, shaman, tell me who works here." I observed with care until the energy of a young man appeared. I had learned in the spirits' clinic that people leave stagnant energy in the places they frequent every day.

"It's a young man. I see him thumbing through the pages of a manual in an enthusiastic manner. He's also got dark hair and light-colored skin. He's wearing a white shirt and jeans. He looks very studious and neat," I said.

"Unbelievable! That's Pedro, our programmer. Enough! More than enough, that's incredible. What else can I say? Impressive. Have you consulted with a medium, a doctor, or someone else who can help you understand all this?" Christian asked as he lit another cigarette.

"You have no idea everything I've done to find someone who can give me a logical explanation. I've got nothing. I'm stranded in this sea of doubt. It's a bubble I don't know how to get out of. I'm lost. Maybe I'll never find a convincing answer, much less discover the truth of it all."

Christian held his head in one hand, his gaze not wavering from the workstations we had checked. It seemed like he was trying to see what I had seen. "This is the first time I've seen something like this. I remember having heard of paranormal situations, talking about spirits and such, but I never had the opportunity of seeing someone demonstrate these abilities in my presence. I knew that we all have energy, but I always thought it was something intangible. I never imagined that someone could see and much less recognize people without them being present." He pulled on the cigarette and let out a deep breath before putting it out in the bronze ash tray.

"Don't worry. I've felt as flustered as you do for a long time. If before I thought I was ignorant, now I think that I'm even more ignorant than I imagined. Energy can be seen; it's something real. It's even been proven by science, or so I've read."

"Come on, let's get out of here before a specter of some sort shows up," joked the thirty-something year old.

We left the eighth floor, stopping to say our goodbyes in front of the building.

"I have to admit that this experience surprised me. Maybe there is something beyond what we see and I've never noticed," Christian reflected.

"We live clinging so tight to capitalism in an unhealthy manner that we can't see the beauty in a drop of water falling from a leaf. There, in that drop, we can see the entire universe. The day that we give it value and go back to living a simple life, we won't need to go out to look for the beauty in nature. It will seek us out on its own," I said, speaking from my heart.

We said goodbye with a warm hug and the promise to stay in touch.

CHAPTER XIV: THE MEDIUM

Time went on. One day after running errands, Graciela came back home feeling tired. Nevertheless she looked happy, as if she had good news.

On one hand, our three children had gotten used to their father's permanent paranormal stories and all the daily situations that I lived through with the holograms. I hadn't lost hope that I would find the truth I searched for. The quest for answers wouldn't stop within me and I wouldn't give up until I found them.

"Daniel, I found someone who I'm sure can help. She's a really good medium that someone recommended and that I went to see yesterday. She lives on the road to Lonquen. I talked to her about you and she's interested in meeting you."

"What? I don't want to hear any more about mediums. You know how many I've seen without anything to show for it. I don't have any more money or time to throw away," I reacted with evident distaste.

"Using your picture and birthday she determined that you have psychic gifts that you need to channel in the appropriate fashion. If not, you could get even more mixed up." Anything related to mediums had me fed up. Each time the subject was mentioned my stomach would churn.

Graciela tried to convince me for several days that we should visit the supposed medium, but it was in vain. I was so sick of hearing that esoteric term. It was more than enough for me.

"Please! Do it for us. We need to put up with your daily stories and confusion. At least we'll feel better knowing exactly what's going on with you." I saw Graciela felt so desperate that I agreed to go see the medium, though it was a begrudging capitulation. I decided that it would be the last visit I ever made to see someone with supposed paranormal abilities.

Graciela managed to book an hour with the so-called Lonquen medium, though it wasn't without complication. Rumor said that her schedule was packed.

One afternoon we got into the car and drove toward an area with abundant suburban country plots. On the way, I meditated on the numerous people who I'd consulted and from whom I'd gotten nothing. Would this be another one? The thought that this wouldn't be the exception was stuck in my head. Who was the woman that was so talked about in Maipu, where I lived?. Of course she must have had some high-profile, isolated instances of success, but she wasn't going to impress, let alone scam, me. I'd had enough with so many charlatans saying they could see beyond what we see every day.

No sir, I'd determine at once if her story was just a way to gain economic benefits of some type or, in the least probable case, if it would help channel the so-called gift that I'd received out of the blue and had changed my life in a radical way.

We got lost on the way. Graciela had forgotten how to get there since all the access roads to the plots were identical.

"I think this is the place. You'll be surprised when you see the huge house and land that she's got. Judging from that alone, her gifts have brought her good returns," Graciela said.

"I don't know. I just want her to be trustworthy and for her to have the power people say she does. I repeat, this will be the last time I'm going to deal with this type of person." I felt foolish consulting with another hypothetical medium.

High brick walls blocked the view of the mysterious house. Graciela stopped the car next to an impressive and elegant gate made of wood and steel. After ringing the bell a couple of times and registering our entrance, the remote-controlled lock opened to reveal a dazzling, beautiful house located on a piece of land so large that you couldn't see the property limits.

The dwelling built in a North American architectural style rose up with huge windows that were impeccably clean. The garden emulated a luxurious park adorned with beautiful trees and splendorous flowers. The field was embroidered with acacias, petunias, gladiolas, and well-kept lawns. The ostentatious installations reminded me of the impressive mansions in the high-class neighborhoods, very uncommon in the suburbs.

We parked a few feet from the front door. When we got out of the car our jaws dropped when we got a closer look at the house's admirable and imposing beauty. Before we could knock on the door, it opened from inside. A short woman with large eyes and a heavy sprinkling of gray hair walked out to meet us. I calculated she was around her seventies, maybe a little less. She radiated tranquility and natural charm, an angel that I don't remember ever having seen reflected in another person before.

"Hi! How are you? Welcome. You must be Daniel, right? I was waiting for you. Did you have a hard time finding the place?"

"Could this woman really be the medium?" I wondered.

"Hi! Yes. I had a hard time convincing him to come, but we're here now. Let's see how it goes," said Graciela in a relieved tone.

"Good. Can I offer you anything? Water, coffee, or tea?" the woman offered with commendable hospitality.

"Nothing for me, thanks. I had something to drink earlier," I replied as I observed the interior of the house with care.

"Me neither," replied Graciela.

"Come with me, please, while your wife waits in the main lounge. Please make yourself at home. There are some magazines here for you to read if you'd like. I need to speak with Daniel alone," the Lonquen medium explained to Graciela.

The gentle pythoness exuded jovial energy. Her eyes were wide and her face animated. We walked along a short hallway and soon entered her office. In it was a desk and a couple of chairs that looked like they were arranged for a patient and their companion. "If she told Graciela to wait in the lounge she probably has something very personal to say," I thought.

"Please take a seat and relax so we can have a pleasant conversation. I'll be right back," the serene older woman indicated, leaving me alone in the room for a few minutes.

As I waited, I focused on observing the office's décor. There were several dark brown bottles on a table. They looked like some kind of medication, so I didn't touch them.

Oil paintings hung on the wall. The design and subtlety of the paintings displayed the artist's great skill. I sat fascinated by the intricate details until the woman came back.

"Alright! I'm back. Are you curious about the bottles?" she inquired with an evident smile on her lips.

"What? Oh, yes, they're eye-catching. Do they contain some kind of medicine?"

"Sort of, but they're natural. I also work with Bach flower treatments. They're very effective for certain pathologies. The other day your wife took some to use on your youngest son, Gabriel. I understand that among other developmental disorders he also suffers from extreme hyperactivity," the woman commented after seeing that I had paid special attention to the numerous eye-catching bottles.

"Yes, she came home with a couple of them. I hope that they help my son. We've tried everything with him, but nothing has worked so far," I commented.

"Well, shall we get started? Your wife told me that you've been carrying some unexplained problems for a while and you haven't been able to solve them, leaving you preoccupied more often than not. She said that you haven't been yourself for a long time and that you don't know what to do. You feel overwhelmed." I raised my hand to my chin in a defensive but at the same time humble gesture. The gray-haired woman transmitted peace and serenity which made me feel comfortable in her presence.

"Well, it's kind of hard for me to talk about this with people I don't know, but I'll try to explain it despite my insecurities. I think I can see supernatural things." I was ashamed to talk in absolutes. "I consider them hallucinations caused by lesions on the brain that I believe developed after a bout of severe depression. I've been dealing with it for the last four years," I continued. A certain degree of distrust snaked its way into my consciousness when I heard her speak. It was strange. At times I trusted her and at times I didn't. The specter of prejudice reared its head again and again. What was I doing there? She noticed my discomfort as I spoke.

"Daniel, please don't second-guess yourself. Talk to me freely. I'm here to help. I think I know exactly what's going on with you but I want to hear all the details direct from the source."

"All of your colleagues have said the same. There here to help, but they haven't been able to. It's not easy for me to talk about this."

"I know, but please don't give up. This could be the occasion where you can leave with something that puts your mind at ease."

As the conversation went on I was more convinced that at long last I was in front of someone serious, professional, and trustworthy. I relaxed and started to tell her everything in great detail, starting with the day it all began. I had the vague hope that after the visit ended everything would be wrapped up. I'd never have to talk to anyone about it again. It was my silver bullet.

She listened with care. Her silence reached the point where it felt uncomfortable while my verbosity droned on, worthy of a prime-time news anchor. I didn't want to leave out a single detail. I needed to make the context crystal clear so that we could reach the best possible conclusion and she could give an accurate diagnosis about the best path forward.

It took about an hour, during which time she asked a couple of questions, though nothing too complex. The absence of any expression of surprise even when faced with the story of some unconventional experiences suggested that I was in the presence of someone who was used to the inexplicable.

"After listening to you, I can say with all assurance that you're an indigo adult. This type of person always goes against the established system because they fight for their spiritual instead of material progress. Also, they have some common psychic attributes. In order to prove what I say, it would be good to have a test. You've told your wife that you see spirits, correct? Would you be willing to do an experiment here in this room? What do you need to see them?" she asked, looking me in the eyes. Her request didn't seem strange. I was willing to go along. After all, I didn't have anything to lose. The word indigo and all the supposed special characteristics made me feel unique but uncomfortable at the same time. Depression had made my self-esteem plummet and, as such, everything that had happened before and after my collapse didn't seem respectable of someone with supposed exceptional gifts. I was unworthy.

"Yes, I don't have a problem with it. I just need you to turn off the light and let me concentrate for about fifteen seconds or so."

She reassured me that she believed in everything I had told her. However, I thought I saw a flash of skepticism on her face, though I didn't pay much attention to it. The die was cast and there was nothing to lose.

"Excellent, then let's get started." She stood up and walked toward the switch near the door to her office. She flipped it and the lights went out.

I adjusted my position so I could concentrate without moving from the chair. After twenty seconds the divine spectrum of the room flooded my senses. Whatever lay beyond this world was close. Little by little the room was clouded by mist. Within minutes we were in the middle of the divine dimension.

I observed every corner of the darkened room. The beautiful oil paintings on the wall looked fuzzy. Within the mist I saw the unmoving silhouette of the woman who in total silence seemed to be waiting for my reaction.

A few minutes passed before my eyes almost bulged out of my head due to shock at seeing something that I had never imagined I would see. I grabbed onto the armrests of the chair and thought that I would faint on the spot.

Just a few feet from the woman two very tall men - more than six-and-a-half feet tall - stood next to her. They had long, thick hair down to their shoulders, and their hair as well as their beards were the same shade of gray. Their eyes were brown and their pale faces emanated a sense of indescribable purity. They wore resplendent white tunics. There was no doubt about how special their presence was. Brilliant white light surrounded their bodies, extending outward around them.

I was astounded. I remembered that as a child I had seen this kind of person in the Book of Mormon of the Church of Jesus Christ of Latter-Day Saints, a congregation that my mother had taken us to for some time to study.

The celestial beings were constant in their observation of her. They didn't look away once. Their faces made me feel profound peace, like a country lake, and were comparable only with the lovely woman in the green tunic that I had seen on my first night at the spirits' clinic.

Under the attentive though invisible stare of the Lonquen medium who I could barely make out in the dark, I started to relate what I saw down to the smallest detail.

"What do you see, Daniel? Can you see anything?" the medium asked.

"Yes. I see two very tall men standing a few feet away from you. They're dressed in impeccable white tunics and have gray hair down to their shoulders. Their beards are exuberant and their noses have a perfect shape. They have brown eyes. They're beautiful. It's clear that they're no ordinary beings, and they're looking at you with so much peace that it would calm a fiery giant. They're surrounded by white light that flares from their bodies." I spoke as if in a trance, overcome by extasy produced by the incredible beauty of the vision. It was as dazzling as it was incredible.

"Please, Daniel, go on. What else do you see?" the anxious woman asked.

I tried to see her in the dark to try to make out the expression on her face. I could barely see her. Next to her there was a child, about five years old, who held on to her arm as if begging for protection. The child's eyes gleamed like a cat's eyes in the dark. They were huge, eager for love and joy.

Who were these people? What were they doing there? What did they want? Many people say that they're protected by angels or teachers. This particular event just managed to increase the unending list of questions that I had been trying to get off my back for years. What is life? Who commands us? Are we the only expression of life on this globe? How many dimensions are there? How do they interact? Mankind searches for life outside of our planet when it seems like millions of life forms coexist here.

The presence of those men with their distinctive tunics and the boundless beauty of their faces spoke without words of the undeniable similarity with our dimension. With everything I'd seen up to that point, I concluded that differences in race, social standing, and intellectual coefficient also existed in the other plane. Excluding the tunic and an apparent mission of peace, what connection did the girl dressed in green have to the giant, bearded men in white?

The number of questions multiplied in my head. Once more, I felt like I was going to go crazier than I thought I already was. Even so, it was all fascinating in the extreme. It would be tremendously valuable information to continue my investigation with and move forward with my daring pretentions of bettering my spiritual illiteracy.

"That's it. That's all I can see." The woman stood up and hurried to turn the light on. Then she went back to her seat and put her face in her hands. She leaned on the desk and looked at me in astonishment before taking a deep breath as if she couldn't get enough air.

"What? Don't look at me like that. Is what I said really that crazy?

Let me guess, you're now going to prescribe some of your famous flowers? Either that or there's nothing you can do." I smiled a few moments to ease the mood that I though was way too tense.

"It's incredible, Daniel! I can't believe it. I have the ability to feel and hear presences. I see them like small clouds of fog, without any human shape or form. You, on the other hand, can see them but can't hear what they say," she commented.

"Are you saying that what I just saw isn't a hallucination?" It was the first time that a medium confirmed some aspect of what I could see. But, how? How could she guarantee that what I described was real?

"Daniel, the first thing you need to do is believe in what your eyes show you. What you saw is real, there's no doubt about it. Up until today there have only been two people who have described what you just did. For about a decade I've been holding workshops on the weekends for children. One day, a five-year-old boy came up to me and asked, 'Who are those two giants dressed in white?' A year later, during one of the workshops, a seven-year-old girl asked me in a frightened voice, 'Why are those two huge men with beards and dressed in white with you?'" When I heard her confirmation, my shoulders relaxed and I lay back against the chair and stretched my cramped legs. A feeling of relief and relaxation took over my body. The person speaking was a medium, and the most believable one in the area at that. The jigsaw puzzle was starting to show how to put it together.

"You're the first adult to confirm what the children said they saw. Believe it once and for all, you gave a gift that's been given to you for a higher purpose: to help others. You have the pleasant responsibility of being an indigo adult," the eloquent woman assured me.

The word "responsibility" brought with it an immediate sense of revulsion. I felt that I had been too persistently responsible for a large part of my life, and it had brought me more than enough problems and too little rewards.

Maybe because I had been too responsible I had taken up causes that weren't mine to defend. I fought battles I shouldn't have fought. I thought that this tendency in addition to my perfectionist personality had ruined my life.

Besides, not knowing how to say no and wanting to please everyone around me hadn't been gratifying in the slightest. Responsibility of being indigo? No. I didn't want to hear anything more about being responsible. Whatever it was, good or bad, give it to someone else, not to me. I wouldn't fall into that trap again.

"I'm sorry, but there has to be a rational explanation. I've never inquired about the supposed paranormal gifts people have. I refuse to believe that it's something exceptional or divine. What you say is too much because, to be frank, I'm too ignorant in this matter. I think I should see a neurologist instead. This has to be caused by a lesion on my brain due to the severe depression that I went through some time ago. Maybe it's a tumor, though I hope it's not. And finally, if what you say is true, I never asked for the damn gift that you're talking about. I don't want to have it. I'm fed up with the whole stupid game. I want to return it right now to whoever gave it to me," I ranted. My values and earthly upbringing posed a ferocious resistance to accepting what I had just heard.

"If you don't accept it, you're rejecting a divine mandate from God. I'm sure you wouldn't want to disappoint him in that manner, would you? Please think about it. Take your time. I understand that it's not easy for you, but I have to say something. I'd really like for us to work together. I can hear what they say and you see them. We complement each other. What do you say?" I remained silent a few moments and checked the time on my cell phone. It was almost ten p. m.

All in all, the visit had been a good one. I had new and valuable information that I needed to analyze to see if it was possible to move forward in my persistent search for answers.

As an agnostic, there was no point in convincing me that it was a gift given by a supposed god. For me, there had to be logical explanation and I was going to find it no matter what.

The woman was surprised. There was no doubt about it. I saw on her face the whirlwind of questions that occupied her mind. They were in all probability the same questions that consumed me. For that same reason I didn't feel ready to accept an invitation like the one she gave me that day.

"I'm sorry, but no. I'm not interested in devoting my time to this. Everything that's happened has worn me out. This is the last time that I'm willing to visit a medium to look for answers as it's more than likely that I'll never find any. You've helped me, it's true, and I thank you, but it's not enough for me," I said, getting up to go look for Graciela.

"Think about it. I'll give you my number in case you change your mind. Call me and together we'll be able to help a lot of people in need." I took her card and put it in one of my pockets. After all, I didn't have the slightest intention of seeing her or stepping foot in her house again.

"Thank you but I'm no saint willing to take on this responsibility," I laughed in irony.

"I never said you were a saint. I just said you are an indigo adult with certain characteristics that allow you to help others. Saints are much more evolved compared to us, and by the way, aren't on Earth. They're in Heaven."

"Well, that's a relief! I know that I'm a long way from obtaining my place in heaven. They might not even want me there. It wouldn't be a surprise after I rejected their offer."

On the way to the car I didn't say a single thing to Graciela, and she didn't ask me either. It was already dark.

When we got to the car, I opened the passenger seat and got in. There were several minutes of silence. Graciela still hadn't asked anything. She was afraid that she'd driven her crazy husband into a new crisis. I looked out the windshield and gave a small smile.

"Enough! Tell me everything! How did it go? Was the trip worth it or did we just throw our money away?" She knew me. I think she had a feeling that something had happened.

"It wasn't what I expected, but I got something more to help me keep investigating," I replied. In the meantime I was piecing together how to structure my investigation to give it a wider scope. An elusive thought snaked through my mind, telling me that the story was just beginning.

CHAPTER XV: INVESTIGATION AND TECHNIQUE

In effect, the meeting with the Lonquen medium had reactivated my motivation to investigate the subject. I would focus on the story of the children that, according to her, had seen the same thing I did. But what was so special about these children that they could see the other dimension? I included my son Gabriel in the question as he had also shown an ability to see these transparent spirits.

My nightly routine changed to me staying in my room with my dog, a laptop, a notebook, a pencil, and a thermos of coffee. I started to do simple analysis on the information, looking up and reviewing statistical medical data from several universities and research centers from around the world. It took me back to the time I worked as a biologist.

One of the aspects of my study centered on the eyes and their relationship with the human brain.

Studies said that certain defects are present when a human is born that the body repairs during childhood and that, at times, may need external treatment. If not, then these anomalies persist until death.

I wondered what caused some children to have imaginary friends. Why is it that it's common for them to see things that no one else believes? When faced with something unexplainable, adults usually say that it's someone's imagination. However, the phrase "from the mouth of babes" implies they speak the truth. I spent months going over all the information I could find on the internet about children who said that they had witnessed paranormal events.

On the other hand, I had always been curious about drunk people who had sworn that they had been witnesses to disconcerting visions that they then shared but no one believed them. That was also how I heard about many stories of drunk people who had become stone-cold sober after witnessing these supernatural events.

I invested a significant amount of time going over online stories of people who had been under the influence and who were sure they had seen things beyond our wildest imaginations, usually related to encounters with spirits or otherworldly beings.

It was a situation similar to drug addicts when they hallucinate and say that they can see beyond what's evident.

As a result of the drugs I had taken to combat my depression, I had also been an involuntary witness to these apparitions. The difference was that I had taken charge of the events and tried to find human as well as other coincidental, and less conventional, witnesses such as animals. Because of this I was determined to find a logical explanation.

What did these three types of people have in common? First, in a society like ours, they usually lack credibility, in particular when it comes to fantastic stories of paranormal events. Second, the three types of people had a high probability of having of having problems with their vision. I started to read through the available literature to confirm some ideas.

Why? Children start to go through a stage of ocular instability, frequently up until the age of ten. For example, some of them have amblyopia or lazy eye and need to use patches in order to correct it. If not, then the condition remains throughout the rest of their lives and, in the worst case, gets worse to the point of needing surgical correction.

At certain levels of inebriation a person has a hard time keeping their vision focused, a condition known as diplopia or double vision. This piece of information allowed me to infer that they are also prone to losing control of their eyes, kind of like a compass getting lost in the Bermuda Triangle.

During the course of my investigation I also found out that drug addicts or those who take antidepressant medication such as amitriptyline and fluoxetine, can also experience diplopia. In addition, ocular defects come with a series of disorders related to the information that these organs relay to the brain. They can incur in errors while processing and generating the images we use to interpret our reality and the world around us. It's similar to what happens when a TV antenna isn't placed correctly, resulting in distorted images on the screen.

Ocular stability doesn't stabilize in children until they reach the age of ten. Before that, their eyes are like balls in an unstable optical roulette. Maybe that was the answer I was looking for, one that was far removed from the supposed gift that had been conferred to me by a supposed generous supreme being. Even so, the path towards complete truth was longer than I could imagine.

After conscientious reflection, I arrived at some conclusions. I remembered the medication I had been given before going to the room I stayed in the first night in the spirits' clinic where everything happened. On that occasion, I felt that my vision was unfocused when I lay down. It felt like they moved all over the place until I was able to focus them. However, a few minutes later it would happen again, each time in different positions until I could focus on one point. That was when the divine dimension opened before me. The portal to the afterlife. It was an unknown and fascinating space that can't be escaped from. There were several reasons to not avoid the divine perspective, and in my opinion, the main one was being able to be a witness to something that in this dimension is usually interpreted as a fantasy, something impossible or improbable to see by most people.

We tend to believe that we live in a world of certainty with tangible and rational aspects. See to believe is our culture's motto. This is because the vast majority don't have time for it or to think. If we're lucky, there's only time to act. In an implicit fashion, the political construct that regulates the common citizen seems to be created in such a way that its central purpose is to obey. There is no chance to think or even question each one of the events that surround and affect them, happening during their short and downtrodden life.

One of my friends used to call it the culture of idiocy, where everything is superficial, disposable, and volatile. Here, the only thing that matters is individual wellbeing and comfort. It's a place full of narcissism, envy, egomania, and unbridled, absurd, and unceasing competition that ends up destroying us and the irreplaceable ecosystem around us.

The time in the spirits' clinic is the only occasion that as an adult I've had the opportunity to observe what's around me. In my daily routine, as a slave to the system, it was impossible. How could it not be? Being in the information systems sector, which is its own world of bits and bytes, it seemed that I was in another existential orbit where time passes three or more times faster than ordinary.

The virtual environment is a fascinating but cold and unanimated ecosystem depending on human intelligence, though I don't know for how long. One of the many pathological human vagaries seeks to generate artificial intelligence. Though it may sound apocalyptic, it's the prediction of a life-or-death struggle that will be fought for control of the world that will result in nothing other than self-destruction through the third and last world war. It is another threat in addition to the biological one that has us in the grip of a pandemic.

I locked myself in a dark room. Standing still and with my mind blank, I focused my senses on achieving a state of maximum concentration. According to my calculations, it was the most effective way of reaching the divine dimension. I wouldn't concentrate on the stage but on the technical aspects so I could determine what position my pupils were in. I considered they were the key to opening the magical door, the portal to the afterlife, a fascinating gateway to a world of spirits present in an undetermined time and space.

I spent the next several months like that. There were days when I would delve with great passion into the two concentric black universes full of mystery and intrigue, windows to a starry infinity, hostages of an iris that knows well how to establish limits. They're universes that are like a fountain that traps a splatter of a restless sea and shows stunning textures, mandalas formed by a supreme being.

After carrying out many tests I believed I had found the perfect position in both direction and distance. Then I came to the conclusion that both pupils needed to focus on a specific point, with the lines of sight crossing each other at the midpoint between the first solid part of the background and the observer's body, forming a thirty-degree angle at that point after which I named my theory. In effect, the simplicity of the technique compared to the complexity of the result was disconcerting. All that was needed was to focus in a similar fashion as when looking at a 3D image though without the need for special lenses.

Once this position is achieved, according to my studies, somewhere between thirty second and a minute should pass for the brain to fix the precise points in space and open the sacred curtain that separates the divine dimension from ours. In that manner the observer could start to visualize the occult from that unknown but captivating perspective, all without needing supposed extraordinary gifts. A parallel universe would open to them where the amazing plane home to the holograms and vital energy like auras or chakras vibrate in freedom and peace in a marvelous paradise where few people can venture.

After finding the recipe ad practicing, I finally thought I had a logical answer to the multi-dimensional mess in my head. The most complex challenge was yet to come. I needed to prove my theory, which would demand additional effort. It would be a difficult mission to carry out, though not impossible. I needed a volunteer that could accompany me in a spiritual journey that would either give me greater certainty or, on the contrary, utter disappointment.

Who would be brave enough to walk with me in the dark, looking for an apparition? It would have to be someone with a very open mind, with no prejudices, devoid of fear, and a high level of sensibility. This last quality was in all probability the most relevant. In all honesty, the requirements wouldn't be met with ease by those around me. Conscious of the act of living in a society like ours, with a high degree of materialism and superficiality that I had been a loyal follower of for years, I started to see that my expectations came crashing to the ground and I became discouraged. Soon my motivation to continue the analysis also waned, and with it the intensity that I had shown for several months.

I entered a state of apathy. No, I needed to find the right person.

If fate had decreed it, the person would show up on their own. It was a matter of time, but how long? Would I have to go to a medium to prove a theory that existed only in my mind, based on a couple of conjectures? Who would want to be involved in something of less importance than helping people with problems? No, the candidate needed to be someone with little to no experience in paranormal situations. It had to be someone innocent, with no prior knowledge in the matter because that way they could treasure an unforgettable and unique moment. They would transform into a living witness of something extraordinary.

Time went by. If I couldn't find the right person, I would go to the grave without being able to corroborate my discrete but special studies. Several times I thought I had found the perfect companion. However, after not much time the possibility would vanish. After getting to know them more, I would detect in them attributes that without a doubt would interfere with the success of the experiment. On the other hand, there were others that would accept the invitation to participate with enthusiasm but then when it was time would, for varied reasons, desist, the most common of which were either fear or lack of time.

After studying some anthropological concepts to minimize the risks of not finding the ideal candidate, I realized that in our society there were two types of people: those who conformed and those who were ambitious. Both types complemented each other, but as with everything in life, they needed to be in perfect equilibrium. If not, it produces an imbalance that sooner or later leads to social entropy. Maybe that's where the four political cycles that humanity has navigated in a recurrent fashion come from: revolution, civil war, dictatorship, and false democracy.

The ambitious person always wants more and the conformist, consciously or not, contributes to the former's objectives.

Extreme ambition exists in our neoliberal society, ambition that will never have its hunger for money and power satisfied. It is usually associated with a pathology known as chrematomania, which is an obsession with accumulating money and material goods, even to the point of ignoring their family.

In the same vein, extreme conformism also exists, manifesting in advanced cases as vagrancy. Both social actors, people with extreme ambition and conformism, use manipulation as their main emotional tool to submit those around them to their miserly benefit.

Moderate conformists restrain their effort to the minimum needed to survive. They are honest and charitable. They don't try to accumulate great fortune but just want to have enough to live in peace and harmony. In contrast to those with extreme ambition, many conformists are not guided by cold head but by a timid and doubtful heart. Maybe that is their biggest weakness since more often than not it allows the ambitious person to subjugate them without remorse to their deepest and most peculiar desires.

In order to test my theory, I needed a moderate conformist because, as is obvious, someone with ambition would never be interested in an emotional experiment. In general they don't act with genuine feelings or sensitivity. Rather, they use this instrument as an effective means of persuasion.

CHAPTER XVI: THEORY

Five years went by after I had come up with my theory. I had written down the description in a notebook that I took with me wherever I went.

I stopped practicing the technique as time went by. I had recovered from my depression and dove back into my normal life with all the implications that came with it. Far from melancholy, I had decided to stop seeing what was to me a heavy burden that I wasn't willing to carry for the rest of my life. It wasn't from lack of willpower but rather from never having been able to discover the precise manner to channel its ethereal hypothesis in a generous and altruistic manner.

After lots of meditation I accepted that I wasn't prepared to receive the apparent divine knowledge. I also didn't feel enough motivation to delve into its fundamental tenants. I thought I needed a long time to assimilate what had accidentally been revealed to me. There's a reason why people who dedicate their lives to the study of everything holy and unknown exist.

As opposed to me, they were born with a certain disposition to see the spiritual side of life. I, on the other hand, at the age of thirty-five and driven by rampant capitalism, had taken a nosedive off a cliff which resulted in me discovering that there was something else beyond what I could see. I discovered how things really were thanks to a brutal physical and psychological collapse that had left me both dizzy and disoriented.

Even through all of this, my desire to prove my "Thirty Degree" theory never dissipated. I was always present in the deepest recesses of my subconscious. However, it was not a priority for my conscious mind for a long time.

I had changed jobs. Now I worked at another technology company located near 333 Teatinos Street, where I had been the victim of the impetuous hostile hologram. How could if forget the painful internal lesion on the left side of my body? I never forgot the enraged and defiant expression on the dark-skinned hologram's face when he saw me in the darkened corridor.

Now my workplace was located in a nine-story building at the intersection of Cathedral and Teatinos streets. I got the job thanks to a good friend who had been working there for a few years.

The financial systems department where we worked was on the fifth floor. It was a relatively modern area with several well-defined though narrow office and workspaces.

My stress had come back along with my heath. After all, it was a necessary drug for those of us who grow accustomed to its demands. Despite the hard times during the past five years, I hadn't learned the lesson. I had forgotten what I had learned, and I say it full of remorse. To top things off, I went to work as a manager in a place where everything moved faster and with more intensity than before.

There I learned that the world of the free market doesn't leave any openings for doubts, providing fertile soil for speculation and forming cold and calculating people. If the market finds you not firmly grounded, it will take not only your money but your life and essence as well.

The financial department was full of commercial and information engineers whose priority was to work for money even at the cost of their health, time, effort, and family. The financial market exacerbated the basest human instincts of people who failed to realize that it places a mortgage on their lives and the lives of those around them.

I was witness to how colleagues would faint in the office like sparrows poisoned by 5G, victims of oppressive stress caused by long and tiring hours spent in front of a computer. They were gullible, trying in vain to satisfy in time, cost, and form the impossible demands of clients just as or even more desperate than same service providers.

I made some good friends there. Michael, a guy from one of the southern suburbs of Santiago was a young extrovert, direct and sometimes with no sense of what was appropriate. At the end of the day, though, he was a good man, good husband, and good father. He won my trust because of his charisma and sensitivity. As he told me, his childhood had been unhappy, unpleasant, and worthy of being used as the inspiration for a book about social disparity.

"How is Michael a Chilean name?" I joked on a hot summer afternoon when we went to have a drink with some other colleagues after a long day of work.

"Well, we have the Chilean Michael Jackson, don't we? Juan Antonio Labra!" and then he hummed a tune with a forced, though no less funny, falsetto. Both at work and outside of it, there was little to no time for sadness with Michael, but lots of time for laughter.

After having spent a few hours at the table, Michael touched on a much more unhappy subject.

"My mom is a hard-working woman. When I was little we were

very poor. We lived in Pincoya. You can imagine how we were treated all my life. That's why my family today is proud that we could make it out of that hole. I almost lost myself to drugs," he affirmed with damp eyes as he took a sip of beer.

"What about you, Daniel? What's your story? You're the oldest one here," the others laughed as they waited to hear me share a story of my life.

"Well, my story isn't very entertaining. I'm a man of few words." They looked at me in astonishment, not believing what they heard. Then they laughed again.

"Are you kidding? You're busted. You've got more experience and a way with words that none of us here have and now you're acting like it's nothing. We know that you were the director of an important company. Do you not have the guts to tell us? Or are you too shy to share your experiences with us poor average joes?" a dark-skinned man asked who I had just recently met.

His words were less than friendly. There was a small silence put the sustained smiles on the faces of those present suggested I should take the phrases as nothing more than a joke. I decided to follow along.

"Well, now that you mention it, I was a director at Microsoft. I even hung out with Bill Gates. In fact, I approved the world-wide distribution of Windows. I left the position when I got offered the chance to come work with you in this little company," I said in a sarcastic tone. Laughter exploded as soon as I finished talking, but the dark-skinned man didn't seem to think it was funny.

"Let's leave the sarcasm for another time and enjoy the night out," said Michael, trying to smooth things over.

"Do you know how many people in the financial systems field have died due to heart attacks in the last couple of years?" asked someone else. He was a thin, pale man with almond-shaped eyes. His large hand wrapped around his glass of beer. His second job could have been as an auto mechanic.

"No, tell us. Why did you ask, Diego?" Michael inquired.

"We need to be more aware. Several have died. Not too long ago, Patricio died, a workaholic manager. They say that he had just gotten home after a long day at work. He picked up his little daughter and answered a call on his cell phone due to a problem one of his clients had with futures, forwards, and swaps. He had a heart attack right there. Dropped dead on the floor," he commented as he tipped back the half-liter glass to take another drink of beer. He cleaned off the vestige of foam left on his lips with a wrinkled handkerchief he took out of his pants' pocket.

Because of the heavy investment in his work, the unfortunate man described by Diego for sure had left part of his vital energy impregnated in the building, especially on the fifth floor where he had worked for years. However, I had no intention of proving it as it had been a long time since I had moved away from searching for the divine dimension and its portal to the afterlife.

Employment in the financial world came with stressful and on occasion endless days of work, many of which lasted far longer than what was allowed by law. I have to say that it wasn't always the employer's fault. Some workers stayed of their own free will long after the workday had finished. Sometimes I was one of them, but others seemed to spend all night at the office on a regular basis.

I had gotten used to being aware of when the lights were on or off at any establishment I found myself in. For me, the day was the dimension of flesh and blood living people while the night and its darkness belonged to the holograms and vital energy.

Every day at around seven P. M. the lights were operated by the security guards in the office. They would turn off the lights in select areas of the building. Their objective was to save on the electric bill due to the forced blackouts that were in effect in the central area of the country. Only a few emergency lights and specific areas were left with the lights on to facilitate the work of those who stayed late at the office.

After lights out, the building took on a macabre aspect in contrast to the other buildings around it on Teatinos and Cathedral streets. For several years, the area had boasted of a decent amount of activity at night.

Many times I believed that I was being watched by holograms. The constant shivers running up and down my spine let me know they were there. However, I was very stubborn in my decision to refuse to use the "Thirty degrees" technique. I had imposed the decision on myself to ignore the other plane because I was oversaturated with everything relative to it.

Two years went by after I started working at that company until one day I found out that they had hired a man by the name of Richard Rodríguez. He was an information systems guy who looked friendly, , good-natured, and affable. He was a tall man with thin hair, a wide face, light-colored skin, a hooked nose and pronounced jaw. Richard was there to take over the role of the chief of information services projects.

He had been married for several years but, according to him, his marriage had been in a steep decline for a long time and he was sure it wouldn't be long before everything ended. He was a father of two and always stood out for being honest and caring with those around him. He looked after everyone, no matter who they were. This gained him the trust of everyone who worked there because it wasn't in general an easy place to maintain a good sense of humor in the extreme stress of our workplace.

With time we became good friends, so much so that every so often we would go to a bar on Friday nights after work to unwind with a good drink, music, jokes, and laughter.

"This week was so much more stressful than usual, Daniel. I can't wait to escape and spend at least a day at the beach, getting some sun and fresh air. Man, I wish I could win the lottery. That way I wouldn't have to worry about work anymore," the robust engineer said after a long drink of his rum and Coke.

"Do you believe in miracles?" I asked while laughing.

"No, but they do exist," Richard replied, laughing heartily.

"Just live life as it comes, but don't let it overwhelm you." He looked at me with a questioning expression.

"Don't get all philosophical on me now. I've got enough to deal with at home when my wife asks why life is like this." Richard didn't stop smiling, as was usual for him. It made talking to him a pleasant experience.

"I'm sorry I wasn't clear enough. Well, there's nothing new under the sun. I'm the only one who understands me, and even then it's not a given." I tried to reach with my right hand one of the mints I carried in my jacket pocket. At the same time, I observed the atmosphere of the bar we were at. La Alcusa was located near the Santa Ana metro station, in downtown Santiago. I had become good friends with the owner, Pedro. The balding owner would invite me to play domino until the wee hours of the morning with several other clients who were involved with politics.

Richard got up without warning and almost ran to the bathroom. He took a few minutes to come back. When he did, he brought up a topic of conversation that I thought I had buried in my memory, under quadruple lock and key and that I didn't have the slightest intention of dredging up again. However, my imposing friend would soon make sure to start a raging debate.

"Have you ever noticed that the bathroom is a source of ideas and a great space for reflecting? As I was taking a leak, I don't know why but a question occurred to me. What is the spirit world like? There are people who claim to see them. Swindlers going around, looking for easy prey with their supposed paranormal gifts. The only thing I know for sure is that when you die, that's the end. There's nothing else. The beyond or the afterlife is just snake oil to be sold to the masses. It's not for me." He was so earnest in his opinion that I couldn't hold back my own.

"What are you talking about? How can you say that there's nothing there after we die?" I had already had a couple of drinks so, fortified with liquid courage, I went on to share my experience. After all, I was sure that he wouldn't say anything about our conversation to anyone else. Richard listened with care to every detail that came out of my mouth. After a few minutes, he stopped me to comment.

"Your story is interesting, but just let me say that no one is going to convince me of what I can't see with my own eyes. I'm sorry, my friend.

I like you a lot but you probably took too much medication and that made you start to hallucinate. That's all it is. I'll chalk your story up to the rum you're drinking now," he said with a smile.

"Fine, forget it. You're right. Maybe the rum was bad. Let's talk about something else." I didn't waste my effort to explain any further. We continued drinking and laughing until it was time to go home.

Next Monday we worked together without incident. Neither of us mentioned what we had talked about the previous Friday night. We had an implicit agreement among all the workers there: personal conversations, whether in or out of the office, were sacred (except for very rare cases) and as such were secret.

Months later, I sat at my desk, concentrated on solving some work-related problems when Richard came up to me. He looked agitated.

"Daniel, I need to talk to you. It's urgent! Please, help me! I'll wait for you by the vending machines." I had never seen him so upset. Minutes later I walked toward the vending machine area, located about ninety feet away from where I sat.

When I got there, I saw that Richard was very nervous. He held a white, wrinkled handkerchief in one hand which he used to wipe his forehead. In the other hand he had a cup of coffee that looked about to spill at any moment from how bad his hand was shaking.

"What's the matter? Did the bank foreclose on you or something?" I joked with a smile.

"I wish. Remember what we talked about a few weeks ago at the bar? Spirits and everything that you told me had happened to you?" He couldn't calm down or even try to hide his agitation.

"Of course, I remember. I wasn't as drunk as you were. You made fun of me, and truth be told, I didn't appreciate it, you damn giant," I replied in a playful tone, smiling all the while. I grabbed a cup to prepare my coffee in.

His quavering voice started to worry me. He insisted that his house had been visited by spirits. They'd scared his children and his wife. He was out of his mind with worry and didn't know what to do.

"My wife called me, crying. The worst part is that since we can't see them, we have no idea who they are or what they want. Are they family? What do you think?" he asked, hoping that I could say something that would make him feel better.

"What can I say? Good luck, since you don't believe in spirits and they're livelier than you are. Can you still doubt it now that you have them in your home?"

"Please help me! I know that you know a lot about this because of everything you told me before. I know you can help me. That's why I wanted to ask if it's possible for you to see these spirits? I swear I won't breathe a word of this to anyone else. I'll do whatever you ask. It'll be the best-kept secret in the world; I promise!"

"Richard, like I told you that day, I left all this behind me. I don't want anything else to do with spirits at all. If I try to intervene, they'll start chasing after me again and I don't want that. Just forget it." I walked back to my desk. Out of my peripheral vision I saw Richard wipe his forehead once more.

All week long Richard sent message after message to my inbox and left notes on my desk saying, "Don't be cruel to your friend. Come on, help me! I believe in them now and I need to know how to handle this. They won't leave my family alone!"

We frequently had lunch together, and he never missed the opportunity to talk to me about it. He'd close one eye to look at me with the other and would plead, "Help me, my friend!" A few weeks went by with me ignoring his request.

One day, as I was walking down the building's stairway, Richard stopped me to say, "Alright, Daniel, let me buy you a drink. We need to talk, and please don't say no. I'm at the end of my rope. The spirits have started to throw things and bang on doors in my house. I'm sorry that I didn't believe. Friends are supposed to help each other. I hope this isn't the exception to the rule." His pained expression and the hand on my shoulder let me know how desperate for help he really was.

When we got to the bar, Richard let all his worries out in a torrent. "Daniel, I know that I underestimated you and I said a lot of nonsense. I'm not a spiritual person. I like tangible things. It is or it isn't; I can see it or I can't. That's why I want to apologize. I need your help and understanding. Please, from the bottom of my heart, I'm begging you to teach me the technique that you told me about. I want to know what's in my house so I can have some idea of what to do."

"Alright, listen. The technique that I told you about is a simple theory, one that I've always wanted to try. If it works, then I'll feel like Einstein when he proved his theory of relativity. You'd be the first person in over six years of investigation that I could prove this with. You'd be the one to make me write a book," I said, tired of his unwavering insistence. Richard focused his full attention on me and rested his chin on his hand. His other hand wrapped around the almost empty glass of beer.

"See? It's a win-win situation. I want to be your Guinea pig so you can test your theory. What's better than a credible witness?" He persisted in trying to achieve his goal, using his not-inconsiderable powers of persuasion. According to my definition of people, Richard didn't seem to be a conformist but rather showed die-hard ambition.

"You're going to make me dig up things that I thought I had forgotten and that I'll have to remember if we want this to work. You've got to be more worried than you let on to insist on it this much. You've been on my case for weeks. Fine. I don't know if I can help you, but at least I'll give it my best shot."

"That's the spirit!" Richard exclaimed before swallowing the last of his beer.

We agreed on the date and time when we'd start his training, treating it like a grand event. Truth be told, it had been such a long time since I had seen the divine dimension that I didn't have much hope. What's more, just the thought that it might work was enough to light in me the fire of motivation.

We'd do the experiment in the office where we worked. The dim lighting that remained after lights out at seven o'clock seemed to be the perfect setting. It was ideal to see the divine dimension and its portal to the afterlife with clarity now that Richard was willing to believe.

According to my calculations, I had found the ideal candidate. My friend took on the mantle of student and practiced with me for several weeks. I tried to teach him as best I could. Both of us were dedicated to achieving the memorable event.

At first, Richard's attempts were unsuccessful. However, he was determined to not give up.

"When I try to use the technique, my vision gets cloudy, Daniel. Do you think that me being short-sighted has anything to do with it?" he asked. I had started to think of him as an elephant. His imposing stature and serene disposition brought to mind being next to a huge elephant. But there was something in his life that for some reason worried me.

I'd heard a story that says that elephants would leave their herds in the last days of their lives and go die in an "elephant cemetery." I'd even seen a book about it. There all their bones intermingled, with nothing to distinguish them as different beings or individuals.

We would often talk about his future, both personal and professional. At his age in his fifties and seen through the lens of my way of thinking at the time, his conformism was inconceivable. I saw in him a kind of failure, which at the same time I saw in myself. Living month to month, which at the end is nothing but living of credit, was something degrading in my opinion. People with ambition say they don't work for money but rather money works for them.

"Just like old elephants do in Africa, you've come to this company to die. Instead of thinking and starting to work for yourself, I suppose that when you get to retire at the age of sixty-five you'll lament no having done something different in your life instead of coming here - like many others - to leave your bones here in this cemetery."

The nickname fit him perfectly, though my analogy for his life choices was a bit of a stretch.

In other words, I criticized him for not leaving the company were we worked in order to fight for his dreams and not the dreams of the company's owner. His age and physical condition were exacerbated by the stressful daily routine. The idea of watching him die in tragic circumstances of a heart attack, as had happened with other workaholic colleagues in the field of financial systems, bothered me.

"Instead of going out on your won and working toward your dreams, you've chosen this brick-and-mortar cemetery. I know that deep down you inside you know that you came here to die, despite how little they pay. Don't be a coward! No one with half a brain would continue working in this company for more than a couple of years," I insisted, half in jest and half serious.

The Elephant would look at me and laugh. I don't know if he ever got tired of my dark humor. In any case, he already knew what my personality was like. He knew that my caustic criticism was intended to be constructive. I had grown to appreciate his character, but I kept seeing him old and alone. I didn't want him to suffer the disheartening future in my head.

The big day finally arrived. We had anxiously waited for the great event. Being sincere, I wasn't very optimistic but deep inside I felt a tiny bit of hope. It was difficult to try to predict if a person like Richard, skeptical and impatient, would be able to see what for so long I had been able to.

If he couldn't, then the Lonquen Medium would be right. It was a gift someone, I don't know who, had given me. I would be greatly disappointed if that were the case. The thirty-degree theory would crumble into dust, meaning that no one else could corroborate the existence of life after death by using a simple visual technique.

Everything was ready that day. The Elephant would practice in the dark bathroom during work hours. Though he had no guarantee that it would work, the robust man was willing to mark a spiritual turning point in his life.

The day went by fast. Seven o'clock rolled around and, as usual, the lights were turned off. Richard and I continued working after our normal schedule.

Once seated, the panels that divided the cubicles obscured the view between desks, which is why during working hours we would communicate using electronic media such as phones or voicemail.

"Daniel, are you there? I hope you didn't go home, you coward! I know that despite whatever you say, you're scared. Your chin is shaking," the Elephant whispered in a relaxed manner. In an effort to calm his nerves before the experiment, Richard joked openly. In all sincerity, I was nervous as well.

"Yeah, I'm here. Did you think I'd make a run for it? My name isn't Richard; it's Daniel, a braver and more respectable name."

"But your last name is Gonzalez, which is a lot worse," he rallied.

"Are you ready, Elephant? Or are you going to bail? If you do, I'll let everyone know about your feathers, you big, mangy chicken. Get over here. The show's about to start." We'd prepared as much as we could for that day. Nothing could go wrong, except for him not being able to use the technique.

A few minutes later Richard showed up next to me. He carried a backpack with him.

"What's that? Are you going on a field trip? Or are you ready to hightail it to the Lo Vasquez church in case we do meet a ghost?"

"What are you talking about?"

"Your backpack."

"Oh, I forgot to tell you. I've got some stuff my kids asked me for. I'll just leave it here on your desk." He was frightened. I could tell by the way he kept rubbing his hands together. His movements gave away the undisguisable anxiety the old man felt. I started to worry that everything could end in a tragedy. I'd heard about people who couldn't deal with the apparition of spirits and had died from shock.

"Richard, before we go on, are you sure you want to do this? We can still stop. I'm serious. I don't want to have to carry your corpse out of here."

"Of course I want to do it. I didn't spend a month practicing for nothing. I'm the one who asked you to do it, remember? Besides, as far as I know I don't have a heart condition, if that's what's worrying you. Trust me, we'll find the new world, or rather, the divine dimension, as you call it." His words were categorical. There was no room for doubt on his part.

"Alright then. That's my Elephant. Let's get things started." We walked toward the building's south wing, near the entryway. "I'll go ahead and you follow behind me. Are you ready?" I asked.

"Yes, captain," he replied with a sure voice.

"Okay, let's go."

I took my place and focused my vision on the thirty degrees, applying the technique to the letter. We started our walk of truth.

The dim light was perfect to visualize energies in. With a bit of patience, I knew that we wouldn't walk away empty handed. We'd for sure see something.

We walked a bit along the hallway. After a few feet we reached the first set of desks, each one of them with their respective computers and other elements used by the people who worked there.

Some of the narrow desks had family photos on them, marked with colorful decorations that were a bit hard to see in the scant remaining light.

I spoke to Richard in the dark, assuming that he was right behind me as I had instructed. "Elephant, are you there?"

"Yeah, Daniel. What's up?"

"We've reached our first stop. Let's see what the energy in this place has to say. Look carefully. Can you see who lives here? You have to concentrate and apply the technique with diligence."

"This is exciting. My trial by fire. Let's see if it works." In the dim light I saw him concentrate and fix his sight on the target. At times I could see his face and his eyes looked unfocused. It looked like he was applying the technique well, though I didn't see any expression of surprise, which made me expect his reply.

"No matter how hard I try, I can't see a thing. What is it I'm supposed to see?" he replied, disappointed.

I took a good look around us. I stopped in front of one of the desks and I could see the energy of one of our colleagues clear as a bell. It was Rodrigo Olivares, a grumpy man with few friends, though at times he acted in a kind manner. His hologram had his back to us, sitting in front of his computer. His characteristic long hair was tied back, letting a fair amount of grey show among his thick hair.

The hologram would bend down over and over to grab a carton of milk and then pour the contents into a ceramic cup. After that, he lifted the cup to drink it all. Then he took out and sliced a bun before putting two slices of yellow cheese in it. The scene repeated without interruption and never deviating from the script, which indicated that the hologram wasn't a spirit but the remanent energy of someone still alive. Rodrigo was without a doubt alive.

"Elephant, do you see anything here? Concentrate," I insisted.

No matter how hard he tried he still sounded like a broken record repeating the same phrase over and over. "No, I can't see a thing. I swear I'm applying the technique just how you taught me but I still can't see anything. I see some small cloud-like shapes, but I'm not sure," explained my first disciple. The preliminary results make him feel disappointed.

In any event, I was fascinated. After ages without taking any medication I could still see the divine dimension just as well as on the first day. Because of that I was convinced that the technique was effective. However, Richard said something that gave way to a budding sense of discouragement.

"Daniel, it's no use. I can't see a thing. The bases of your theory are crumbling before your eyes, my friend."

"I think that you're not concentrating enough and not following the principles of the theory." Was it possible that the thirty degrees technique was part of a misconceived theory? Yes. It was very possible that after five years of study my analysis and conclusions had gone in the wrong direction. Even so, I was willing to go on. Mi investigation was backed by information that was tracked and tallied with precision during long hours with little sleep. However, I also had to consider that my studies in the matter lacked a formal scientific base. They were supported by the analysis and deductions arrived at by a person with formal education in technological engineering. In that sense, what I had done was not much different from what someone who was ignorant of the subject could do.

We carried on. There was a workroom a few meters from where we stood. Its architecture was made up of numerous small glass cells. It was called the aquarium because of its looks, and it was possible to see everything that happened inside when observing from the outside.

We wandered along the halls of the fifth floor like Don Quixote and Sancho Panza looking for giants that didn't exist. I'm sure that for Richard I was Alfonso Quijano and the titans were simple windmills. How ridiculous!

This time we went to a different work area. The design of the cubicles was uniform. All of them looked much like the other. After a few steps, we stopped in front of a desk that stood out. It was decorated with some family photos and some small oil paintings that differentiated it from the rest of the cubicles. It still had some objects related to the recent Independence Day festivities. Next to the computer there was a pen made with ice cream sticks, presumably a gift from the owner's children.

"Moto sits here" said Richard to my surprise.

"What? How do you know that? Did the technique work?" I asked, anxious to hear his reply. He started to laugh until he ran out of breath. His fillings flashed in the dark before he answered.

"Because I work with him and I know that this is his desk. What were you thinking? That your theory had been proved?"

"Not funny. Can you see anything? Please concentrate and put your eyes in the position I showed you."

"I still can't see anything, Daniel. Oh! Oh, wait a minute! There's something there. Daniel! Ah! I can't believe it. I think I see a silhouette where nothings supposed to be there. Could it be Moto?" It sounded like Richard had at last managed to do the impossible. In effect, the man's energy was there, sitting at his desk. He seemed to be using a cell phone. He moved to one side and opened the first drawer where he would take out an object that looked like a set of keys.

"Are you sure? What do you see Moto doing?" I asked to compare his apparent vision with mine.

"I'm not sure, but it's sitting down. I can see part of its back. The image is very hard to see," he commented. His description was nowhere near conclusive evidence.

"Please try to see some more."

"My eyes hurt." He used both hands to rub his eyes before trying to see again. His face showed that he was getting tired.

"Well, it's a step in the right direction. Let's keep going and visit some other workspaces. There have to be over a hundred on this floor alone."

We continued walking. The sounds of the motors from the vehicles moving outside on Cathedral Street were the only interruptions in the night's silence.

"I feel bad because I can't help you. Also, I won't be able to contact the spirits that are scaring my family at home. I thought it would be easier. Well, we're not done yet. There's still some hope that things may change," he said in a soft voice.

Our eyes had become used to the dark. It made our walk much easier. Richard kept walking behind me, following me where I lead until a few minutes later when we decided to walk back.

"We've gone far enough and haven't seen anything interesting. Let's stop here," I suggested.

"Yeah, let's head back."

On the way back we walked past the Aquarium again. The door was open when we stopped about six feet away. The only windows in the atypical room looked out on Cathedral Street. Green blinds and a translucent curtain covered them. Through the curtain we could see the streetlights and the headlights belonging to the cars traveling westward at that hour on the street outside.

Out of instinct I looked into the room through the glass wall. About ten people worked there during the day, members of the quality control team in charge of the systems developed by the technical team.

A subtle movement at one of the cubicles in the room caught my eye. The light from the street outside let me see something more than the simple curtains hanging there.

"Wait a minute, stop. I just saw something in there. I want to know what it is." Richard stopped a couple of feet behind me. I started to apply the technique in order to look inside. As I did, I started to see a feminine silhouette seated at one of the workspaces in the central part of the office.

I was sure that it was a hologram, but I didn't know if it was someone who was alive or dead. I made sure not to share any of the details I saw. Similar to what happened with Graciela the night my son's picture changed on its own in front of our terrified gazes, I need to avoid at all costs influencing my robust companion with my description.

"Richard, come closer. I want you to look in and look into the aquarium with care. Look through the door toward the middle of the room," I requested with as much seriousness and sobriety that I could. Richard noticed the change in the tone and volume of my voice, assuming that it was something important. He looked towards the place I had mentioned, using the technique with adequate concentration.

"Daniel, I'm applying the technique but, as usual, there's nothing there. It's useless." He continued to try for a few moments until he exclaimed, "My God! It's not true. I swear I'm not lying. There's a woman there!" His voice trembled with each word he spoke.

"Shhh! Be quiet!" I whispered to Richard. The feeling of terror was evident on the Elephant's face. His face vanished into the darkness intermittently as the light from the cars outside shone through the curtains before reaching his troubled visage.

"Are you sure it's a woman?" I asked in order to make him verify that he was seeing the same thing I was.

"I swear as God is my witness that I see a woman sitting at the desk in the center of the aquarium. She's about nine feet away from the window," he confirmed without a shadow of a doubt.

As the seconds ticked by the hologram had noticed our presence and, showing profound sensitivity, our gazes as well. She turned to look in our direction. As soon as she saw the look of terror on Richard's face she stood up with disquieting calm. I let him relate everything that he saw so that I could minimize my intervention.

"Daniel! She stood up! Fuck! Tell me what's going on, please!" he exclaimed in desperation. For a few seconds I thought that he would take off running and leave me to my fate.

The woman wore a two-piece dress, which was peculiar for female office workers. The brown outfit looked to be from the nineties. She was around thirty-something and had olive-toned skin. Her poofy hair was shoulder-length, and her sleepy eyes with minimal make up made her look captivating.

"Oh, God, she's walking this way. Daniel, what do we do? I don't know if I'm about to run or faint on the spot!" He looked to be losing it fast. His face was bathed in sweat. When I saw that I thought I should tell him that we needed to leave so to avoid a tragedy in the form of a heart attack. However, it was too late as running could result in either his end or mine. My heart raced at full speed as well.

"No, wait! I've waited more than five years to prove this, and now you're going to run away? Are you insane? You have to stay here with me!" I grabbed hold of his arm and pulled him toward me. As this happened, the woman continued to walk towards us at a sedate pace. As she came closer, I felt Richard's large hand grip my forearm tighter. We were two chickens frozen in place with fear, waiting for our necks to be wrung.

"What does she want to do, Daniel? If we don't make it out of this, God have mercy on us." Richard couldn't hide his terror anymore. I tried my best to cover mine up.

"Richard, please try to calm down. You're shaking. You look like an elephant scared of a mouse. Listen. Don't look her in the eyes. Just observe her out of the corner of your eyes. Don't say anything and don't move. Nothing bad will happen if you follow my directions. If you look at her, she'll think that you want to communicate and she'll follow you wherever you go, even to your house. Do you want that to happen, or are the spirits you already have hanging around your family enough?" Richard shook from head to toe. He took out his usual wrinkled handkerchief to mop up the profuse perspiration on his forehead. Though he was still aware of what the woman was doing, he avoided her gaze as I had indicated.

The woman stopped less than a foot away from us. The cold air around her reached out about a foot and a half from her body. She moved in a deliberate manner and made a circle around us. First she looked me in the face and then did the same to Richard. The poor man was at the end of his rope. I thought for sure that he'd take off running at any second. Either that or drop like a sack of potatoes on the floor, victim of a heart attack.

"She's too close, just watching us. What does she want with us? I'm cold. She's colder than a penguin in a refrigerator," Richard said to try to lighten the mood. He wanted to regain his composure, but it was almost impossible.

The woman continued to study us, walking behind our backs. We stayed still, almost holding our breaths. Her objective was clear: she was trying to meet our gazes but neither frightened man was willing to acknowledge her request.

I remembered that not far from there, at 333 Teatinos Street, I had learned a valuable lesson, though in the worst possible way. If we didn't want to run the risk of being trampled by a disoriented hologram, we had to avoid her gaze at all costs.

"She wants us to look her in the eye, with the hopes of communicating with us and asking us for a favor. But we can't do much for her. Richard, do you understand?" The Elephant was still perplexed, submerged in his fear. Little by little he started to calm down as he saw that nothing happened if he followed my instructions.

After about ten minutes of unsuccessful attempts at communicating, the woman seemed to give up.

"Daniel, she's going to give me a heart attack. I can't sweat anymore, and my muscles are tired from shaking so much," said Richard before heaving a big sigh.

"She's sad because she realized that she's not going to get what she wants from us."

After walking a complete circle around us, the woman stopped right in front of us for a few minutes. She looked at us for a while. Then, with the same deliberation she had shown before, walked a few feet back into the aquarium before making an abrupt turn to look at us one last time. At long last she turned back and walked to the place where we had seen her first appear.

She sat down at her desk after she got there, as if to continue her work. Just like her, we stopped watching the scene and walked back to our desks. After a few minutes of silence when we tried to assimilate what had happened, Richard said, "This has been the most extraordinary experience of my life. I have an impressive story to tell my grandchildren before I die. You proved your theory. You've got to tell the world because everyone needs to know that there is life after death, and that it's not necessary to visit cemeteries or haunted houses to prove that spirits exist. People don't even need to be clairvoyant or a medium. You have no idea how excited I am. Words fail me to express how thankful I am for this valuable opportunity." His eyes were bright, glistening in the dim light.

"I don't know if I'll ever right about this. I'm not a writer, but you can be sure about one thing. I'll spend every day of the rest of my life talking about it to whomever wants to listen." I sat down and held my head in my hands. It was so noticeable that I was overcome with emotion that Richard put his hand on my shoulder to show his empathy.

"It's alright, Daniel. You did a good job, my friend. You deserve congratulations. No one is generous enough or even brave enough to risk being called crazy. Someday everyone will open their eyes. Mine were opened today. What comes next? I imagine that you've got a ton of questions without answers."

"Speaking of, this is just the beginning for me. I'd left the divine dimension, the portal to the afterlife behind, but you came to help me. I'm serious. Thank you with all my heart. If it hadn't been for you, I wouldn't have been able to have this incredible experience. The next step would be to try to communicate with them, to try to hear them. If most of them want to talk to us, it's because they've got something to say. I don't know what it is, but I have the feeling that it's going to be something of transcendental relevance. My theory still has a lot of points that need to be cleared up. I'll keep investigating."

"I'm afraid that in the divine dimension there's a world like ours, with the same dogmatic fallacies and maybe with similar practices. I need to find out if it exists before ours in the hierarchy of dimensions or in its distribution in the universe. If that's the case, then I can deduce that though they don't have the same organic and biological problems that we do, their political, social, and emotional system has much more of ours in it than what we imagine. We could be the mirror of what they're building in what Einstein called space-time. I just hope that they don't have anything similar to what money is in our dimension," I continued.

From that day in 2010 forward, with my theory proven and for various reasons, I decided to not use the thirty-degree technique again. One of the motives behind this decision, and maybe the most powerful one, is that I never felt I had evolved enough spiritually to give with an acceptable level of maturity some kind of help to those souls that were, according to me, less evolved.

With deep pain in my soul, knowing that some spirits were desperate for help and others were disoriented and sad, I gave up a probable promising career as a medium. I don't know, just time would say if my decision was the correct one. At the moment, I would let the subject matter experts do what they knew how to do best. Who knows if in the future I would regret that decision.

Richard Rodriguez and I parted ways in 2011 when I decided to exchange the world of finance and the stock market for a non-profit entity with a noble cause, such as the volunteer fire-fighter's association of Chile. I left the stressful job in technology and gave priority to my quality of life and spiritual growth.

I met up with the Elephant seven years later. The corpulent man was walking out of a restaurant on Society of Jesus Street in Santiago. He looked the same, just with a little less hair.

"How's my generous Elephant? Did you escape the cemetery? Do you remember me?"

"Huh? Daniel? Man, what a surprise! It's a miracle! Where have you been? What have you been up to all these years?" he exclaimed with joy.

"One question at a time, please. Don't overwhelm me as it's early and I've got a lot to do," I laughed. We gave each other a big hug and a firm handshake.

We talked like great friends who hadn't seen each other in years. People walked around us as we stood in the middle of the sidewalk. The happiness in both our eyes at meeting again could be seen a mile away.

"After you left, I tried several times to use the thirty-degree technique, but it never worked. Hopeless. A few years later we formed an esoteric group on the fifth floor, but it only lasted a few years. I told them of our experience and they were over the moon. We tried to contact you a few times to invite you to give us a talk, but we couldn't find you. But that's just like you, Daniel, as unreachable as a celebrity."

"And it's just like you to exaggerate, you great big lout. I'm always available for anyone who wants to talk a while. I'm at your order, don't forget it. I've got a lot of people to be thankful to, and you're one of them."

"After our great discovery, were you able to make progress in your investigation?"

"Not much. I've gone back to the most neoliberal stage of my life.

My investigation was put on the back burner because I've got to work to live. The spirit may not eat, but this handsome body does." He burst out laughing.

"I assumed as much. Don't lose sight of your goal and share your theory with the world. I'm still working at the same place. The elephant cemetery is addictive and it's waiting for me."

We talked for over an hour. We said our goodbyes and promised to meet up again, a promise which, by the way, we still haven't been able to keep. Such is the life of those in information technology.

CHAPTER XVII: YAMIL, GUARDIAN ANGEL

In 2010 I decided to never use the thirty-degree technique again, but when you spit at Heaven it comes back to hit you in the face.

After my divorce and having lived with my friend Lali and her son for a little over six months, I decided to move out. It was time to abandon the temporary shelter that she had had the kindness to offer me.

"You don't know how much we'll miss you. You were always respectful and courteous during your stay. Thank you for all your advice," said Lali.

"Not at all! I'm the one who's thankful. You made me feel like I was at home. You're a wonderful person. Thank you for everything you've helped me with."

Another friend, Beatrice, had found a couple of alternatives as to where I could live to continue the process of adaptation to my new life alone.

"I found two places you can live. They're close to one another, so we can go see them whenever you want and you can decide where your new home will be," she said over the phone one day.

"I'm grateful for you looking out for me. I think that I'd like to go visit both places tomorrow," I replied.

Beatrice was a forty-nine-year-old woman, separated from her husband. She had large, expressive eyes and dyed curly hair. She was short and stocky. She had become my confidant. We'd known each other since elementary school and now she was the mother of two adult children, product of her first marriage.

After three decades we saw each other in a school reunion at the school in Pudahuel, on the intersection of Serrano and Saint Daniel streets, where a large part of our childhood and teenage years took place.

It had been over thirty years since I had looked for a place to live. We went to see the buildings where the rooms to rent were located.

The first residence was in an elegant condominium. It had two stories and a large garden. The room that they offered was on the second floor and was spacious, with good access, comfortable, and it looked well-cared for. It was an ideal room for a person who was fastidious about the decoration and comfortableness of his surroundings, which I wasn't.

"The people who live here are very relaxed. They usually go to sleep early so they can go to work the next day. What do you do for a living?" inquired the realtor, a thin red-headed man of medium stature. He looked me over from head to toe. As a good friend would say, first impressions count.

"I work in the technology sector," I said as I observed the architecture of the house. In a country prone to seismic activity like ours, it's of great importance not to ignore that detail.

"That's great. The other renters here also have advanced degrees, usually accountants and professors."

"Yes, it could be a good place to start over in."

"Don't say another word. I bet that you're recently divorced." I looked at him in surprise. Was he psychic?

"Something like that," I replied, looking at Beatrice.

"Most of the current renters had the same problem, so you should have a lot to talk about. What do you think?"

"Thanks, but I don't usually share my personal matters."

"Please don't feel offended. It was a joke."

I left the house with a sour taste in my mouth. Once outside, Beatrice noticed my discomfort.

"I don't think that this is the place for me. Let's go on to the next one, please," I proposed.

"If you ask me, I suggest you stay here and not at the place where we're going to next. This one is much more comfortable, spacious, and safe. The other one is much more unassuming and I don't think it's the right fit for you."

"Let me decide that for myself and we'll see if we agree on it."

We soon reached the second residence, a few blocks from the elegant room where the nosy redhead had made his inappropriate remarks.

The building looked impressive thanks to its two stories. The front walls were covered with vines, some of which dangled in a languid fashion over the large windows. When we knocked on the door, a tall, thin man with glasses came to greet us.

"How are you? Please come in. We've been waiting. My name is Jose Miguel and I'm one of the owner's sons. My mom lives on the central coast and she's not here right now, so she asked me to show you around. Come this way, please." He acted very respectful towards us. I guessed his age at not more than forty. He was cordial and kind and tried to give us the best impression possible. After a few minutes we heard steps coming down the stairs. It was his wife coming down from the second floor. She was a young woman whose abdomen showed an advanced state of pregnancy.

"Oh, congratulations! How far along are you?" Beatrice asked the young woman.

"Hi. I'm just a little over six months. How are you? I'm Maria, but everyone calls me Mary."

"My name is Beatrice. Nice to meet you." They smiled at each other and we started the visit together. We talked as if we had known each other all our lives.

Maybe their warm welcome made me feel positive energy, a very different feeling from what I had sensed in the previous house. Jose Miguel and Mary were in tune with my own weak vibrations.

There were several ornaments in the large main room: small statues, bronze vases, and paintings of rural landscapes. Large mirrors filled the space on the walls, multiplying the number of objects in sight.

"They're to ward off bad energy," the house's owner hurried to explain after seeing that the reflection from all the mirrors had caught my eye. "This way, please. Which one of you is interested in renting here?"

"Me," I said as I raised my index finger.

We walked into the room. It was small, somewhat modest, but cozy. I looked over every nook and cranny. I made up my mind. I preferred the peace that I could breathe in this room and the hospitality of the owners over the evident comfort displayed in the other house.

"This is the bathroom. There's hot water and everything else needed. Now let's go see the kitchen. It's my favorite place," commented Jose Miguel. Beatrice followed after him.

"How large is the fridge? Is it shared?" Beatrice asked.

"Yes, but don't worry. No one will take what your brother stores there."

"He's not my brother; he's my friend." Beatrice smiled at me with a conspiratorial look on her face.

"That's right. No way she'd be my sister. She's way more rebellious than I am." Everyone laughed.

"What do you think, Daniel? Do you want to stay here or in the other house?" Beatrice asked in front of Jose Miguel and Mary. I turned to look at them as I had been distracted trying to find the dogs that I could hear barking in the patio.

"This is nice. I'll think about it over a cup of coffee. I think that I'll have my answer later tonight."

I walked out the door having made my decision. The man and his wife, who had remained silent for most of the visit, had transmitted enough confidence to believe that living together would be harmonious. The other house with the various professionals and its comfort had been relegated to nothing more than a quick visit thanks to the redheaded realtor's blunder.

We had a cup of coffee at Beatrice's house that afternoon. My decision aside, the large-eyed woman had expressed her content at knowing that my new home was close to hers.

"I've got the feeling that you want to stay at the married couple's house. Or am I wrong?"

"Yes. It's a nice place. Did you see the pool and garden? Summer is coming and I don't like to go out that much, so I'll be fine there."

"You threw me a curve ball. I thought you'd like to live in the other place. It's much more elegant and comfortable. Why'd you choose the second one?"

"Comfort and elegance don't guarantee peace."

"I rest my case, your honor," she replied laughing before taking another sip of her coffee.

A little before sundown Beatrice sent a message to Jose Miguel's mother, accepting the offer. The house and its surroundings seemed to be a good place to live.

The next day, a generous friend and his car helped me move my things to my new home. A new life full of adventure waited for me, the path having been cleared by capricious destiny.

The months in my new home went by fast and we adapted well to living together. Mary, Jose Miguel, and I fit together like a ring on a finger. I came to consider them as part of my family.

Not much later I met the house's owner, a seventy-year-old woman with unparalleled charisma. She was tall, blonde, and had cinnamon skin. She was enchanting and generous. Tuca, as her friends called her, had been a widow for more than thirty years. She had had to raise both her children, Jose Miguel and Francesca, on her own.

Life had been cruel to Tuca from early on, but in response she had risen to the occasion. She overcame all the obstacles life threw at her. As she would say, she was determined to never back down, no matter what the cost.

"Look, Daniel, here's a picture of my husband. He left us when our kids were small and I was very young. He had a heart attack while out on his bike, not too far from here, on Pajaritos de Maipu Street," the blonde woman told me during one of her visits from Las Cruces, where she had moved to four years ago. She looked with nostalgia at the old picture hanging on a wall on house's second floor.

"It must have been hard for you. But you're as strong as an oak."

"Yes, it was a difficult time of my life. Just imagine it. I didn't work because I took care of the kids. He was the one who went out to work. Everything changed in the blink of an eye and I had to leave home and work to feed us."

"Your bravery and strength are admirable, Tuca."

Live gave her a second chance at love. She found a new partner, Yamil. He was a large man who worked as a chef. They lived several years together and he had loved Tuca's children like his own. Unfortunately, they had separated not long ago. Unreconcilable differences had worn the relationship down. Even so, she thought of him with affection.

"Yamil is a good man. He comes from an Arab family. He really likes to cook and is a chef. Every day he would make wonderful food, but nothing is forever and we had to go our own ways. We lived together in this house for many years. It was our home and our life."

"What happened to him?"

"He lives with his sister. His health isn't the best because of his diabetes. In any case, I hope our lives work out for the best for both of us."

"It's nice that you still think of him in an affectionate way."

One night someone knocked on my door just as I was about to go to sleep. I got out of bed and opened the door, thinking that maybe I had forgotten something in the bathroom and the person had gone to give it back to me.

"Hi Daniel, how are you?"

"I'm alright, Tuca. Hope you are too."

"I came to give you a special invitation. I hope you won't say no."

"Wow! An invitation to what?" I thought to myself.

"You're cordially invited to celebrate my birthday. It's next Saturday. There'll be a lot of surprises and guests, so you can't not come. If you want, you can bring your friend Beatrice. I've been told she's very pretty." Her friendly smile left me little to no chance of saying no. She blew out a large puff of smoke from a half-finished cigarette. Her invitation took me by surprise. I hadn't lived in her house for long and she was already treating me like one of the family.

"Thank you very much, Tuca. You didn't have to bother. This makes me feel special."

"Don't worry about it. I was told that you can sing, so it'll be a good opportunity to get to listen to you. See you there."

"Who spread those lies?" I wondered, smiling as she walked away, her dress flowing around her.

Several people arrived the day of the party, including her children, family, and close friends. She looked elegant in her splendid white and yellow clothes and was happy as she took care of her guests. Everyone was happy as they talked. Soon, it was time to dance.

"I'd like to dance Cueca, as it's a traditional dance, but I don't know how to do it. Daniel, do you know? I saw you dancing in a video on Facebook for the Independence Day celebrations. Come on, let's dance. Please show me how. It's my seventy-first birthday and I want to do something different," said the charismatic woman in front of her children and guests.

As soon as she'd finished speaking I made an improvised handkerchief and we started to dance. She was beside herself with happiness. I observed her slanted eyes and expansive smile as we danced. We did the best we could, and the guests clapped and laughed along as the dancers twirled and moved. I tried to use original dance moves to give it a playful touch that would make everyone laugh.

When we finished, the elderly woman sat down to rest. Someone brought her a glass of water, which she took her time to drink. She was occupied doing this when she got a call on her cell phone. The interruption made her stand up. A feminine voice spoke on the other end, informing her of an important event. I thought it might be someone who wanted to wish her a happy birthday. I watched her for a moment as I sat a few feet away. The expression on her face spoke of something other than a simple birthday wish, and fast changed into something else. She tried to cover her mouth with her hand as it fell open in surprise at what she heard.

"Oh my God! Yamil just died! No! Oh, God! Couldn't it have been a different day?" the blonde woman exclaimed, looking at the sky.

The guests were all in shock. In an instant several went from laughing to crying. In less than a minute the party had become a wake. Life is too short to live in pain seemed to be the message the elderly woman tried to convey as she tried in vain to cover up her grief and continue with the celebration.

Her shocked expression said it all. The joy in the celebration vanished like a tropical shower and soon the guests stated to leave little by little.

"He'd been insisting on calling me but I didn't answer. He always called to talk about irrelevant stuff from our past. Yamil knew that I wasn't going to take him back ever because everything between us was over," I heard Tuca say as she said goodbye to one of her guests.

"Don't feel bad about not being able to say goodbye to him. There'll be more than enough time to make up for it when you meet again." I gave her a hug to try to cheer her up.

Early that morning Tuca and her children went to see Yamil at the funeral and say their goodbyes. As for me, I never had the chance to meet him, not even in pictures. However, everything I had heard about him made me think he was a good and generous man.

Months later the heat of summer and the social outbursts that happened in Chile on the 18th of October in 2019 gave me insomnia. Gunshots and the stampede of furious crowds could be heard at the Parcelas de Maipu metro station four blocks away. A colossal battle had started between protesters and the police.

The voracious behavior of the current system, working against individual dignity, couldn't be tolerated anymore. For a long time, the government institutions couldn't meet the expectations of the majority of the population. The political apparatus was left naked and abandoned by its representatives. The populace took away their credibility and they were tried as accomplices of the apparent legislative apathy and its vices, as well as the excesses at every level on behalf of the Executive branch, led by a president that couldn't live up to the circumstances.

A bilateral political agreement to stop the violence left a large part of the populace unhappy as they thought that the agreement between the official party and the opposition had been written up and signed behind the peoples' backs.

It was close to four in the morning and I still couldn't sleep. Hard as I tried, it was impossible. I kept tossing and turning without finding a comfortable position to rest in. Thousands of thoughts drifted through my mind, none of which were conclusive. I wanted to take advantage of how active my mind was at that time in order to plan some things that, in the end, ended up as nothing at all.

I lay face down on the bed, shirtless, with the covers up to my waist. Without any warning I started to perceive something very strange in the air in my room. It was the same sensation I had felt before the paranormal event that had left me astonished at my grandfather's country home when I was twelve. The feeling of something out of the ordinary came to mind as an unpleasant memory.

Someone was watching me from the doorway to the room. I stayed in the same position I had switched to a few minutes earlier. I paid special attention, waiting for the strange sensation to dissipate. All of a sudden an abnormal force took hold of my legs and back, paralyzing them. I didn't try to get away. I wanted to see what the bold entity was up to. I wasn't afraid at that point. The sound of someone breathing started to be heard in the dark. It came from the door and began to move up towards my head. For the first time in thirty-five years I felt fear of the unknown. Even so, I remained calm and didn't resist.

At times I thought that would be it. However, I was very wrong. A large, thick hand took hold of my shoulder in a brusque manner and started shaking me as if trying to wake me up.

The entity had blown past all of the acceptable limits of physics. The circumstances were alarming. I was alone in the room with the door locked. Jose Miguel was in the house, sleeping in peace on the second floor. Who or what was trying to attack me? I tried to take control of the situation and stay as serene as possible. I worked up my courage and started to talk to the shameless entity. I wanted to let it know that I wasn't afraid and that I could see it whenever I wanted to.

"Who are you? What do you want? Leave me alone; that's an

order." The silence was nerve-wracking. A few seconds went by and the hand landed on my shoulder, shaking it again, though this time with even more insistence.

"Damn it! Are you so determined to not let me sleep?" I hadn't even finished speaking when the hand shook me for the third time, this time almost pulling me from the bed. I panicked. I stood up and turned on the light. For a moment I thought about using the thirty-degrees technique to see who it was, but almost immediately I decided against it. If I did, and it was a hologram looking for help, it wouldn't leave me alone for the rest of the night. Who knows, maybe it would even act like Glasses and stay with me for a while. Besides, the rash ghost had broken all the rules when it touched me. I had no reason to think that the intruder would stop using the same strategy.

I tried to get a grip on my nervousness. To my relief, the physical aggression stopped. The behavior that someone or something was very strange and aggressive. The experience I had had at 333 Teatinos with the hostile hologram had been worrisome, but this, in Tuca's house, was extreme to say the least. Up until that day I had never felt a hologram's body with such force.

I started to fix the covers on the bed with the intention of lying back down. The thin blanket had been pushed down towards the foot of the bed. As I straightened it out, I saw an unusual fold on the white sheet at about the same place where my chest had been a few moments before. I straightened the fabric, and when I did, a terrifying, aggressive, and enormous recluse spider jumped out from under it. The movement was so sudden and vicious that my heart almost beat its way out of my chest.

It tried to escape, running away with characteristic speed. In my desperation to not let it get away, I lifted my hand in disgust and smashed it against the spider until it was dead. The poor arachnid left a huge black stain on the sheet and my hand, as if a new pen had exploded there.

"Oh my God! All that venom would have been for me!" I exclaimed. I sat on the edge of the bed, dropped my head into my hands and felt a huge lump form in my throat. I choked up. My inability to understand the entity's motives to alert me to danger generated in me a feeling of impotence but at the same time gratitude towards the intruder.

"Why did you do that? Who are you to stop things that need to from happening? I don't know your name. I don't know who sent you. In any event, I'm thankful. From the bottom of my heart, thank you." Immediately I cleaned up the viscous liquid that had been left on the bed as irrefutable proof of the tragedy that had been avoided. I replaced the thin sheets and then inspected each and every corner to make sure that I was safe. After a while, I turned the light of and lay down.

Sunrise wasn't too far off. I was still awake. Who, in my place, would have been able to fall asleep after everything that had happened? I had to find out who had worked in such a selfless manner to save my life. Experts say that the recluse spider's venom is fifteen times more potent than a cobra's. It was time to use the thirty degrees. I lay face up on the bed and started to concentrate. It had been many years since I had used the technique, but it didn't take long for the person behind the brave and noble deed to appear before me.

He was a robust man with prominent cheekbones, round eyes, thin lips, and thin hair. He moved towards me and started to move his hands. The man wanted to say a thousand things but at the same time said nothing.

"Who are you? Why did you do it? Who sent you?" were my exact questions. The old hologram didn't answer any of them. All he did was convey that I should have been more careful with the spider.

He placed his right index finger under his eye, pointing at it, as if to say, "You were lucky this time. Next time, be more careful. Keep an eye out." I memorized his unmistakable face.

In truth, it wasn't the hologram of Miguel, Tuca's late husband, who I had seen a picture of not long ago. I had been told that the departed had appeared to a couple of delinquents who, even though they were from the neighborhood, had tried to break into the house. The guys had almost died from freight when they saw him standing in front of the door, blocking the way into the house. This fact had made me think that the former owner wouldn't have had any qualms about manifesting in front of me, but if it hadn't been him, then who?

That morning, I fell asleep wondering about what motivation the hologram could have had to go through with the unusual behavior. What had I done to deserve such consideration?

I woke up the next day still wondering. I told Mary through WhatsApp what had happened. Jose Miguel's young wife and her young daughter Florencia had taken a few weeks to visit Chillan, where Mary's mother lived.

Florence was a very intelligent girl. She had turned six not long ago. Months earlier, a paranormal even that happened in Tuca's house had terrified her mom. The event described by the girl affected everyone in the house. She said that she had seen a man's hand come out of one of the large mirrors in the living room . It waved at her and motioned her to come closer. She was so frightened that she ran up the stairs and ended up crying in her grandmother's arms.

Now it was me, the crazy renter, who shared the physical traits of a supposed spirit that had saved my life. Mary didn't reply. She tried to think of someone who could match with the description I had given her. She didn't hide how worried she was.

"Who could it have been? The only souls that could have

manifested in Tuca's house are either her dead husband, Miguel, or her later partner, Yamil," Mary commented.

The small, young woman who was around six months pregnant was amazed. Someone who she barely knew was telling her about a disconcerting paranormal event that happened in the house she lived in.

"I've seen Miguel in pictures, and it wasn't him. What did Yamil look like? Is there any way you could get a picture of him?" I asked, trying to figure out the identity of the daring ghost.

"I don't know how to describe him, but I know who could have a picture. It's Francesca, his stepdaughter. I'll talk to her."

When I received his picture on my cell phone, my astonished expression was impossible to hide. There was no doubt about it; it had been Yamil.

"Yes, that's him. Yamil saved me from a life-or-death situation. I feel better now. After that, he hasn't shown up in my room again." Mary listened with attentiveness on the other end of the call.

"I wanted to ask you a favor, Daniel. Florencia and I are very easily frightened. If you see Yamil again, could you please ask him to go rest in peace? I'm afraid that the hand that my daughter saw a few months ago was his. I don't want him to scare her again."

"What you're asking isn't easy, but if I see him, I'll try to talk with him and let him know how you feel."

I didn't want to get the young mother's hopes up, so I didn't agree to have the eventual talk with Yamil's hologram within a set timeframe.

As luck would have it, I was able to talk to him the following night. For the first time I felt enthusiastic at the idea of talking to a hologram. He was my hero, a savior. How could I be scared? As soon as he arrived, I thanked him again, but the news I had weren't the best for him.

"How are you, Yamil? That's your name, right?" The hologram smiled but didn't say a thing. He just looked at me with kindness. "I want you to listen to me carefully. Everyone in this house loves you. You were a great person in life, but it's time for you to go to the place where you should be. Mary, Florencia's mom, gave me a message for you. She wants you to leave and not haunt this house anymore. Both she and her daughter are afraid of spirits, so, please, when you can, leave this home. We all wish you the best and will never forget you and your generosity."

As soon as he received the message, his expression changed. He looked at me for a while, his face serious. After that, he disappeared without saying or expressing anything at all.

From then on we didn't hear of any other supernatural experiences where he was involved. I didn't look for him either. I had the healthy sensation that after having conveyed Mary's message to him, he left for good.

THIRTY DEGREES – Portal to the Afterlife

After the last encounter between use, I still wonder about the reasons that motivated him to save the life of a complete stranger like me. Maybe it's one of the questions that I'll never be able to answer.

CHAPTER XVIII: THE PRESENTATION

In the large auditorium, in front of the attentive audience, I started my talk. I was nervous. It was the first time I presented anything about the subject and there were high expectations around my talk. I had to be clear and precise. I walked up to the podium and took the microphone on the illuminated stage that contrasted with the darkness covering the seating area. I looked out at the first couple of rows, dimly light by the stage lights and the dark ochre of the upholstery. I felt shocked when I noticed that among the audience, seated as if he were a special guest, was Glasses, the bearded hologram. He observed the atmosphere in a thoughtful and relaxed manner as he hugged the backrest of the seat in front. I ignored him and started to talk.

Since 2005 many years of incredible spiritual discoveries have gone by. There is no material wealth on the planet capable of paying for the secrets that were revealed to me. Whether it was by accident or on purpose, to this day I still don't know. That's why I'd like to tell you that I'm grateful for it and I will be until the end of my life. My goal is not to convince people to believe what this story leaves evident. Each person can think what they like. Having the opportunity to write about and share this treasure is too great a reward for someone like me.

I learned that humans need to live to the fullest each of the situations that destiny has written for their lives, which is nothing but the path that each person has charted for themselves - within a finite margin- before coming to Earth.

No person can take over another person's experiences. There isn't a single person on the planet that has the power to intervene in the destiny established for someone else. Whoever does so not only expresses their selfishness by defying the laws of life, but they also demonstrate their arrogance and indifference towards things that are not pertinent to them.

It may seem contradictory, but even overprotecting a loved one is a selfish act. Who are we do stop someone from experiencing what they want or have to live? Whether good or bad, when the destiny of an event is defined, there is no way to send it back to the source. Fate will come about though to the eyes of those who are less evolved it may seem like tragic or unfair events.

There is no God to punish us as many believe or have referred to. The one who made us isn't the type of supreme being that they describe: egocentric, narcissistic, or vengeful. No, the real God is very different.

In this dimension, most of us act influenced by our souls, that is, ruled by emotions, feelings, and earthly decisions. If we knew that the spirit is what in reality connects us with everything, we could overcome any problem, pain, or outside pressure felt by either the body or soul.

But what is the spirit? In essence, it is the energy that allows us to understand that there is something more extensive, divine, capable of lifting our thoughts and giving us what we want without any limitations or restrictions. Some call that power God. Others say it's the universe or the inner self.

In the end, your spirit is what needs to achieve the inseparable attachment to the infinite cosmic energy through the absolute reparation of love and the useless desire for the material world.

Irrefutable proof of having attained this state of magnificent evolution manifests when we transform into unshakeable beings. The spirit is vertical while the soul is horizontal.

In our life on Earth there are two paths to choose: the first consists in delegating our destiny and its events to a third party, whether God, the universe, saints, wandering spirits or others, so we can avoid our responsibilities and let events happen in a random fashion. This option always ends up minimizing the probability of achieving our earthly goals. The second alternative is to become empowered and take responsibility for our destiny, and in consequence, our reality. It means taking absolute control of ourselves and proclaiming us as the owners and masters of what we want to happen: what, how, when, where, and with who. This will allow us to achieve a hundred percent of our desires because we understand that the true power to administer at will the places and events that affect us, as well as our own bodies, is within us. It's like signing an irrevocable contract with our mind, knocking down the philosophical approach of stoicism and its cosmological determinism.

If we can modify our mental structure, we can change the reality of our bodies and with it, for example, our health.

The energy field commands matter. Therefore, the spirit and energy field are the same thing. Albert Einstein said, "the field is the sole governing agency of the particle." That is to say, the mind is the sole governing agency of the body. This means that, without fear and resorting to permanent positive thoughts, cancer or any other illness would not affect us.

Moreover, "there's no time to lose time" is a phrase as well-known as it is simple, but it contains a concrete message that's as true as the sun rising every day.

In this plane, time is more valuable than gold, but in the divine dimension it's worth less than a grain of sand. In all truthfulness, nothing that happens here is good or bad. It's just necessary.

We're subject to earthly roles that we have been entrusted to carry out as part of a universal process of equilibrium between positive and negative energies, both of which are necessary and complement each other.

We came to feel in every sense of the word. Yes, as simple as that. To feel. Every experience and, consequently, wisdom stems from those feelings. That is to say, here on Earth the spirit develops a unique ability that is only possible through experiences as a human being. Everything happens through earthly camouflage articulated by vulnerable thoughts and subject to stimuli from the environment around each person.

According to the type of feeling and what it produces in each one, both on a physical and psychological level, in the assigned ecosystem is what motivates us to live in a determined manner each of the different stages and challenges of life.

The result is that each event can be classified as good or bad, depending on the perspective of the observer and what is known as common sense, a phrase coined by the soul but not by the spirit.

It means that the soul limits us and makes us hostages of a controlling system that is needed to give a complacent relative order to the whole of our experiences on Earth. However, it is the spirit and its thoughts that makes us free.

In other words, we could ask is life a play where we're all actors carrying out the role of a character? For example, someone takes on the role of murderer, rapist, thief, and so many other negative roles? Yes. From the perspective of the spectator submersed in the plot, the antisocial roles mentioned could be seen as abhorrent or damnable in the context of the play, but in the consciousness of real life, we know that it is only a staged scene following a predetermined script. Therefore, we refuse to judge the actors as good or bad people when they interpret these roles, as we know it is an act carried out in an artistic setting.

The same happens if we compare life in flesh and blood to the spirit. In the eyes of someone with an earthly mentality, blinded by the judgement of the soul, a person could be the most detestable murderer to have ever walked the Earth. However, on the spiritual plane, that same murderer and their despicable acts have no relevance, much less transcendence whether negative or positive. Like it or not, it is the role they came to play so that other events could so that others could fulfill what they wanted to come to this world to feel or experience when they were spirits. In this manner, the universal energetic equilibrium is maintained.

When this statement is compared under a theological framework to what's written in the Bible, we can infer that if Judas hadn't betrayed Jesus, the Messiah's mission wouldn't have been accomplished in the manner he had stipulated, independent of all the suffering he endured to free the world from sin. Therefore, Judas wasn't a good or bad man. He just came to carry out his task, and once it had been completed, chose to end his life.

It is probable that if Adolf Hitler hadn't been defeated by the Allies, the Jewish people would have not received the land that Great Britain gave to them three years after World War II ended. For that to happen, though, many people had to die.

The secret I witnessed was an accidental gift that I will never stop being thankful to whoever it was that gave it to me. For me, it will always have an unmeasurable value, worthy of all my respect, happiness, and maximum responsibility.

Even when my spiritual evolution is, to this day, inferior to that required to put the thirty degrees technique to good use, I will be convinced that, if it hadn't been for my tragic depression, I would never have been freed from the oppressive way of thinking that I had been under for so long in the current system and its self-deceiving culture.

A phrase that struck a chord with me is, "A body can be held captive, but the mind never. It is a free bird, impossible to cage." Under normal circumstances it depends on us whether our reflexive and critical thinking is restricted. In the same way, a people that is educated with their own ignorance can never overcome their material, much less spiritual, poverty.

As the years went by, I assumed that the holograms' recurring visits to the spirits' clinic had been the work of persistent prayer and love (fundamental for my recovery) that friends and family gave me during my short but intense stay in the old residence on Rodrigo de Araya Street in Macul.

As Einstein said, "there needs to be a balance between rationality and intuition." Love, in essence, is a powerful energy that we underestimate. It's not strange that thoughts of love have helped people recover from what seemed to be terminal illnesses. We still haven't learned to use that powerful, but at the same time simple and elemental, energy. It should be as easy as training the right side of the brain where intuition and spirituality reside. Love is able to heal and save lives. On the other hand, stress and hate can end a person's tangible existence.

The beautiful young woman's visit, dressed in a green tunic, turban, and medallion, to the spirits' clinic at the height of my depression made a lot of sense after I was told by reputable psychics that green is the color of healing.

It took me five years to recover from my severe depression and get back to living a normal life. After all, it wasn't easy to find a new sense of purpose for my terrestrial journey. As fortune would have it, I was able to do it with the appropriate reflexive will. However, some latter studies worried me. For example, some state that the prolonged consumption of fluoxetine, an antidepressant with a fluoride component, can have an adverse effect on the pineal gland. Prolonged consumption can calcify it to the point that it inhibits its paranormal abilities.

The pineal gland, like the pituitary, is part of the endocrine system. Among other things, it is responsible for the production of melatonin, which regulates sleep. Its spiritual function can be adversely affected if it becomes calcified, even up to the point of dehumanizing the person.

Our society has discredited intuition, classifying it as something illogical and inexact. Conversely, it has elevated rationality as the only tool to understand life and the world around us. The social paradigm has made us think that if something isn't proven by science, it has no value in any proposition. It is hard to try to speak about something intangible without being labeled as crazy. As such, our credibility in the eyes of rational people would be comparable to someone who tells a religious fanatic that God doesn't exist. The fanatic will believe the other person is possessed, someone despicable, demon spawn, unworthy of trust.

There is a narrow connection between souls in the spiritual state and those who inhabit human bodies. We are all souls that have interacted in one way or another in one or several of our past lives. We meet and go our separate ways over and over, in varying scenes, because we are twin essences.

Based on the premise that there are uncountable dimensions, we can say that we have more than one mirrored soul interacting in different cosmic planes. One of those planes is the divine dimension, which is the closest one to the human plane.

True happiness is within us and not on the outside. In consequence, it is a choice. It is a journey, not a destination. Happiness doesn't pay attention to where it begins, but to where it can go, according to Seneca.

In the material, there are people who are very rich but are unhappy and people who are poor but tremendously happy.

We live thinking about the mistakes of the past as well as worrying about the future but spend little time concentrating on living in the present, which is the only thing we have certainty about.

This is also related to the architecture the current political, economic, and social model that rules us is responsible for. It is a paradigm that has us convinced that the most urgent thing is to worry about the plans for the future. Otherwise, they say, our failure is right around the corner where grave problems may arise without warning, leading to ruin for us and our loved ones.

However, if we focus on the real essence of life, valuing the effective growth of the spirit and not the unrestricted acceptance of an overwhelming model, we would understand that the latter will only make us easy prey to uncertainty, fear, and paranoia. As such we would be susceptible to modify or change when and where we want.

The consolidation of our repressed way of life has been sustained in the diverse unpopular measures and reforms that every so often are applied to the masses at the most critical moments of crisis.

In other words, it's as if we were trying to continuously perfect the model with the purpose of prolonging it. This, through a partial or total, subliminal or explicit application of a disturbing doctrine to shock people.

The past can't be changed, which is why we need to learn from it and they say goodbye and turn the page. The future can be organized and planned for, but we shouldn't worry about it. True happiness is in the present because it is here and now where our consciousness perceives everything with the most clarity. Everything else is just an ingredient of a good imagination that can or cannot be a component of our reality in the measure that we have the required evolution to change it at will.

Wanting to satisfy everyone and putting off our own needs can lead to the abyss. There is no way to please everyone and investing our energy in that purpose is a simple and self-harming idea.

Depression is a state of extreme sensibility that makes us see things from another perspective, one that is more critical and reasonable. Overcoming it doesn't happen by medication alone because it is a generalized and integral problem that includes mind, body, and soul.

Many people view this pathology with compassion and up to a certain point that's fine. However, as in everything, it's not good to reach hasty conclusions with respect to the consequences of that condition because most depressions are temporary and not always disabling.

We live a life saturated with anxiety and hyper productivity that just allows us to exist, not really live. This way of life favors depression, though it can open new and unexpected spiritual perspectives for the individual, many of which can be misunderstood by a society that is less evolved and in general interprets them as something anomalous or imaginary.

Evan with all the complications an episode of depression can have in a person, this experience left me with consequences that were positive in the extreme. I lost my fear of death and the fear of taking risks. If you know that your existence is infinite, you won't fear anything or anyone. That is to say, when you know that life is eternal, it doesn't matter if your body goes back to being dust.

I never acted like a money-making robot. I also didn't exchange my time for it. Each hour that we waste is one hour less in the account of our lives.

The day when money can buy everything is when we'll be immortal. As this will never happen, we'll have to continue dying as it behooves us to on this terrestrial plane.

Freedom to do what we want with our time is a countless treasure. We may have a lot of money, but what good is it if we don't have time to spend it?

Time is the fuel that moves our lives. However, in the whirlwind of existence it's hard for us to be aware of this. That's why with only minutes to go before it runs out, we realize that there are no gas stations where we can refuel. Is it necessary to wait until that moment to give value to that scarce resource? It is recommended that it be used for substantial rather than superficial reasons.

The system such as it is, is far from being able to meet the fundamental rights of a human being. This is public knowledge. If we want rights, some say, we need to pay for them. The problem is that the rich in Latin America and the world in general don't want to pay for anything. That's their first sin and the inconsistency that doesn't allow many nations to rise from the precarious conditions they're in.

The social revolt in Chile left exposed how fragile the constructed model is, the weakness of the foundations our institutionalism is built on, which, by the way, is already cracked so much it may be beyond redemption.

Among several consequences, the imminent collapse of the system has shown the spiritual vacuum that has been the reason why we've been blinded, forgetting what is really important, which is to live.

Many times we behave more slave-like than we are: beings without the capacity to stop and think, question, give kindness. We need to value those moments of reflection as they are necessary to find ourselves, our consciousness, and others.

Not everything in life can be dedicated to the production of wealth. Spare time and lack of discipline can give way so creativity and philosophical thinking may flourish. They help connect us to these invisible forces that daily wander among us but we can't see due to our spiritual blindness. We need to ask what we seldom or never do, all because of the belief that there has to be an order to things. What importance could terrestrial entropy have when the entire universe is chaos?

"Working to live and not living to work" is a phrase that holds many life messages that we rarely want to understand. The system demands it, it's true, because it is firmly adhered to the culture of a society that, for the most part, has low self-esteem and serious structural problems that none of us have taken care of or have the least intention of taking care of.

I understood that there is no point in judging others though sometimes it is very difficult not to. However, just as with the thirty-degree technique, it's a matter of practice. Elevating our thinking and removing the nefarious programming of fear from our minds is a must. Fear? The tool of choice for those with ambition to make the ones who conform live a pauper's life of control and submission in exchange for a few crumbs.

I thought I had understood the meaning of life and its objectives in several aspects, especially in regards to respect and acceptance of our destiny no matter how unfair or disagreeable it might be, remembering that we can change it when and how many times we want.

Reality is a process that requires our consciousness to be. That's why if we suspend our disbelief, we can modify it using only our thoughts. Religious faith helps in the measure that it is able to convince our subconscious about what we really want to achieve.

The latter is supported by science. Reality varies according to the observer (as in the experiment with the atom and the two slits) which is why it is generated according to what the observer decides. All this is subjugated to their levels of prejudice, fears, or certainties that they may have.

Death doesn't exist. It is only an illusion. What happens is that we remain here in spirit and soul together with people of flesh and blood. Our bodies become less dense to the reflection of light in a dimension perpendicular to ours called the divine dimension, where life is very different in some aspects but very similar in others.

Once there, our state of transition remains immutable until something makes it change withing the space and time that we have been assigned to be there. This something can be a ritual through which a portal is opened and through which the journey to infinite eternity, the encounter with internal peace begins.

Everyone has supernatural power and we don't know it. Therefore we don't use it. For someone it may be hard to see farther because, seen in a literal and scientific sense, everything depends on light. That's what allows us to see truth or mirages.

In their writings, all cultures present and past refer to the divine dimension and its inhabitants, spirits. Some of them have been assigned to help us when we need it. Those closest to us are the ones who in past lives played a large role in our evolution. They inspire, guide, and help us. Like them, there are others who can have certain beneficial or detrimental influences in our lives.

Lastly, remember that the most profound universal secret isn't found on life on Earth, but in a spiritual cosmic plane where humans as a race come from. We were created in their image to reproduce here on Earth with a higher motive, the same which has us now fighting an all-out cruel and brutal war. Our destiny and the manner in which we live and exist depend on this. The final battle will be decisive and it will be determined in the war of spirits.

REFLECTION ON THE PANDEMIC

Covid–19 has shown us that, in this system so far from equality, measuring success and happiness according to how much money and goods we can accumulate not only makes us look naïve, but much more vulnerable than what we believed. The evolved spirit understands that the simpler life is lived, in harmony and with respect towards the environment, the happier and more successful we can come to feel.

ABOUT THE AUTHOR

Miguel Ángel Camiletti Sáez is an engineer with dual nationality (Chilean–Italian). He was born on August 9th, 1970, in Santiago, Chile.

As a child he loved arts and literature but it was in his adulthood, after graduating from the university, when he started his literary-artistic exploration.

His childhood and adolescence took place during the seventies and part of the eighties in the suburbs of the eastern part of the capital city.

From his youth he started to acquire abilities in the business world where he undertook several business ventures related to technology.

Due to his tireless investigative, analytic, and intellectual spirit, in the nineties Miguel Angel became one of the most ideal people to combat IT viruses in Latin America. He was part of the executive staff of some companies in the tech industry in Chile, where he became the main proponent of innovation and digital development.

After the tragedy in Antuco on the 18th of May 2005, in the city of Los Angeles, and in memory of someone dear, Miguel Angel created and directed the now-closed website Héroes de Antuco (Heroes of Antuco). On this site in addition to remembering the 45 victims, harsh criticism and analysis of the political and social contingency at the time took place. The page became a benchmark for public and private agents, both national and international, such as the Minister of the Interior or the New York Times, who used it as a source for ideas of varying depth such as sketches of plans and strategic proposals of social interest and sensibility.

He was a professor of technology in several public and private institutions of education. He also collaborated with non-profit organizations, some of which are related to overcoming poverty and the rescue and rehabilitation from drug addiction.

In 2011 he led and developed the technological implementation of the first national registry of firefighters in Chile. It was the first in the history of a noble institution with over 160 years of traditions. The initiative included the University of Chile, along with a staff of engineers from the Faculty of Information Engineering of this prestigious house of studies.

Miguel Angel was also involved in politics, where he developed leadership roles adhering to constructive criteria that won the recognition and appreciation of his colleagues at a time when traditional Chilean politics had lost credibility due to high-visibility cases of corruption.

Now, and for more than 25 years, Miguel Angel resides in the Maipu neighborhood of Santiago.

Leaving behind the whirlwind of business and politics for a while, he has focused on diving deeper into the study of metaphysics, spirituality, and energy. This set of subjects is something he has been working on since 2005 and talks about in an open manner in his novel "Thirty Degrees." This work suggests an alternative perspective to understanding the known earthly and spiritual systems.

Made in the USA
Coppell, TX
29 July 2024

35311057R00132